Salt Skin

Michelle Rhodes

Salt Skin

ISBN: 978-0-473-38188-2

editkitten.wordpress.com

For Daphne, and all the women who came before me.
In love and light.

"For the moon never beams without bringing me dreams."

—Edgar Allan Poe

Prologue

When I was four I drowned.

For years I didn't think about the events that had taken place on the lonely stretch of beach. I'd pushed them into the quietest part of my mind, where they stayed undisturbed for over a decade. But it seemed such things could never truly be forgotten, however much I wanted them to be.

I started having flashbacks that left me breathless, fearful. They were so real to me I could almost feel the sting of salt on my lips. Without warning I'd be pulled beneath the surface, struggling, helpless, watching bubbles burst like millions of diamonds around me.

I couldn't understand why after all those years the shattered memory had begun putting itself back together.

As if something inside me needed to remember.

Chapter One

Despite the moonlight, when I looked across the field our house was lost to darkness. The pine forest behind it swayed in the wind and pushed shadows up over the roof. Inside, my mother and sisters slept.

I crossed the silver lawn, thinking it almost looked lovely. During the day it was merely a dying stretch of grass. I slunk around the side of the house, climbed a giant pine, and clambered through my open window. Nothing ever happened on my night-time missions. Sometimes my friend Miriam and I would jump the fence that separated us from the abandoned factories and drink cheap wine. Usually I just went walking.

Still wide awake, I plugged in my speakers and climbed onto the roof. My coffee intake that day had been excessive. I should have been finishing my English essay, but I pushed that thought aside. Lying back against the lichen-covered tiles, I watched the moon rise high above the trees and flood everything with light. It clung to my clothes and to the branches that pressed against my windows.

I stared out across the lawn, then behind me to the dark forest, and the familiar sense of urgency that I should have been elsewhere clawed at me. It was a strange sensation, a pulling of sorts, only I didn't know how to follow it. More than anything I wanted to, but it was much more complicated than getting in my car and driving towards the horizon. My heart began beating recklessly because I was aware of missing something vitally important. The moon always did this to me.

☼

"Sunny?" Brie's whisper jolted me awake.

I was momentarily blinded by the morning light, and the room tipped as I tried to untangle myself from a particularly disturbing dream. What time was it?

When I realised it was still early I took a steadying breath and flopped back onto the pillows.

My younger sister eased the door open, which made it creak even louder than usual. I tried to ignore her. She inched into the room, tripped over a half-finished cup of coffee and landed in a heap on the ground.

"Morning," I sighed.

"Sorry if I woke you," and because she genuinely meant it I couldn't be angry.

She threw open the wardrobe, and I watched her methodically sift through my clothes, looking for an outfit.

4

The hangers clinked against each other as she chattered, and her conversation moved so quickly I found it hard to keep up. When she mentioned a boy's name I groaned inwardly. Had Mum's countless failed relationships had no impact on her at all?

"Perfect!" She yanked a top from my wardrobe.

I sat up, pressed my fingers to my temples and peered in the mirror. Sleep had evaded me until the moon was low in the western sky. It showed in dark circles beneath my eyes, making my skin appear paler and my irises even blacker.

Tonight would be no different.

Outside it had started raining. I heaped an extra spoonful of coffee into the filter, slumped at the counter and tried not to remember my dream. But it followed me all morning, coming back in fleeting, disjointed fragments. I'd dreamed of an ocean that was dangerous and rough. It shouldn't have unsettled me as much as it did.

Rain splattered against the kitchen windows and flooded the shallow drains in our driveway. Maybe tonight there would be enough cloud to hide the moon. Mum had already gone to work and she'd left a letter that had come for me where I'd see it — tucked under the corner of the coffee machine. I didn't need to open it to know who it was from. I had a stack of others, all in the same careful writing, put away in a drawer upstairs. They were from a grandmother I'd never meet, and I knew this one would contain the same question as all the others — would I please visit? I'd responded once, years and years ago, explaining it was difficult because we lived so far apart. But she'd ignored my excuse and kept writing. I ran my fingers over my name. Sunlight West; not ideal for someone who wanted to blend in. I stuffed the envelope in my bag before Brie could ask questions and looked towards the mess she was creating in the lounge.

"Where are those boots with all the buckles?" she called, and I looked down at my feet.

"You mean my boots that I wear every day?" They were heavy and scuffed and gave the impression I might sing in a punk rock band. Brie looked so gloomy amongst the mountain of flats and stilettos that I sighed and switched them for an even older pair of Converses. We ran through torrential rain to my car.

I drive an old Mustang with cracked leather bench seats and a big soft top that folds back. Even though I had nowhere to go, it was freeing to think I could fill the boot with clothes and leave if I wanted to. It made me feel less claustrophobic.

Brie slid in beside me and shook out her caramel-coloured hair. Usually she would have pushed back the roof to let the wind stream in, but not today. I backed out of the driveway and pulled onto the main road while Brie went through my minimal collection of makeup. She was piling on loads of mascara and too much lip gloss when we approached the busy bus stop.

Our sister Emily, who's a year older than me, deliberately looked away from us, the smoke from her cigarette a halo above her. I rolled down the windows and turned the volume on the stereo right up so she'd hear it. Brie stuffed her fingers in her ears as I blasted the Rolling Stones.

I saw Emily glaring at us in the rear-view mirror as we passed. She was so bitter. Even though she didn't have a licence, the fact that Mum had given me the car had been at the heart of countless arguments since, and Emily refused to let me drive her to school—or anywhere. At the time I sat my licence, I hadn't given the possibility of owning a car any thought—the Mustang had been parked and covered in the garage my whole life. Sometimes if something is in one place long enough you stop noticing it. When Mum pressed the key into my palm, smiling, it had taken me a moment to understand the gesture.

At school I was restless yet tired; a frustrating combination. I stumbled through the corridors and fell asleep in history. The teachers frowned as I carved my name into the leather surface of my diary. West—the only thing my father had given me. That's if you weren't counting yet another reason why I don't trust men.

I can't remember him because he left when I was very small. I arrived when Mum was living in a caravan and growing sunflowers for a living. She had a mane of blonde hair and wore rings on every finger—I've seen photos. Emily's dad had disappeared a year before that, and I often wondered how Mum dealt with all the abandonment.

She got rid of her incense and tie-dyed skirts as if she could shed those days like a cicada does its skin. Perhaps if she'd realised her hippy days wouldn't last she would have named me something simple the way she had my sisters. Ironically, anyone in my blonde-haired, blue-eyed family would suit the name Sunlight better than me.

☼

It was the next day, after another night of outlandish dreaming, that Mum told us we were moving. I had yawned my way through school, despite all the caffeine I'd consumed, and made plans to hang thick blankets at my windows the minute I got home. Maybe it would help, maybe it wouldn't. I swear the moon can affect people; I've believed that ever since I googled lunacy.

In the rear-view mirror my face was washed out and tired-looking, my eyes the colour of Coca-Cola. The moon was already rising—huge and pale against the afternoon sky—and somehow I just knew I was in the wrong place.

As we sat waiting for the lights to change, I stared at my reflection until I didn't recognise myself. Panic swelled in my chest. How long had I felt this way? The traffic light glowed green and I floored it to the front of a long line of cars.

If I'd known what was awaiting me at home, I wouldn't have been in such a hurry.

☼

I sensed something had changed the instant my fingers touched the cool handle of our front door. Inside, the atmosphere was stretched tight as if the house knew something I didn't. I paused before entering the kitchen, listening. I couldn't hear any heated conversations or the shuddering of door frames but for the first time in years, Mum was home before us. She was perched awkwardly on the couch, her mismatched socks distracting me for a second.

"Hey." I slung my bag over the back of a chair and glanced around the room. Emily lay, oblivious to everything, on a threadbare rug that adorned the cold floor. Brie bounded past me to the fridge.

"So, guess what?" Mum said as she brushed her fringe out of her eyes.

I braced myself, hoping she didn't have yet another man she wanted us to meet—and perhaps Emily was thinking the same thing because she finally looked up from her magazine, eyes full of suspicion. I knew, to some extent, she resented Mum for her bad choices. We'd witnessed her heart break more times than we could count, and it was because of her I'd learnt to guard my own so closely.

"You've got another date?" my sister muttered tactlessly, but Mum's next words weren't what any of us were expecting.

"I've been transferred. We're moving."

"What?" Emily spat, but Mum ignored her and instead flicked me an anxious glance.

My heart missed a beat when I saw the uncertainty on her face. There was only one place in the world that could be worse than here, and I looked at her in horror. "No!" But I already knew the answer was yes.

Emily found her argument before I did. "What about my friends?" she demanded. "I just made the cheer team, or did you forget that? If you paid even a fraction of attention—"

"Where are we going?" I interrupted, and suddenly all our eyes were on Mum.

"Way up north to a place called Procellae Bay. We have a house waiting for us right on the beach."

My chest tightened and I drew in a sharp breath of air. "As in beside the ocean?" I asked stupidly. When she nodded, the room closed in on me.

"That sounds so romantic!" Brie gushed, twirling excitedly towards the stairs, her head no doubt full of sunshine and shirtless boys. I wouldn't have been surprised if she was going in search of her suitcase.

"Romantic?" Emily didn't try to hide the hysteria in her voice. "It sounds like something out of a bad Shakespeare play!"

"This is the position I've been waiting for! I'll be practically running the radiology department up there." Mum came to stand behind me so she could gather my dark hair into her hands. "I'm sorry, Sunny. I know how you feel about the ocean."

But she couldn't have. Not if she was suggesting this.

An almighty crash from upstairs distracted us, and I knew the contents of Brie's wardrobe had just avalanched into the hallway.

"I need a new bikini!" she called seconds later. I sighed, turning back to Mum who still stared at me guiltily.

"It's fine, really." I forced a smile and cleared the table so she couldn't see my face. I'm a terrible liar.

☼

Later, in the sanctuary of my bedroom, I paced mindlessly, stopping every now and then to gaze out at the wet pines. Drops of rain clung to the needles like tiny fairy lights, and I was bewildered to realise I'd rather stay in this mind-numbing field than move anywhere near the ocean.

Just twice I'd seen it, a glorious expanse of blues and purples that seemed to go on forever. Mum said I was mesmerised by it that first time, my four-year-old self completely enraptured. We'd gotten up before it was light to drive the long, winding road out to the coast. I remember how hot the sand had been and hearing the gulls screaming through the sky. Emily and I had been making castles out of sea foam and then ... what exactly?

I shuddered. If the memory alone troubled me, how was I going to live a normal life with the ocean breathing on my windows? I picked up my car keys, called out to whoever was listening that I was going to work on an art project, and stepped into the night.

☼

I didn't even take art but I don't think Mum knew that. Brie had given me a calculating look from the couch but stayed quiet. She's great like that. I always wondered how she had so much compassion when Emily often had none.

I drove aimlessly. As the landscape darkened and disappeared, my thoughts took over. Under different circumstances I would have been excited to leave this place.

If only they'd transferred her anywhere else. But Mum wasn't to know just how frequently I revisited that day from my childhood, or the dread that accompanied me when I did. Sometimes I felt detached, unsure how to fill my days when I'd been so close to not having a future at all. But I couldn't tell her that—I hardly understood it myself and didn't want her to worry.

A house on the beach ...

As a fresh wave of panic crept up on me, I fumbled around for a CD and slipped it into the player. The Cure came darkly back at me through the speakers, and I turned it up loud to try to block out my mind and the growing sense of unease that had taken over my body. Above the music, I imagined I could hear the haunting call of seabirds and a sighing ocean. Paramedics had called my time of death at eleven minutes past eleven on that desolate beach thirteen years ago. They say I'm a seventeen-year-old miracle child, but really I'm still drifting.

☼

When I got home I flicked off the porch light Mum had left on for me and pushed the door open. The house was warm and smelled like herbal tea. I brushed my teeth quietly and made my way upstairs. Brie was settled on my duvet, yawning sleepily. "How's your art going?" she asked with a lopsided grin.

"I just needed to go for a drive," I said wearily, dropping my keys onto the dressing table and peeling off my jeans.

Brie hugged a pillow to her chest. "Emily told Mum she's not coming."

"Oh, okay." This didn't surprise me.

"Are you all right?" she asked, her pretty features all serious now.

"Yes." I pulled on my pyjamas, hoping she'd take the hint and go to bed, but she was still staring at me.

I cupped my hands on either side of her worried face,

wishing she wasn't so hard to lie to. "Brie, I'm fine."

"Are you scared about moving?" For fourteen she sure seemed to have everything worked out.

"No."

☼

That night the ocean came for me in a starless dream. I walked beneath a giant moon, my feet sinking into wet sand with every slow step. The water tied ancient ropes around my ankles, and even though I knew I shouldn't, I went deeper. It was so pretty, so persuasive. If I listened closely enough it whispered my name.

I tripped and the waves rose up to catch me. Fear pulsed through me; the kind that should only accompany something truly terrible, not just a regular nightmare. I was swept out, pulled under; saltwater poured into my lungs. I tried to claw my way to the surface and woke up screaming, a foreign word on the tip of my tongue.

"Pytheus," I whispered, and was afraid because I didn't know what it was or where it came from. Rain was beating relentlessly against my windows, and I could just make out the dark shapes of the pine trees being pummelled by the wind. I unravelled my twisted sheets and took a ragged breath, thankful that tomorrow was the weekend.

I was getting used to these dreams, as terrifying as they were.

☼

On Monday I woke with a headache and only got up because I needed to drive Brie to school and empty out my locker. We weren't leaving for a few days but I'd decided my time there was over. I'd been getting straight As up until recently, but at some point my concentration had floated far off into the universe where it had dispersed and become unreachable. I repeatedly told myself that change was good; however, during a painfully dull history lesson my fears escalated. The ocean swirled across the classroom floor and filled the building with strange noises. I tried to shake the memory but I was no longer sitting at school in a room full of others. I was four again, wading into the water in my little white dress …

Storm clouds floated dark and ghost-like across the sky. The way Mum told it, the beautiful morning turned bad within a matter of minutes. Before the waves had reached up to pull me under, an unnatural stillness came over the bay. Then the wind started to blow, and rain lashed from the sky. Everything after that is a vague distortion of sirens and havoc and … pain. The pain in my chest had been unbearable.

I sucked in a deep breath as the classroom came back into focus. Mum's recollection of what happened next plays like a movie in my head. The lifeguards pulled me, limp and white, from the ocean twenty minutes later. I imagined my small body laid out on the sand as they tried to bring me back. My pulse was deathly slow until eventually they couldn't find it. They'd already pronounced me dead when I came to. The doctors said I would never recover, that the brain damage would be too severe—yet I was back to normal the following week. Mum said people called me her little mermaid. I shuddered as the bell rang, and headed for the lockers.

Brie was there swapping books. Her locker was a collage of photos and colourful stickers, and I knew she wouldn't empty it until the last minute. I punched in my combination and waited for the door to open, but it didn't. I looked around for any teachers and then started pounding on it with my fist. They hated me doing that. There was a dent just below the keypad from where I had done it so many times, and the person before me too. It swung open and I was greeted with the usual dull grey space. The only decorating my locker had ever undergone was when Miriam had tagged our names across the back of it with a purple marker.

She was the one person I'd miss when we left. Even though we had nothing in common she was like a sister to me—not that I needed another one. When I'd told her I was leaving she'd offered to give me a tattoo so I wouldn't forget her, but I had gently refused.

I emptied my locker of rubbish, swept my stack of books into my open bag and let the door bang loudly shut.

"Do you think Em really will stay?" Brie asked, and from the window I could see her on the field. She was jumping around in a tiny skirt, clutching red and white pompoms as if they were her lifeline.

This was Emily's second attempt at her final year. Mum had begged her to try again, and I think the only reason she'd agreed was because some of her friends had also been held back. It wasn't about grades for Emily, but a social life.

Brie was looking at me, wanting an answer, and I shrugged. Emily was still adamant she'd be staying in the city with her boyfriend. She and Mum had argued about it all weekend.

"I feel sorry for her in a way," Brie said, and I knew what she meant. I'd once heard a teacher say to Mum she'd never met three sisters who were so completely different.

I blame it on our fathers.

In the days leading up to our move, I got up early, chucked an empty schoolbag on the back seat of my car and drove Brie to school. Then I snuck home. I knew Mum wouldn't approve of me missing even a single class. She was big on things like that. Her education had been disorderly, her twenties much the same, and she wanted better for us.

I parked the Mustang, peered through the garage window to double-check that Mum had actually left, then stretched in the early morning sun. My moment of peace didn't last long. The kitchen window was thrown open

17

and the smell of cigarettes burnt the air; beyond it, Emily shouted incoherently.

I stomped inside and slammed the door, expecting her to head for the stairs when she realised I'd come home. Instead she stayed put, sobbing, the tear-streaked phone clutched in her hand. I slipped past her, hoping she'd ignore me, but she started up when I was heaping spoonfuls of delicious, crushed beans into the coffee filter. "He's cheating on me!"

When I reluctantly turned to face her she looked awful. Dark shadows sat beneath her eyes and only now did I notice how thin she'd gotten.

"Hayden?" I asked, and even though I'd thought him half decent, I wasn't surprised. What surprised me was that she'd thought it could ever end well.

"With Chloe, my best friend! How could they do this to me?" Tears were streaming down her face, and I crossed the small space over to her and sat down.

"Probably quite easily," I replied, vaguely recalling an exotic, skinny girl with legs that belonged on the runway. All she had talked about was her recent nose job and trip to Paris.

Emily looked up at me and for a moment I thought she was going to defend her, but instead she just nodded glumly.

"So where are you going once we've gone?" I asked, pouring her a coffee.

She looked at me like I'd asked the dumbest question.

"I'm coming with you!"

Unbelievable.

"What about cheerleading?" I couldn't make sense of her rash decisions and sudden mood changes.

"Trust me, when I'm finished with Chloe I won't have a place on that team and I'll want to be as far away from here as possible."

I didn't ask questions. "Well, Mum will be pleased." It was all I could think to say.

Chapter Two

According to the internet, Procellae, when roughly translated from Latin, means storm or violent winds. When I read that, I wished again that we weren't going there. The town rests not far off a lonely highway. It's situated on rugged coastland — a wild stretch of beaches with the sea eternally restless on its shores and not much else for miles.

I flicked the switch on my computer and watched the screen fade. Hopefully I would like it, because either way it looked like I'd be stuck there. I peeled down my music posters, emptied out Hercules' tank and put him into a plastic travelling bag I'd picked up from the pet store last week. Sometimes I felt sorry for my lone goldfish — how he'd swim round and round his bowl — but Brie told me he only has a three-second memory span, so I found a certain reassurance in that.

It took me ages to pack. I spent hours procrastinating — sometimes staring unproductively out the window at nearby factories for minutes at a time. They were stark and ugly against the grey sky, and I couldn't think of a view less inspiring. No wonder I felt like life was slowly passing me by.

Eventually my attention moved to the piles of junk that had cluttered my room for years. I binned half of it and stuffed the rest into boxes. I put my beat-up old guitar into its even more battered case, and then pulled my diary out from under my mattress.

I shook out the newspaper cutting that Mum had kept from after my mishap. Until recently it had remained untouched, resting beneath old schoolbooks and forgotten things, but a couple of months ago I'd turned my room upside down trying to find it. I'd read it over and over as if maybe it would shed some light on what had happened that day at the beach.

I held it carefully, the soft paper familiar in my hands. The words were almost completely worn off from where the crease was, but I knew them by heart. I skimmed my eyes over the article. Freak storm, lifeguards, an ambulance—then the random bystander's recollection, which always gave me shivers.

One moment she was so lifeless, gone. Then she just sat up, rubbing her eyes like she'd woken from a deep sleep ...

Mum had resigned herself to the fact that only two of her daughters would be accompanying her. We were almost ready to go when Emily began carting her boxes down the stairs and out to the moving truck. The casual way she went about it made you think it had been the plan all along, but when Mum looked on with confusion, I knew Emily hadn't bothered to mention her change of heart.

"Are we dropping you somewhere?" Mum asked, baffled. "I thought Hayden was picking you up tomorrow."

"I'm coming with you," Emily said silkily, settling herself into Mum's car. "The bastard's run off with my best friend."

Oh, to be our mother.

She and Emily left five minutes before Brie and I were ready. The gravel road was still clouded with dust from their departure, another thing I wouldn't miss. When I drove the Mustang down our road for the last time, I didn't look back. The only bad thing about leaving, other than our actual destination, was that Miriam wasn't escaping with me. We'd said our goodbyes late last night, and she'd promised to come visit.

Brie, however, was twisted right around in her seat, watching our house until we turned a bend in the road. "Goodbye," she whispered and I thought maybe she was going to cry, but she looked at me with a wicked grin.

"What?" I asked and couldn't help returning her smile.

She wound down her window and let out a wild howl. "Bring on the beaches, baby!" Brie loved the water; she'd spent practically all of last summer in her friend's pool.

She sifted through my CDs. "Sunny, this is all ancient," she complained half-heartedly as she flicked past the Rolling Stones, the Yeah Yeah Yeahs and the Cure. She chose one at random and began talking non-stop, unfazed by how little I joined in with the conversation.

I was getting nervous. The only other time I'd set foot on a beach was last year, when our teachers planned a camping trip out to the coast. It wasn't until we actually arrived that I realised how much I didn't want to be there.

Just seeing the ocean had made my heart beat faster, and it must have been enough to awaken my elusive memories. I stayed dry the entire trip, excluding myself from every water-based activity. From the banks I watched the girls flirt shamelessly with the boys. It seemed insane to me that anyone would volunteer to take a class of hormonal sixteen-year-olds on a co-ed camp. The worst thing about that trip had been the sleepless nights. While my classmates snuck down to the beach, I'd stayed in my tent — unable to block out the sound of the waves.

Then, just a couple of months after that, our school got a load of funding and by the time we'd returned from holiday there were two brand-new, full-length swimming pools beside the fields. It turned out I wasn't just afraid of the sea, but of water itself. Up till then I'd been lucky that none of my schools had had pools and I'd never had to face the idea of trying to swim.

The first week I forgot my gear, the second week I conveniently had a bad cold, and by the third I was writing lines. However hard the swimming coach tried to force me to swim, I always resisted. I developed a variety of different medical disorders, my most effective being female-related because our teacher was a man and just hearing certain words made him want to change careers. I had a never-ending supply of excuses. In the end he gave up and instead of arguing with me he would just hand me paper and I'd write lines. It was a win-win situation.

The highway snaked for hundreds of kilometres up the country, and pretty soon I was further from the city than I could ever remember being. We stopped driving at dusk, staying at the only place we could find—a derelict hotel with lumpy mattresses and no hot water.

We left early the next morning, Mum extra chirpy to try to compensate for Emily's evil mood, and me desperate to be back on the road away from her bad vibes.

"There is absolutely no way I'll be re-enrolling in a new school!" my sister snapped.

"Then you're getting a job," I heard Mum insist as Emily slammed her door.

By the second night I was exhausted; driving ten hours through an unchanging landscape was tiring. I could have slept anywhere, but Brie spotted a cute bed and breakfast. It had great showers, and big blue flowers in vases beside the beds.

My dreams were full of storms and ocean as if even in sleep I was worried about where we were going. I couldn't forget them when we started out early again. We'd left the sprawling cities far behind us now, the landscape turning into a mass of rock-strewn paddocks. We drove like this for days, stopping at night and starting out early in the morning, chasing the sun. It took much longer than we'd predicted.

When Mum finally announced we were on the home stretch I was well and truly over it. We'd driven for hours without seeing a single house, but then barns and packing sheds began to appear in the orchards, and I knew we were getting closer to civilisation. To my disappointment the sun soon disappeared behind solid cloud, but Brie didn't seem to notice. She was bursting with energy, making me stop at one point so she could take photos and then again to pat a cow wandering on the road. We pressed on, and I zoned out after a while, dangerously tired from my endless chain of dreams each night.

Suddenly I was aware of Brie staring at me.

"Huh?" I'd been far away.

"I said did you see that sign?" she repeated, and when I shook my head she pointed.

"There's a petrol station, and your fuel light is on."

I hadn't even seen the garage, but she was right; I was on E. I flicked on the indicator and pulled off the road.

A guy in faded overalls filled up the tank and checked all that other junk I knew nothing about.

"Nice car!" he said enthusiastically.

Like I needed a guy to tell me that.

"You can never beat the classics." He was trying to make conversation but I couldn't be bothered, even if he was ridiculously good-looking.

"Are you from around here?"

Incredibly, the guy wouldn't even take a hint, but his beautiful blue eyes stopped me from being too mean.

"We've just moved from the city," I told him.

"Well, I hope you like rain," he said cheerfully, and in the distance I saw towering mountains blanketed in mist.

There was an awkward sort of silence then, because I didn't know what to say. Brie was watching us from the front seat, no doubt over-analysing the situation. I didn't understand how she could have a different boyfriend every week and still not think they were a total waste of time.

"How much further is the town?" I asked.

"About ten minutes. You're nearly there."

"Thanks." I paid inside and walked back to the Mustang, trying to convince myself I hadn't just felt a drop of rain.

"He liked you," Brie started, but I killed the conversation and asked her to get out the map.

We drove for a few minutes in silence, the road taking us into some rocky hills. It was narrow and I hugged the middle of the road, too scared to look down. We were getting really high up, the cliffs plunging down into dark forest.

"According to this we should see the bay any minute now."

Yay. We rounded a sweeping corner and there it was. A vast rolling ocean that made me grip the steering wheel too tightly. I felt breathless. All I could imagine was being stuck out in the middle of it with the seabed miles beneath my feet and who knows what lurking in the deep.

I wasn't used to so much space, as if we were on the very edge of the world. Brie was winding down her window, inhaling deeply. I swear I could smell the salt.

"Wow," she breathed. "Take this turn up here."

I sighed, changed gear and swung onto a road that led us straight down into the valley. Houses perched on the cliffs, their hooded windows and slate roofs dating from a whole different era. The wind picked up as we got closer to town, flinging leaves in our path and pulling the unmistakable smell of ocean into the car. We passed magnificent old buildings that appeared empty and unused, the brickwork stained with age.

"This must be the older part of town," Brie said as she stared down a cobblestone alleyway. "I read how it was built in the late seventeen hundreds, then almost totally abandoned."

We wound through deserted streets into the newer part. There was a strip of shops and cafes, half of which were closed, and a smoky little pub on the corner. Suffocating black clouds hung low in the sky. I wasn't trying to be negative, but the place had already given me a reason not to like it.

"Look at the sky," Brie said, and I figured now wasn't the time to tell her it rained three hundred days out of the year here. She looked at me with uncertainty but I smiled, determined not to bring her down. It started to rain—a light drizzle that settled on our clothes and hair. *Welcome to the bay.* I parked briefly to pull the roof back over us and zip up my leather jacket. The street was empty apart from a group of pallid teenagers pushing their way out of a huge library. We carried on driving.

"Down here," Brie muttered, and I turned onto a road lined with ash trees and dark houses. Most of them were really old—Georgian, maybe? I should have paid more attention in history. Peering through the rain towards them, I tried to get a closer look. Boughs of ash had been nailed to their front doors, and I realised this was an old place with even older beliefs. The lawns were large and gardens unkempt, their lemongrass and water mint sprawling beyond the footpaths. I hadn't known such places still existed outside of horror movies.

"These houses give me the creeps," Brie whispered.

"What?" I laughed, turning onto yet another road and doing my best to be cheerful. "Just because they're old doesn't mean they're creepy."

She shrugged unconvinced, and I tried to ignore the horrible feeling that she was right.

☼

When we reached our street, Brie let out a breath of relief. The houses here were much newer. Maybe she too had envisioned walking long, haunted hallways to the bathroom at night. So we'd been relocated to the middle of nowhere, but we sure had a nice place.

I pulled into our new driveway, got out, and stretched beneath a massive tree. It was in flower, the grass beneath it a splash of purple. "Pamphlet perfect," I heard Mum telling Emily as we walked over to them.

Suddenly Brie was running across the grassy lawn and out towards a jetty. It was supported by great wooden posts, where fishing boats could dock. I watched uneasily. Surely she wasn't about to do what I thought she was. Her blonde hair streamed out behind her like corn silk and I wanted to yell at her to stop, but the words caught in my throat. She hurled herself off the planks into the water and then I was sprinting to her, my heart leaping wildly in my chest.

"Brie?" I tried to keep the shrillness from my voice but I could see where the surface had swallowed her and I was panicking.

When she finally appeared, Mum was laughing. Laughing! Brie hauled herself up the ladder with the biggest smile on her face, and I took a couple of deep breaths. She leaned against some twisted railing, struggling to pull off her wet jeans.

I turned shakily back to our new home and followed Emily inside. It was completely different from our old house beneath the pine trees – the carpet was soft under my feet, and I knew there'd be no damp wallpaper here. The front was all glass. On good days I imagined it would fill with soft green light off the ocean. The kitchen was big with white marble countertops, and Mum couldn't stop raving about it. A carpeted staircase led to a second storey. Emily claimed the biggest room as I knew she would, and I wasn't fussed due to the fact it faced directly out to sea. Mine backed onto hers, which meant I had a view of the southern end of the beach. This was bad enough. My other window overlooked the backyard. The tree I'd just stood beneath pressed its petals against the glass, and I gazed into its branches before heading back downstairs.

The movers had arranged our furniture and left their business card on the living-room table. There were boxes everywhere. We unpacked as much as we could and settled on the floor in the lounge, tired.

"See those islands there?" Mum asked, and we looked out over the dark ocean.

"Apparently they're called the Hidden Islands because half the time they're shrouded in mist and you can't see them."

Brie's eyes lit up. "How mysterious!"

I stared out at the land that was only sometimes there, and Mum opened a bottle of bubbles. The uneasy feeling within me subsided in a strawberry haze.

☼

I lay wide awake that night, listening to the wind pick up. It blew lazily around the house at first, whispering through the open window. I could hear the waves slapping unevenly against the jetty and knew I wouldn't fall asleep for a long while.

Fat drops of rain started to splash against the glass, and a gust of wind made the lace curtains billow inwards. I kicked off the bedcovers and went to the window, pulling it shut and wrapping my arms around myself to stop a bout of shivering.

The weather became wilder and the waves darkened. Lightning ripped the sky apart in blinding white streaks, illuminating the islands. The wind was thrashing so hard against my windows I was afraid the panes would shatter. I swear I could feel the house moving.

I dragged a spare blanket out of the wardrobe and settled back into bed. It felt as though the ocean had come right inside the house. The glowing green digits on my alarm clock said it was past three o'clock. Great, my first day at a new school and I'd have huge black circles under my eyes.

I slipped out of consciousness and woke to Brie stroking my damp face. I'd disturbed her by sleep talking, which wasn't so unusual. She was used to my nonsensical ramblings, but now she looked at me strangely.

"I'm okay, Brie, go back to bed."

"That was so weird. You were singing a lullaby Mum sang to us when we were little."

I frowned. "What lullaby?"

She looked into the distance, trying to recall the words. "Dark waves, like a blanket," she murmured. "Rock me to sleep in your gentle currents …"

Suddenly I remembered, shuddering. "And never let me go," I whispered.

Chapter Three

My alarm clock went off almost as soon as I'd fallen asleep, and when I opened my eyes I was relieved to see the house was still firmly in place — that we hadn't been swept out to sea. Light burst through the windows, and I wondered if the weather was always this inconsistent.

I stumbled out of bed and over to the wardrobe. I hadn't bothered unpacking much the day before, and now I struggled to find a decent outfit. I was half dressed in black when Brie rushed in.

"Wow, you look tired," she said as she went over to my dressing table. "Can I borrow your makeup?"

I nodded and pulled a tight top over my head. She frowned into the mirror when she saw what I was wearing.

"You're not going to school like that, are you?" she asked.

"I was planning to." I plugged in my straightener and dragged it through my hair, readying myself for her fashion advice.

"It's just all ... black," she said carefully. "The top's good but you should wear these." A pair of faded jeans came hurtling towards me. I didn't have the energy to argue—and I didn't want to make any dark impressions on my first day at school—so I pulled them on. Brie was looking at me jealously.

"What?"

"If I had your legs I'd be wearing my shortest skirt."

"That's not your shortest?" I asked incredulously, and she stuck her tongue out at me before flopping onto my bed and painting her nails a multitude of colours.

☼

We swung into the school car park just as the bell was ringing. A grassy lawn led to several large brick buildings and I noticed another big ash tree near the courtyard, its berries a pool of blood beneath it. I grabbed my bag from the back seat and wound up the windows, feeling slightly envious of Emily, who still lay tucked up in bed.

There were a few curious glances in our direction. At first I think they were eyeing the Mustang but when Brie stepped out, their attention moved to her. A couple of guys stared openly at her and she glided in front of the car, revelling in it. I walked quickly towards the main gates, which made her hurry along behind me.

As we pushed through a pair of double doors, Brie looked at me nervously. We were in a long, dark corridor with high ceilings and old windows. Wads of blackened chewing gum were smeared across the floorboards, and sheets of paper littered the ground, though some still hung from the walls where they'd been carelessly taped. The same photo of a girl smiled from each one.

"No one's seen her for weeks."

We turned to see an ancient caretaker leaning against his mop, and I peeled a flyer off my shoe for a closer look.

Sophie. Sixteen and missing.

A group of white-faced students swept past us, their startlingly green eyes giving us the once over.

"Come on," I muttered to Brie, almost expecting to feel her hand slip into mine as it had so often when we were younger.

We made our way to reception, where a woman with frosted blonde curls spoke patiently to a tall, dark-haired boy. He took a seat and she turned her attention towards me. "Name?"

I always hated this part. "Uh, Sunny West."

She flicked through some papers and then looked at me questioningly. "As in Sunlight West?"

I fixed an indifferent expression on my face as I once again silently cursed my mother for this ridiculous embarrassment. "Yes." I could hear the receptionist's thoughts as clearly as if she had spoken them aloud: *Poor girl, got to wonder about some parents.* I vowed that when I had children, in the very distant, almost unforeseeable future, I would give the naming process a lot of thought.

"Here you go." She handed me some forms and began talking to Brie. I looked around. There were only a few seats in the small room and they were all side by side. I realised I couldn't avoid sitting by the boy, who was now looking at me with raised eyebrows. For a confusing moment I thought I recognised him, but that wasn't likely — I'd only been in town five minutes. I made my way over and scanned the forms with feigned interest.

"Sunlight?" he queried, and the way he said my name was somehow intriguing. I'd heard that the further north you travelled, the stronger the accents became. His was barely noticeable, but when he spoke I thought of red wine, rich and earthy.

I nodded and kept my eyes on the paper.

"Ironic — you brought the good weather with you, huh?"

I didn't know if he was being serious or sarcastically referring to the wild storm last night, but I'd heard enough jokes about my name to last me forever. I looked directly at him in the hope he'd be silenced by my icy stare; instead he flashed me a mischievous grin, revealing perfect, white teeth.

"I'm kidding," he said.

"How original." I gave him the most disdainful smile I could muster, but he looked totally unfazed. I turned away from him and began filling in the forms with dark ink.

☼

I walked into first period late, which was an error on my behalf. I braced myself for the awkward introduction as the teacher ran his finger down the register.

"Sunlight!" he announced enthusiastically, and I cringed at how stupid it sounded. Someone cleared their throat loudly from the back row and as I prepared to unleash my well-practised death stare for the second time that morning, I saw it was the same guy I had spoken to just minutes before.

He looked at me with a hint of sympathy as whispers spread audibly through the class. A blonde girl sitting noticeably close to him giggled and turned towards him, seeking his approval, but he was already gazing uninterestedly out the window.

"Welcome to history, which in fact—" the teacher was now looking down at his watch " —started five minutes ago."

Give me a break.

I mumbled an excuse about getting lost and took the empty seat closest to me. I could see the students looking me up and down, taking in my dark hair and porcelain-pale skin as if maybe it were some kind of joke. At least physically I didn't stand out. None of them were tanned either, and most of them had hair blacker than mine. Again I heard someone mutter about the weather. If my name wasn't weird enough, it was just my luck I didn't even suit it.

☼

At lunch I headed outside and passed tables crammed with laughing students. Although it was still early in the year, everyone knew where they belonged. Part of me wished I was brave enough to introduce myself, to join in with their conversations and private jokes, but I sat alone. The sky was pastel blue with no hint of a cloud, and people lay sprawled on the grass, stretching in the warmth. Brie was on the other side of the green, surrounded by people you'd think had been her friends for years, but that was just her. She was a people person. I uncapped my bottle of Coke.

"Hey!" A girl with bright pink nails and heavy combat boots swung her bag onto the table and slumped down. "It's Sunlight, isn't it?"

I nodded, relieved someone was talking to me, and told her everyone called me Sunny.

"I'm Amber." There was a pause as she took a long swig of her drink. "Everyone thinks you're using a fake name." Her tone was cheerful, and I laughed at her honesty.

"You must have very imaginative parents," she stated decisively.

"Something like that," I agreed.

"But you brought the sun with you and that's a good thing," she smiled. Another stab at my name, but I was beyond caring. Amber flicked her eyes heavenward. "This town doesn't get much sun. Today is perfect."

Oh, great. What I'd been afraid of had just been confirmed. A girl with thick eyeliner dropped down beside us and introduced herself as Lexie. Her eyes were amazingly green, like they'd been injected with liquid emeralds. I was aware of her watching me before turning to stare up at the sun. It was like she'd never seen it. "He must be happy," she said matter-of-factly and began scratching off her nail polish. Little black flakes fell onto her ripped stockings.

"Lexie, please," Amber begged.

"Who's happy?" I asked, confused, but before Lexie could answer, a boy came over to Amber and slipped his arm around her waist.

"Go away, Aaron," she said coolly without turning around.

He looked taken aback. "Come on, Amber, let's just talk about it."

She turned to face him then, smiling sweetly, but even I could sense the danger behind it. "There's nothing to discuss. You cheated on me, remember?"

He flicked his hair away from his face, and I could tell he wasn't used to being rejected.

"What? So you're breaking up with me?"

"Yes. I need a man, not a boy."

His face darkened, and he took a step towards her before stopping abruptly.

"Punky never liked you." She was holding something

39

in her hands but I couldn't see what.

"You're a freak, Amber," he said, backing away.

"That's what they tell me," she replied suggestively.

He walked off looking shaken and she turned to face me. "Sorry about that." She tipped a black-and-white rat onto the table. "Sunny, meet Punky, the coolest rodent to ever walk the earth. You want to hold him?"

I shook my head.

"Go on," and before I could protest, the rat had run across the table where it sat staring at me. Lexie continued to watch me as I stroked Punky with one finger.

"It's okay, he's very friendly," Amber told me, smiling.

A skinny guy from the next table wrinkled his nose in distaste.

"That thing is disgusting. He shouldn't be here."

She stuck up her middle finger at him and focused her attention back on me. "So, you want a rundown on life in the bay?"

Chapter Four

I stood at the lounge window, facing out to sea. For a split second I wondered what it would be like to dive beneath the surface and feel the cool water against my skin. Goose bumps sprang up along my arms and I rubbed them away.

There was a rusty old fishing boat anchored near one of the islands. Great red stains ran down the sides, and I could see men hauling up their nets from the turquoise blue. Again I was pulled back to my first memory of the sea, reliving the fear I'd felt when I couldn't touch the sand beneath my feet, the crushing weight of the saltwater drowning me.

The back door swung open and Mum came in loaded up with groceries.

"How was school?" she asked excitedly, dumping bags on the kitchen counter and flicking on lights.

"Great!" Brie smiled. "I've joined SAN and the debating team."

"And what exactly is SAN?" Mum asked.

"Save Animals Now," she declared, pulling out a thick

wad of forms from her bag.

Their conversation soon faded into the background, and I stared back out over the cold waves. Seagulls were busy circling the boat, occasionally landing to rest on the rails. I had an unsettling feeling that wouldn't go away.

"Sunny?"

I spun around and they were both staring at me. Mum had a slightly worried look on her face.

"Huh?"

She came to stand behind me and rested her hands on my shoulders. "Are you okay?"

"I'm fine," I lied, glancing once more out the window and then heading for the stairs. "I have heaps of homework."

Upstairs I finished unpacking. I hung up all my clothes and to my dismay discovered Brie was right—nearly all my clothes were black. Maybe I would have to go shopping.

I tacked up my posters and put Hercules in a shady spot on the windowsill. My room was cute. The ceiling sloped almost to the floor on one side, and white lacy curtains hung at the windows. I stood my guitar in a corner and went back to staring at the ocean. The wind was tracing delicate patterns across the surface, and I suddenly shivered. Would I ever get used to this place?

I grabbed my car keys off the dressing table and headed back down the stairs. Mum and Brie were now resting on the verandah, sipping iced lemonade and admiring the bay. To them, this was paradise.

"I'm just going for coffee," I called, stepping outside and hoping Brie wouldn't decide she wanted to come.

I drove through badly set out streets until I reached the main road and then turned north out of town. The road was pitted from years of rain and it went inland for a while before snaking back towards the coast. My mind soon went blank. Eventually I came to a lookout and pulled into a little car park that was scattered with cigarettes and broken glass. As grungy as the place was, the view was breathtaking. I got out of the car, my shoes crunching against the gravel, and made my way to the graffiti-scarred barrier.

Wind gusted in, the salt strong in my nose, and I felt a strange sort of ache right inside my bones. How was it that this view felt so familiar to me? I fixed my gaze on the fine line that separated the sea from the sky. What would have happened if I'd never been found that day? How long would my tiny body have floated on those lonesome currents? It seemed about the only thing I could think about lately.

The sun had turned the ocean pink and sunk to the west when I finally went back to my car. I flicked the heater on high as I drove the winding road home. Dusk was setting in quickly, and I was completely zoned out when I caught movement on the side of the road. As I got closer I saw it was somebody hitchhiking, and was just thinking what a crazy time it was to be trying to get a ride when I realised it was a girl. All Mum's spiels about crazy murderers raced through my head, but I pulled over anyway.

She turned, shielding her eyes against my lights, and walked cautiously towards the passenger door. Bright pink nails rested on my half-open window, and in her other hand she held a helmet plastered with stickers.

I recognised those nails straight away. "Amber?"

I heard a sigh of relief. "I'm so glad it's you!" she said happily, opening the door and climbing in. Her heavy boots had dry clay up the sides and she looked freezing.

"What are you doing way out here?" I asked, pulling back onto the road.

"My scooter broke down. I'm so stupid—that's the second time I've run it out of petrol this month." She tore off a bit of thumbnail with her teeth and looked over to me. "Began to wonder if I'd be walking all night. There hasn't been another car go past in over an hour. What are you doing up here?"

"Just felt like getting to know the place."

She nodded. We were quiet for a moment and she held her hands against the heater vents.

"So, what does Sunny listen to?" she asked casually, turning up the stereo. Her eyes lit up at the sound of the Rolling Stones and she bopped her head along to the beat.

"You want to go and get some petrol for your bike?" I

asked.

"Don't worry about it. I can get Dad to drive me out tomorrow."

"Honestly, I don't mind." I needed at least one friend in this new place, and I still didn't feel like going home.

☼

It was late when I turned onto our street. All the neighbours' houses were dark, and I filled their driveways with light. A couple of deathly pale teenagers on the other side of the road obviously hadn't been expecting anyone to come past. They were holding baseball bats, and my lights reflected off shattered glass at their feet. By the time I'd parked the car they'd taken off.

I walked over to where I'd seen them standing and peered down the street at the row of smashed path lights. Some were blinking feebly but most were too damaged. They lay dented and deformed on the asphalt.

I looked up at the quiet houses, wondering how it was possible none of the neighbours had heard.

☼

When I got up the next morning, Mum was sitting in the lounge with her back pressed against warm glass. It was early—I'd woken from strange dreams and hadn't been able to get back to sleep. There had been a girl. I could still

45

see her swimming for the rocks, her skin wet and splattered with moonlight. What a weird dream.

I poured myself a coffee and sat beside Mum. Behind her the sea was blue and still, like an endless sheet of glass; another perfect day.

She leaned her head back against the window and rubbed her eyes. "I didn't hear you come in last night," she said sleepily.

"It was pretty late," I admitted and she yawned. I could tell it was too early for her to commit to giving a lecture.

"You didn't hear the path lights getting vandalised, did you?" I asked, suddenly remembering, and she shook her head.

"Come and look at this," I said, pulling her to her feet.

We surveyed the damage from our doorstep.

"I wonder if anyone's rung the police," Mum said as I finished my last sip of coffee. She wandered down to the letterbox, and I headed inside. I really could have gone another coffee but didn't have time.

"Brie, are you nearly ready?" I called up the stairs.

She flounced down in a brightly coloured dress and twirled on the spot. "Ready," she sang.

I threw a pile of books onto the back seat of my car and watched as our neighbours opened their curtains and got their newspapers off the lawns. They cast their eyes briefly over the ruined lights, but not one of them looked perturbed. I raised my eyebrows in surprise. Surely they weren't used to this kind of destruction? Brie must have been thinking the same thing.

"Won't be a sec," she said before jogging over to a woman who was trimming something in her garden. Her footsteps made the elderly lady look up, and I watched as she put a hand to her eyes, protecting them from the brightness.

"Hey, my name's Brie. I live just across the street."

They looked to where my Mustang sat idling in the driveway.

"Yes, I met your mother last week. Works at the hospital."

Brie smiled at her, then looked at the shards of glass that had fallen onto her lawn. "Someone smashed up these lights real bad, didn't they?"

Our neighbour frowned and turned back to the vine that was strangling her roses. Her pruning shears made loud slicing noises in the quiet morning air.

Brie tried again. "My sister saw them doing it when she came in late. There were two of them. Didn't you hear anything?"

"No. The waves were loud last night."

Amber caught up to me in the corridor, out of breath and with her bootlaces undone. They were still covered in clay from her hike the night before and she bent down to tie them up. She wore her blonde hair in teased pigtails, and a big pink bow was clipped into her fringe.

Lexie hovered at her side like a shadow, dressed in black. "Isn't the weather strange?" she said slowly, looking up at the sunlight filtering through high windows.

Amber ignored her and told us we were going to be late. I hadn't even heard the bell—I'd been too distracted staring at a poster of the missing girl. I wondered if something terrible had happened to her or if she'd just run away.

"Where are we going?" I asked as Amber pulled me outside and down a long, covered walkway.

"PE." She pulled a face as if she too would rather be stuck in any other subject.

I stopped dead in my tracks, rummaging wildly through my bag for a timetable, and the person behind us almost crashed into me.

"Sorry," I gasped. How could I have over looked this? PE held the terrible possibility of swimming.

"I can't take this subject," I stuttered.

Lexie gave me a weird look. "Why not?"

"I don't swim. Ever. I'll have to change classes," I told her, turning around and heading for the main office.

"It's compulsory." Amber reached for my sleeve and steered me towards the fields. "None of us love it but it's not so bad."

It was bad.

The teacher marched us over to a massive swimming pool that glinted in the morning sun. "Changing rooms," he bellowed, and when I didn't move he pointed to where a couple of squat concrete buildings sat. I stood rooted to the spot. "Is there a problem, miss?"

"Uh, I don't have my gear today. I didn't know we'd be swimming," I said, focusing my attention on him. He had his hair cut military style, and judging by the look he was giving me, I knew I had a problem. It would not be so easy to get out of swimming here.

"Make the most of this weather," a boy said before diving into the pool.

"But don't get used to it," someone else added.

The teacher held my gaze and pointed to a wooden box beside the pool. "Plenty of old swimsuits in there."

I must have looked horrified because he let out a great, booming laugh and told me he'd let me off this one time but that was it. Next time I was to bring my gear or I'd be writing lines.

☼

All day I heard people commenting on the weather. Were they seriously that sun-deprived? As I navigated the crowded corridor between classes, I caught snippets of conversation I didn't understand.

"I wonder why the sun's shining," a dark-haired girl said to her friends. She dropped her voice and bent closer to the pale group huddled around her. "There's only one thing it could mean, right?"

Chapter Five

I sat at one of the scarred wooden tables in the library and flicked my eyes down the list of books the history teacher had given us. I frowned, sure I would never get around to reading them all, but stood up and began searching the shelves anyway. By the time I'd found the recommended texts, a daunting pile of books teetered on my table. Reluctantly, I started drafting an essay.

Out of nowhere a lithe figure appeared and slipped into the seat opposite me. I was the only one in the room besides the librarian, which left at least fifty other seats available. I sighed as I looked up.

He had dark hair, messy like he'd just rolled out of bed, and his eyes were such an intense blue it took a moment to realise I was holding my breath. It was the guy from reception that first day, and I prepared myself for some clever remark about the weather.

"Hey, new girl, how do you like the bay so far?" His voice was slow, sexy—and once again I wondered where I'd seen him before.

"It's beautiful and terrible," I answered, shocked at my honesty and the way he now looked at me.

"How so?"

"I don't like the ocean."

I could tell this interested him but he didn't push it. Perhaps he saw the fear that danced in my eyes at the mere mention of it. He leaned forward across the table, so close I could feel every exhale of his breath.

I had the strangest sensation that if we were any closer I might faint. "What are you doing?" I demanded shakily.

He scanned the room as if to make sure no one was around, and I found myself doing the same. I flinched when his fingertips grazed my cheek and again as he lifted a handful of curls away from my ear. "Just thanking you for the sunlight," he whispered.

My hair fell back into place, slipping over my shoulders and catching the last of the afternoon light. I was speechless, hardly noticing he'd made yet another crack at my name, and he rose from the table, chuckling — at what I wasn't exactly sure. As I watched his retreating back, I felt the slightest of shivers run through me.

☼

I left the library not long after he did. To say he'd distracted me would have been an understatement. He reminded me of heartache and everything I should stay away from.

A cold wind stung my face and I walked quickly to my car, which was on the far side of the car park. The smell of him seemed to linger in the air around me — a combination of cinnamon and the cherry-sweet scent of dried tobacco. I searched through my bag for my keys and in the end had to empty the contents onto the ground to extract them from under the mountain of books.

A red sports car was parked close to mine and it wasn't until I heard someone coughing that I realised it was occupied. The driver's door flung open. Some students I recognised from PE stumbled out, red-eyed and giggly. I was engulfed in a cloud of smoke, and the pungent smell of marijuana hit me as I unlocked my car. One of the girls had long blonde hair and eyes like a cat. She turned to stare at me, and I knew I was looking at the high school's queen bee.

"You're that girl with the weird name," she declared.

Hating her already, I raised my eyebrows and said nothing.

"Midnight or Sunset — what is it again?" she asked. Her friends were in hysterics behind her, and she was smirking at me.

"It's Sunny." I chucked my bag onto the back seat and drove home, my mind back on the history essay.

As I swung into the driveway it was getting dark. Usually

the path lights would have been glowing by now, but tonight our house blended into a puddle of darkness. Brie was staying at school late with the debating team, and Mum had left a message on my phone saying she was tied up in a meeting. I briefly wondered where Emily was as I unlocked the door, but she wasn't much company these days anyway.

A quiet house would be good, I thought, as I turned on lights and settled at the counter. Mum had left a stack of menus and a note saying she would pick up takeaways, but I wasn't hungry. I laid the essay guidelines in front of me and began flicking through history books for inspiration.

Half an hour later the tiny black words were swimming on the page, and I still hadn't written anything. My blank sheet stared back at me expectantly. I sighed, frustrated. I used to be able to churn essays out in under an hour—actually enjoying the challenge—but now I rubbed my tired eyes and yawned. It wasn't like me to be so unfocused.

Outside, the gentle swell of a high tide lapped rhythmically. The combination of reading a complex article and listening to the waves must have lulled me to sleep because within minutes I was slumped at the counter, dreaming of her again.

It was really late or really early—I couldn't tell. The sea and sky were soaked in moonlight, and the dreams were so similar I was already searching for her in the darkness.

Then there she was, just beneath the surface—swimming towards the silvery skin of the ocean, her strokes lazy and slow.

Something about this girl was very familiar, and not just because I'd dreamt of her before. She slipped up through the surface into brisk night air. Was it the colour of her hair? The curve of her naked body in the moonlight? Tilting her face to the radiant moon, she became completely captivated. It was impossible to make out her features, no matter how hard I tried.

She turned slowly and I held my breath, straining to catch a glimpse of her face, but then the back door was thrown open and I jerked my head off the counter.

My heart beat wildly in my chest and I struggled to look calm as Mum, Brie and Emily emerged in the kitchen. They were all laughing loudly and placing steaming containers of food on the counter. The smell of sweet and sour filled the room.

"Hey, Sunny!" Mum trilled.

"You're pale," Emily said, pushing a plate of noodles in front of me. She was shovelling rice into her mouth, which was a huge change from her usual picking and missed meals.

Their laughter ebbed around me, and my heart settled, but I couldn't forget the girl in the sea.

☼

Friday afternoon I made the last stop to my locker, relieved to be going home. People had already gotten over the fact that I had the weirdest name of all time, and now I was just Sunny. Through one of the windows I could see Brie waiting for me. She was leaning on the bonnet of my car, chatting to a couple of attentive guys.

I pulled a heavy folder from my locker, at the same time managing to create a landslide of papers and all the other junk that had accumulated over an impossibly short space of time. Compared to my last locker, this one was nightmarish.

The contents spilled loudly to the floor, echoing down the deserted corridor and rolling in every direction. Glad no one could see me, I dropped to my knees.

As I rounded up the last of my pens, I was aware of a tall figure standing over me. I stood up, my face coming within centimetres of his, and swayed slightly. Maybe I'd got up too fast. A familiar scent of cinnamon lingered on his skin, and I took a big step backwards.

"That is one scary locker."

"Yeah." I'd meant to say something much more sarcastic, but right at that moment the sun had hit his face and the blue in his eyes incandesced. It was like looking at the ocean — and just as disturbing, because the stirring I felt within me was not what I wanted. He'd been in my dreams last night, I was sure of it. Blushing, I shoved everything to the back of my locker, and in the process dropped my keys.

"Are you okay?" he asked, sweeping them off the floor.

"Yeah, I'm just tired." I watched as he turned my car key in his callused hands, and I tried not to imagine how they'd feel against my skin. I flushed even deeper. The sooner I left the better.

"Of course!" he exclaimed as though something incredible had happened in the last two seconds. "You're the girl with the Mustang."

Wasn't this already common knowledge? I thought everyone knew that the girl with the weird name drove a weird car.

"When you walked into reception on Monday I knew I'd seen you before," he mused. I looked up at him. So I hadn't been imagining it?

"I talked to you that day at the petrol station." He was looking at me intently, and I was suddenly breathless.

Yes, I'd seen him at the garage and he'd told me he hoped I liked the rain. How had I not remembered those eyes? I realised I was supposed to say something. "Oh, yeah."

Brie was there now, standing at the doorway and staring at me in disbelief. I had forgotten all about her. "Uh, I'd better go," I said hurriedly. It was far too hot inside. I went to leave and cursed inwardly when I remembered he still had my keys. He was grinning when I turned around. I could feel my stomach lining beginning to burn and an obvious heat was creeping up my neck.

He dropped them into my outstretched hand. "See you

later, Sunny."

Brie, who had been trying to make eye contact with me the entire time, started up as soon as we rounded the corner. "That guy from the garage is gorgeous!"

"He's okay."

She almost choked. "Don't play cool with me. I saw how you looked at him!"

I shrugged as I unlocked the car, even though all I could really do was wonder about him.

Chapter Six

It was Brie's screams that woke us. Her desperate cries filled the early morning with dread and caused my stomach to knot up in fear.

I was out of bed before I'd even woken properly, barefoot and running. She wasn't in the house, so where was she? I fumbled with the back door, my heart hammering so hard I thought it might explode, and rushed along the path that led to the beach. I couldn't hear her at all now, which was almost worse. Was she badly hurt? Had someone taken her? Emily was close behind me but I didn't wait for her.

"Brie?" My voice shook terribly.

There she was, standing motionless at the water's edge, seemingly unharmed. The sand was cold and a bitter wind blew off the sea.

"What's wrong?" I gasped as I turned her roughly to face me. She was whiter than death, and her body trembled beneath my hands.

Emily appeared, breathless at my side, and swore softly.

"Look," she murmured.

I followed her gaze and wished I hadn't. A body was drifting in the shallows at our feet, and for a moment I couldn't move. Whoever it was, she'd been dead a while. Long brown hair concealed half her face and where her eyes should have been there were only empty sockets. Bruises, dark and angry, stood out against her pale wrists, and I pulled Brie further up the beach. She seemed unable to look away so I covered her unblinking eyes with my hand.

By the time Mum reached us, Emily was already talking into her phone.

"I need to report a body," she said bravely, and for once I appreciated her being there.

☼

My heart was still pounding when we headed for home. I took my time, knowing I'd feel restless the minute I got indoors. What a way to start the weekend. I turned my face away from the wind and watched as the first police car arrived, then the second and third. The beach would be cordoned off from the public soon.

A couple of men in uniform strode across the shells towards me. Sand flew from their boots and it looked like they were arguing. When they passed me it was in silence. One appeared more worried than the other, so much so that I could almost feel the anxiety alive inside him. He had troubled green eyes and when I turned he was running his hands through thinning grey hair. I'd always thought of cops as calm and grounded, capable of handling anything, but he looked wrecked. They started talking again, in low urgent voices, and I stopped to listen.

"Another body?" I heard the other man whisper furiously. "Seriously, McLeod—"

"That was almost a year ago!" the nervous one called McLeod interrupted. "This is probably a tourist—someone who was passing through and didn't know the currents. It won't be like last time." He didn't sound sure but rather desperately hopeful. Their voices soon faded into the distance.

The grassy banks became crowded with curious locals, and from my bedroom I watched McLeod, who in turn watched a group of pale teens up above the high-tide mark.

I knew they wouldn't be out of there until at least midday, and all Brie seemed capable of doing was following me around the house.

"I wonder who that poor girl is," she kept saying, though no doubt we'd find out soon enough.

"Let's go for a drive," I told her.

She jumped at the offer. But when I started my car, the engine whined loudly and instead we had to drive straight to the workshop that was tacked on to the petrol station. At least I'd gotten her out of the house. While she got us cheap coffee from the machine inside, an older guy tried to explain to me what was wrong with my car. It was way beyond my limited car knowledge, and I was distracted. I found myself carefully scanning the premises for any sign of the dark-haired boy.

Reminding myself I didn't actually want a boyfriend, I made a hasty exit and we hitched a ride back into town. A guy was the last thing I needed, and I told myself this over and over as we wandered past rows of unkempt mansions.

I peered into one of the yards. It was so neglected you wouldn't think anyone actually lived there. Weeds crept out onto the footpath, and a forlorn-looking doll lay face down in the mud. I moved on, keeping my eyes straight ahead, trying not to imagine anyone staring down at me from those horrible multi-pane windows.

Brie started talking again which meant she was feeling better, so we stopped at a café for breakfast.

I picked up the Mustang that afternoon and got in line to pay a small fortune for a stupid car part. The shop was dingy and cluttered—you could tell women didn't work there. I sifted lazily through an assortment of chocolates but when I heard his voice I looked up. He was packing items haphazardly into a box for someone and humming along to a tune on the radio.

To my embarrassment he looked up too, and his eyes held mine. They were so captivating—such a translucent blue—they trapped me like a butterfly in a jar. The world slid sideways just a fraction.

"Excuse me," a rough voice interrupted.

Our gaze broke and the feeling shattered. I could almost see little pieces of intensity shimmering on the floor around me. I turned slowly to face the bored-looking guy who was indicating he was free to serve me. When I told him which car was mine he handed me the bill with grubby fingers.

"Cash or card?" he droned.

The boy was now helping another customer. I'm sure I saw the trace of a smile lingering on his face as he flicked his eyes up to meet mine for another fleeting second. It felt as though the oxygen in the little shop was being quickly depleted.

I wrenched my attention back to who was serving me. "Huh?"

"How would you like to pay?" he demanded.

I thrust some notes across the counter and he rolled his eyes. As I left the shop, I thought about saying something to the boy from school, but he was still busy; besides, I didn't know what I would say.

He's just some guy you don't need, I told myself.

As I drove hurriedly away from the petrol station, I realised I didn't even know his name.

62

☼

The light was fading when I got home, and the first thing I noticed was the leafy branch of ash nailed to our back door.

I ran my fingers over the silver bark, bewildered.

"Who put this here?" I asked Mum.

"The neighbours brought it round," she said, smiling as if it were a normal gesture. "It's said to ward off evil and protect you from drowning. Why are you looking so shocked, Sunny? It's harmless."

"What are these people afraid of?"

She didn't understand what I meant, and I couldn't explain the little comments I'd heard uttered in the school corridors or the general feeling I got from this place.

I went upstairs and flopped down near the window. The tide had come in and gone all the way out again since Brie's morbid discovery. Everything had been washed clean by the waves, except for our memories. That body was something we could never un-see.

There were already rumours it might have been Sophie, the missing girl from our school, but that idea was just too horrible to think about. I'd also heard someone say the girl could have fallen off a boat. Were we the only ones who had seen the discolouration of her wrists? As if she'd been restrained?

No amount of ash branches could save you from that.

The group of pale teenagers stayed long after everyone

else had left. I wondered if they'd known Sophie and believed it was her.

Wind howled through the bay, and I pulled my window shut before slipping into bed. My sisters and I dreamt about the un-named girl that night—of her white, featureless face, and how the ocean had finally pushed her to shore.

☼

By midweek everyone knew. It seemed the only thing my classmates could talk about. I found it hard to focus during our lectures, struggling to piece together paragraphs for complicated essays. I was thankful when we finally got to Friday, last period.

"Can one of you please describe how Romeo felt when he was forbidden to see Juliet?" The English teacher was looking impatient and I didn't blame her. All around her the students were busy whispering about the dead girl, and I just hoped they didn't learn it was Brie who'd found her.

Lexie was sitting next to me. She had ripped a page from her book, torn it into tiny little pieces and was scattering them on the floor.

"Jake," the teacher said abruptly, but no one answered. "Fraser!" she hollered, and my heart missed a beat as the guy from the petrol station finally stirred.

Jake Fraser. His name bounced back and forth in my

mind. I turned slightly, watching him lift his dark head off the desk as he simultaneously removed earphones and hit a button on his iPod. He did it with such precision I think I was the only one who noticed.

"Read me what you've done," she repeated.

For homework we were supposed to have written a diary entry detailing Romeo's intense suffering. I hadn't done mine, mainly due to lack of motivation. Jake's face was expressionless, void from all emotion, but what he said sent little ripples through my body.

"You know not of the hell that's danced through my head, of the rage and fire like hate and desire," he read on and I studied his lips, full and soft as they formed the exquisite words.

Words that bypassed my brain and descended straight to my heart. He looked at me swiftly, as if he knew I'd been staring.

"I will tear down the stars if I have to," he finished, and I hurriedly fixed my stare on the floor.

A couple of guys wearing death-metal shirts snickered quietly from the back row, but every girl in the room had stopped talking and turned to face him. The blonde who had tried to insult me in the car park last week was fluttering her eyelashes and literally holding her hand to her chest. I noticed he wasn't paying attention to any of them. When I looked closely I swore he was trying not to smile, but maybe that was how he always looked.

The bell rang to end the lesson and I headed for my

locker, wondering if Jake was some kind of lost soul. He didn't come across as the type who would spout dark poetry. I entered my code and waited for the door to click open. It remained tightly shut. Great. I put in the numbers again but still nothing happened. I pounded it with my fist. Maybe it was just my luck to have difficult lockers.

"Trying to break into my locker?"

I spun around and Jake was standing there with a bemused smile on his face. He was taller than I remembered, and I could see part of a tattoo where his sleeve was riding up. I struggled to make out what it could have been. A word maybe …

He stepped forward, punched in his code, and the door swung open to reveal an almost empty space. It dawned on me that my locker must have been the one directly beside his. Colour rushed to my face. Typical. This was like a bad high school movie.

"Sorry," I muttered, and he laughed as I opened my locker and shoved in my books. There was an awkward silence while I spent too long getting out folders and looking for non-existent papers. He was standing calmly beside me, watching.

I took a deep breath. "So, that was pretty intense — what you said in English." That made him laugh again, and he nodded his head towards the iPod sticking out of his pocket.

"You mean they were lyrics?" I asked and he nodded.

I should have known he wasn't actually into

Shakespeare. Our eyes met and he held my gaze, unfazed by my obvious discomfort. When I turned back to my locker he smiled like he'd come to some conclusion about me. It was irritating because he knew nothing about me. I rummaged through another pile of papers.

"How's your car going?" He was smiling again.

"Fine." I felt myself trying not to cringe as I remembered back to the petrol station. Had he felt even a fraction of what I had?

This was ridiculous. I slammed my door shut, annoyed, and watched from the corner of my eye as he put his folder in his bag. I could see his arms defined through the thin shirt he was wearing—muscled, as though he was used to working.

He'd opened his mouth to say something when an arm choked with bracelets snaked around his waist. "Jake!"

He turned quickly and I had a violent image of shoving the blonde girl hard against the lockers. She was perfect. Thin, fake-tanned and wearing the tightest jeans I'd ever seen.

"That was beautiful, what you read out." Her lips were redder than spilt blood, and I watched as she trailed her finger up and down his arm.

"Thanks." He nodded but his face was closed, guarded.

She suddenly turned her attention towards me as if she had only just noticed the two of them weren't alone. Her eyes swept over me and a look of revulsion flickered across her features for just a second. "Who's your friend?"

she asked sweetly, even though she already knew.

"This is Sunny." He was looking increasingly uncomfortable.

She nodded and looked me up and down again. Did she really think I was a threat? I could see everything ticking over in her mind.

She turned back to Jake and asked, "Do you think that girl on the beach was Sophie?"

The look he gave her was hard to place. For a moment I was sure it was fury that blazed in his eyes and she seemed to revel in it.

"I have no idea," he said, sounding frustrated.

"Poor thing," she said casually, but I could tell she didn't really care. "It hasn't even been a year since Claire died."

"Sunny!"

I spun around. Amber was walking towards me with Lexie in tow, eyeing the situation suspiciously. "There's a band playing down at the beach. You want to check them out?"

I nodded, glad for an excuse to leave.

"Taylor Santorini," she explained once we were out of earshot, "is the most obnoxious person to ever grace this high school."

The band was average but we stayed for the atmosphere.

They belted out some three-chord punk rock songs while the greasy smell of fast food hovered thick in the air.

Amber asked me what Taylor had been saying.

"She was talking about Sophie."

"That'd be right. Jake's dad is a cop and Taylor's is the detective."

"Who's Claire?" I asked.

"She was another student. Crashed her car off some cliffs up north last year — didn't stand a chance in that little white thing she drove."

"That's terrible," I said, and she nodded.

Lexie was sidetracked, probably not even hearing the cymbals crashing just metres from her. She was absorbed in a thick book and when I asked her about it she looked up confused, as though she may have forgotten where she was.

"What are you reading?" I asked again, and for the first time since we'd met, her expression of constant boredom changed to excitement.

"Don't get her started," Amber sighed, but Lexie ignored her.

"It's about the curse, and this author has put a totally different spin on it. It's fascinating!"

"What curse?" I asked.

"It's rubbish, Sunny," Amber assured me.

"How can you say that?" Lexie demanded and Amber groaned. I could tell they had disagreed about this many times before.

"It's our history, Amber!" Lexie spat. "And the sooner everyone accepts it the better off we'll all be."

"Cursed by what?" I tried again but Lexie was now glaring out to sea. It began to rain, big wet drops, and we had to make a run for it.

☼

I woke up in the middle of the night but not from strange dreams this time. It was windy outside, and trees in the yard were creaking and swaying, scratching at the windows and side of the house.

I couldn't get back to sleep. My room was full of moonlight, and the shadows changed ordinary objects into twisted things of the night.

I felt twitchy. Grabbing my keys, I slipped quietly out the window and into the flowering tree. As I lowered myself into the yard and tiptoed to the Mustang, I thought about how perfect my escape route was.

A cool breeze pulled at my hair and clothes. With the car out of gear, I rolled it to the end of our driveway before starting it. The streets were quiet and empty. For all I knew I could have been the only person awake in the whole town. It was an invigorating thought.

Winding down my window, I breathed in deeply. I wouldn't stay out long—just until I'd had my little fix of free will. The wind rushed through my car but it also carried in something else. I could hear people, riled up and angry.

I pulled over and opened my door, listening. Gusts of wind tugged the voices in different directions, making it hard to work out where they were coming from. After grabbing a jacket from the back seat, I locked the car and crossed the road. Above me the moon was bright and almost full.

I walked quietly, keeping to the shadows while following the voices. Sliding between buildings crammed close together, I rounded a corner and almost walked straight into the uproar. I quickly drew back and crouched down behind a wheelie bin.

A group of six teenagers circled an expensive car beneath a streetlamp. One boy, wearing heavy boots, was crouched on the roof of it, and a girl with sleek black hair was draped across the bonnet, smoking.

"Oh, feel that moonlight," she purred.

I didn't know her name but I'd seen her at school—we were in the same biology class. A tall guy I also recognised took a drag from her cigarette before kissing her deeply. The one on the roof laughed and stood up. He leapt high in the air and came crashing back down, causing the car to shudder and the couple on the bonnet to slide off.

"Screw you, Seth." The girl scowled as she picked herself up.

"I'd love you to, Britta, but you already know that," he responded, jumping onto the road. She flew at him, and the light at that angle set her green eyes glowing. Her nails slashed across his face and she pinned him against the car.

Her boyfriend intervened, looking amused. "Here, beautiful, you can go first." He closed her fingers over the smooth handle of a baseball bat. "Put that anger I love so much to good use."

She swung it as hard as she could into the driver's door, missing Seth by a couple of centimetres. They all howled with laughter as they set about dismantling someone's car in full view of the street.

I stayed until they eventually got bored and left. From my hiding spot I could see the car's irreparable panels and the broken glass that now littered the road. I was stiff from the cold and about to leave when headlights flooded the street. A police car made its way slowly towards me, and I recognised the cop, McLeod, from the beach. I was shocked when he drove past the ruined Mercedes, as if his colourful green eyes had seen nothing at all.

Chapter Seven

Even though I'd only had a few hours' sleep, I woke early with the dark-haired girl on my mind. She'd swum in and out of my dreams for the second half of the night, slipping like a shadow through the moon-sprinkled sea. She moved with such fluidity that it seemed she were part of the ocean, and the moonlight caressed her skin as if they were old friends. Yet I still hadn't been able to make out her face.

I stood up, rubbed the clouds from my eyes and felt a surge of adrenaline as I thought back to my midnight outing. They were never usually that eventful. It would probably be about now that someone was walking to their car only to discover it had been badly vandalised by a pack of delinquents. Why hadn't that cop done anything?

I opened my curtains to a cloudless sky before tiptoeing downstairs. I loved Saturdays and was glad to have the day to myself rather than spend it in a classroom.

Letting the door close softly behind me, I headed down the narrow concrete path that ran alongside our house. I heard it before I saw it, the wind whispering over the surface of the water, chattering as though it were telling a million secrets. The ocean was gentle and calm all the way out to the horizon, broken only by the little islands that looked like they could have been floating.

The tide was coming in lazily. It would swill in higher and higher, then slowly ooze out, leaving little trails of bubbles on the beach. I crouched down and pressed my fingers to the cold sand. The sun hadn't risen yet and the salt clung to my skin. I let a handful of sand slip out between my fingers, watching it cascade into piles at my feet, and as I did this over and over I felt something stir within me. It was just the slightest of shifts, but before I could embrace it fear caught up with me.

I tried hard not to remember but it was no good. I was being pulled out, sucked under, the waves carrying me far from the safety of the beach. I couldn't breathe, water was filling my lungs.

Stop it, Sunny, but I couldn't. I gasped as though the sea really had poured into me, turned my back on the ocean and ran.

I stumbled to the end of our street and along the footpath that would take me around the block. Someone had repaired the path lights. As my shoes pounded against the concrete, I shut out the ocean and instead thought about Jake, but that held little comfort. It made my heart ache a little to know I'd never trust a guy — worse still that someone as beautiful as him actually existed and wanted to talk to me.

I ran faster as though maybe I could run away from all of it.

☼

Hours later, Amber arrived at our house unannounced and said we were going shopping. I'd mentioned to her earlier in the week I needed clothes, and she'd promised to show me around town.

I had some money saved up from a heap of babysitting I'd done last summer. Maybe I'd buy something that would demand Jake's attention.

"You know that girl Brie found?" she asked as I laced up my boots. "It was Sophie Hodgson."

The girl from the poster.

"Apparently it's being treated as a homicide. Do you know how messed up that is? I spoke to her the week before she disappeared." Amber looked miserable as she passed me a spare helmet.

"They'll catch whoever did it," I said, climbing onto the back of her scooter. It was hardly big enough for two people but we weren't going far and she seemed to like the strange looks people gave us.

She drove recklessly and at one point we almost collided with a parked car. I was holding on tight, hoping this wouldn't be the end of my short life, but she was as calm as anything, chatting about this and that and what she wanted to do in town. My legs were still trembling as we walked around the shops.

The pavements were crowded for once. Families swarmed through the shopping centre, and dogs lazed in the sunshine. Amber steered me towards a little shop that I wouldn't have seen at all if she hadn't pointed it out to me. It was dark inside and smelled musty, as though it had been shut up a long time. A crooked sign above the counter read "Pre-loved".

Amber looked as if she'd suddenly entered paradise. "Vintage," she sighed blissfully.

I wandered between the racks while she selected armloads of clothes. She'd already found a pair of red boots that were ultra tacky and was clutching them to her as if they were worth a fortune.

☼

I soon learned from Amber that she was all about two things. One, she didn't like liars, and two, if she wasn't teetering from a dangerous height or going two hundred kilometres an hour then there wasn't any point getting out of bed in the morning. She had "Sleeping is for dead people" etched across her diary in big black letters.

We were a strange pair, and although she did have other friends, she seemed to have taken a liking to me of all people. She was wild and funny and had a tattoo of a ladybird on her ankle. I got the rundown on local hangouts, places not to go in the weekends, and basically the history of every single student in our year.

"What about Jake and Taylor?" It bothered me how compelled I felt to ask, and I hoped I'd sounded nonchalant.

She rolled her eyes, oblivious to my motive.

"Couple question of the decade!" she declared between huge gulps of coffee.

"What do you mean?"

"No one's sure exactly what went on last year but there were a lot of rumours. Jake went all dark for a while but he seems okay now." She swilled the remains of her coffee round and round her cup.

"Are they together?" I asked, and when she shrugged I felt unhappy — and then frustrated that I cared so much.

"Who would know? They've been on and off since kindergarten. I think their families have been friends for ages." She changed the subject. "It's a full moon tonight."

I thought that was just about the weirdest thing she could have said.

"So?"

"I figured I should warn you. Tonight you'll witness human insanity at its worst."

I stared at her curiously. "Sounds fascinating."

"A lot of the locals still believe in the old stories." She looked pained just talking about it.

"Old stories? You mean what Lexie talks about?"

Amber nodded. "She comes from one of the families

who've been here forever."

"What do they do?"

"Every full moon they pay tribute to a sea god," she sighed.

"You're being serious?"

"Deadly. They gather on the beach at dusk."

☼

I knew I had to start my essay, but all I could think about was what Amber had told me earlier. Was there really a group of people about to meet under the full moon?

Determined not to think about it now, I grabbed a stack of books off the desk and settled onto my bed. But before I'd even started I heard footsteps on the landing, and Brie appeared in my doorway.

"Have you heard the stories about this place?" she asked breathlessly.

I shook my head. "Not really."

She threw herself down beside me, eyes sparkling, clearly unaware that I was trying to concentrate. "Apparently this town is cursed," she whispered.

"They actually believe that?" I asked, and she nodded.

"Not a month goes by when they don't stand beneath the moon. They want the rain to stop. A boy in my class was telling me he's done it his whole life!" She was being dramatic.

I stared at her. "So this sea god—" I felt ridiculous just

saying it " — why would he curse a little town like this?"

She shrugged.

"Crazy." It was the only word for it.

I slipped my essay inside the textbook and flipped it shut. It had been a miserable attempt and wouldn't be in on time. My mind was fuzzy, as if someone had blown smoke through my brain. When the light began to fade I made my way downstairs.

"Coming to see what these freaks do?" Emily asked as she eased open the French doors and stepped onto the verandah. Brie followed closely behind her.

I shook my head and instead walked out onto the jetty, watching my sisters make their way along the beach. I sat down, feet hanging over the edge, my toes not quite reaching the black water. Behind the islands a soft glow hovered — first signs of a moon.

I peered along the shoreline. That must be them. From a distance the dark crowd looked just like the people I imagined would live in those huge old houses. The sky was darkening quickly and the moon rose whole and yellow out of the sea.

People lined the shore, and in the light washing off the ocean the scene was just plain eerie. There were the strange, pale kids I'd seen stalking the school corridors, and I thought I recognised Lexie's black, sweeping dress.

Then something happened—a feeling more than anything. A shadowy figure had stepped forward, and in an instant my hands turned clammy and I felt lightheaded. I didn't know what it was about him that made me so uncomfortable. There wasn't anything noticeably creepy about him—minus the whole situation, of course. He was just a man on a dark beach, yet it was so much more than that. Something instinctive made me want to run, but instead I pushed myself deeper into the shadows cast by the gnarled wooden posts and gripped the side of the jetty to steady myself.

He must have been speaking, because every now and then the group would mumble in unison as though they were agreeing on something. Afterwards there was a silence so deep I could hear my heart beating. It went on for about twenty minutes, and although I struggled to see the people through the gathering darkness, I was aware of them just staring up at the moon. Then there was movement, and tiny flames flickered on the beach.

Before moving here I hadn't realised people still had such old beliefs. They were igniting tea-light candles and placing them on the waves. As they floated away I marvelled at the beauty of it, however crazy these people were. Long after everyone had gone home, I watched the lights being taken out to sea by the tide.

A hundred silent prayers sent to the universe.

☼

At school on Monday, Amber told me to prepare for the weird and wonderful. Had Saturday not been weird enough?

But she was right. School had barely started when there was a tantrum in room three, and in second period a fight broke out. Lexie, along with about a hundred other sleep-deprived students, prowled the corridors, restless and agitated. I gave them a wide berth after I accidentally brushed against one of them and was glared at.

"Are they related or something?" I asked Amber on our way to PE. They all had the same smooth skin, and hair so straight it made me jealous.

"They're descendants from the old families. A lot of them would probably be at least distant cousins. If you think this is bad, wait till you see them before the moon. They're like a pack of wild animals."

I hadn't mentioned what I'd seen Britta and her maniac friends do. They'd been out of control all right.

"Why? What's wrong with them?"

"They say the moon affects them, but it's totally in their heads. It's just an excuse to vent their frustration."

I thought back to the trance-like state they'd been in on Saturday night and raked my hands through my hair. It was beyond strange.

"This is their so-called comedown," Amber told me, pushing open the gate. The class was assembling beside the pool.

"They look like alcoholics fresh to rehab," I admitted

and she burst out laughing.

"Good one! You coming?" she asked when I didn't follow her.

I shook my head. So far the teacher and I had argued before the start of every lesson and I'd written pages of lines.

"Have you told him you don't actually know how to swim?" she asked.

"Yeah. He doesn't believe me." Through the heavy mesh fence I could see Mr Jacobs explaining the tasks he wanted us to do. I was not getting in that pool. "I might hide in the library."

"You are going to get so busted," Amber said as I slunk back towards the school. I was hoping to spend the hour wading through my homework.

"West!" he roared, and I cringed. How could he possibly have known it was me from all the way over there?

I considered ignoring him, but that would mean certain detention. Perhaps I could come up with a brilliant excuse in under twenty seconds. I turned slowly and he beckoned me with his finger.

"Diving. The point of today's lesson. Go and change." He pointed to where the other students were filing into the changing rooms.

"I can't swim today."

He didn't look surprised.

"I have a really bad headache."

"You look fine to me."

What did he expect to see? Visible waves of pain exiting my brain? Or did he just assume I was lying again?

Lexie was a couple of metres away, bent down close to the glittering asphalt as she rummaged through her bag. I don't know why but I got the weirdest feeling she was listening in. Her hair had swung forward like a black satin sheet and she had her head tilted towards us just enough for it to look unnatural. The rest of the class had disappeared and she was undoubtedly taking her time.

I turned back to him. "Well, I'm not." I crossed my arms.

"Detention. Tomorrow after school," he said flatly and strode away.

I sighed. At least it was better than swimming.

The sun was hot and already burning my pale skin, but it still wasn't enough to get me in the water. Jake, who was pulling the covers off the pool, watched me as I walked past him to the stands, but I avoided eye contact and instead pretended to send several important texts. Taylor sauntered meaningfully up to him in a tiny leopard-print bikini and forced his attention back on her. She fluffed her hair and stroked his ego until he left for the changing rooms.

As soon as he'd gone she came marching over to me. "What's the matter, Sunny?" she spat. "Allergic to chlorine? Got some horrific mutation you don't want us to see? Or do you think you're too good to swim with the rest of us?"

"None of the above and none of your business," I said coldly.

She glared at me through narrowed eyes. "Whatever. Just stay away from Jake. He's mine—everyone knows that."

"I heard he's not interested."

She looked as though I'd slapped her and took a step closer. "I've warned you, Sunlight," she said quietly. "Who the hell calls their kid Sunlight, anyway?"

I was about to answer when Jake exited the changing room. My heart raced as he pulled his singlet over his head and shook out his messy hair.

Taylor turned to see what had caught my attention and spun back to face me, scowling. "Didn't you hear me? People like Jake don't go out with people like you."

Jake was now watching us in confusion. Taylor flounced off down the stands and pressed herself up against him. They looked like they'd just come from a swimwear commercial, and something in me wanted to tear her to pieces. Jealousy wasn't something I was familiar with and I didn't like it.

He dived into the pool, soaking her in cold water, and when he emerged his skin was wet and irresistible. I didn't take my eyes off him the whole hour. Suddenly I'd never wanted anything as much as I wanted him.

☼

I made so many excuses to revisit my locker that day, but it wasn't until fourth period that I talked to Jake again. He smiled when he saw me, and this time I managed not to drop anything. I'd been feeling restless, my mind constantly reverting back to him, and I wondered what it was that made me crave more. Was this what people called chemistry?

"Hey," I said, getting out books I wouldn't need until tomorrow just so I was doing something.

"You like coffee, yeah?" he asked as he pulled on a leather jacket and extracted keys from one of the pockets.

I was thinking about the unhurried way he spoke, calm and careful, when it occurred to me he might have been asking me out. I nodded eagerly, about to say something, when Taylor appeared holding a stack of papers.

She swept down the corridor, pausing every few steps to tape flyers carelessly to the wall, and glowered at the sight of us.

"The principal asked me to hand these out," she said, thrusting her arm between us and handing me a sheet of paper.

A collage of black-and-white photos showed a radiant Sophie. Below was an invitation to attend the celebration of her life. This may have been how everybody else remembered her, but all I had was the disturbing image of a water-logged body.

I took a deep breath, and Taylor smiled at me patronisingly before addressing Jake. "Could you drive me out to my dad's on Sunday? My car won't start and I really need to talk to him."

He looked wary. "What about?"

I wondered why he cared and why all of a sudden his eyes were full of worry. She shrugged, continually playing with the papers in her hand.

"Sorry, I have plans this weekend." He turned away from her, and I hoped the plans involved me.

"Maybe your dad could take me, if he's on duty and heading north at all." Taylor didn't take her eyes off him as she taped a flyer deliberately to his locker.

I was starting to feel really awkward and began riffling through my bag.

She sighed dramatically. "I hope they find whoever did this. Sophie's parents deserve to know what happened."

It sounded innocent but I detected the undertones of something else, and Jake looked defeated. "I'll pick you up early," he told her and she grinned.

"Great! We can get breakfast on the way."

☼

I wasn't looking where I was going when I made my way to our final lesson—alone. Taylor was becoming more and more painful, like an annoying headache that wouldn't go away.

Suddenly a door to my left was flung open and I collided with the girl who stepped carelessly through it.

"Ow!" I gasped, falling backwards and dropping my folder. Sheets of paper scattered across the ground. With the intention of asking if she was okay I looked up; however, the words caught in my throat.

Britta.

She stood motionless, her bottle-green eyes staring at me in shock.

"Sorry," I mumbled, even though it wasn't really my fault, but she continued to hold my gaze with an expression that was hard to place. It was quite disconcerting.

I began gathering up my papers, and she drew a shuddering breath.

"Who are you?" she asked when I stood and faced her.

I was surprised by her question. Had she not seen me before? Was she totally oblivious to the fact we were in the same biology class? She waited almost hungrily for the answer.

"Uh, I'm Sunny."

Her eyes flashed as she ran a fingertip contemplatively over crimson-painted lips, then she turned on her heel to glide gracefully down the corridor.

Chapter Eight

The conversation between Jake and Taylor played in my head for the rest of the afternoon and throughout the next day. Why had he agreed to help her? I took comfort knowing he felt obligated in some way, and I eventually pushed it from my mind.

"You're free to leave, Miss West," said the woman who was running detentions.

It wasn't until I glanced outside that I realised it had gotten so late. I'd managed to write half my history essay at the same time as copying out a dull sheet on why PE was an important aspect of the curriculum. *Not if it made me have a panic attack every time,* I felt like adding.

It was strange walking through empty corridors. My footsteps echoed and bounced off the walls as I made my way to the lockers. I felt a stab of fear, and all the horror movies I'd ever watched came back to haunt me. I counted the doors carefully, which had become a habit. There was no way I was going to let Jake catch me trying to open the wrong one again.

"Five from the left," I muttered as I ran my fingers over the steel, and then stopped abruptly. Taped to my door was a bright hand-drawn sun, and as stupid as it was it made me smile because there was only one person who would have put it there. Did that mean he was thinking about me? Was that really what I wanted?

Taking a deep breath, I transferred a heavy stack of books from the locker to my bag and walked out to the Mustang. I could hear the teacher locking the doors behind me, and I watched as she practically ran to her car. It looked like she was as eager as me to get away from here.

I wasn't used to seeing stars but there they were, sprinkled across the clear, cold sky. In the city it had been too polluted for me to ever make them out. I fitted my key into the ignition and turned the key. Nothing. I tried again.

Sighing loudly, I searched for my phone. *Please tell me I haven't lost it,* I silently begged. It wasn't until I dumped the entire contents of my bag onto the back seat that I found it. Chewing gum and empty mascaras rolled to the floor and I plucked it from amongst the rubbish.

Great, no signal. Isn't this the part where someone sneaks up behind me with a knife?

Besides a dirty motorbike that stood a few metres away, the car park was deserted. I paced back and forth, trying to find reception, but it was no use.

I stretched out on the bonnet of my car, the windscreen cold where my jacket was riding up. Closing my eyes, I tried to work out what to do. It wouldn't be too bad spending the night here—I'd slept on the back seat before—but I knew Mum would go out of her mind with worry.

Heavy footsteps made me quickly sit up.

"Nice night for it." Jake was standing in front of me with his head to one side, grinning in that lopsided way of his.

I had a fleeting image of him half undressed beside the pool.

"Sorry about yesterday," he apologised. "Taylor really knows how to get under my skin."

"Seems like it," I agreed. "Oh, and thanks for personalising my locker." I kicked my toe against the tyre of my car; being still was an impossibility when I was near him.

"Do you usually hang out here in your spare time?" His voice was tantalising, and I imagined flowing rivers, dark like silk ribbons.

"Only very rarely."

That made him laugh. It was embarrassing admitting to him I must have left my lights on. After several failed roll starts, Jake said we should try jumper leads. "Mine are at home, let's go."

"Where's your car?" I scanned the car park, my eyes landing on the bike.

I must have looked apprehensive because he laughed again. "I see you on the back of Amber's scooter all the time!"

So he had noticed me.

"But it doesn't go very fast," I explained nervously.

He handed me the helmet and I climbed reluctantly on behind him.

"My place isn't far from here and we'll bring a car back."

I was contemplating the dilemma of what I would hang onto, but before I could think about it he yelled over the noise of the engine, "Hold on tight!" and I threw my arms around him as we tore out of the car park. The dark road disappeared beneath us until we could have been flying, and the cold night air rushed past my face. He was fearless and I loved it. I pressed myself against his hard body and breathed his cinnamon-tainted skin, wondering what Taylor would think if she could see us. *Don't think about her.*

From here I could just see part of his tattoo, and I'd been right about it being a word. The letter T stood out dark on his skin. Even though it was all I could make out, my heart fell quickly. Surely he was smarter than to have branded her name on him for life?

We soon entered a neighbourhood I hadn't seen before. Skinny dogs roamed the streets, and the houses were in need of fresh paint. Jake pulled into a driveway, and I followed him inside to the kitchen. A pretty girl was arranging flowers in a vase. She smiled when she saw us.

"This is my sister, Charlotte." She had a lip ring, which I thought was cool, and the same blue eyes as her brother.

A harassed-looking woman bustled in, and her face darkened when she saw us. "Who's this?" Her tone was unusually sharp and I wanted to shrink back out into the night, but Jake appeared unfazed.

"This is Sunny," he said easily, as if her obvious distaste for me didn't surprise him.

She opened her mouth to say something but changed her mind. Instead she turned to a pot bubbling on the stove. Jake gave me an apologetic glance before heading down a dimly lit hallway. I wondered what his room looked like, and it killed me knowing that Taylor would have woken up within those four walls.

As I waited, his muffled footsteps faded into what were the most silent, uncomfortable few minutes of my life. I had no idea what I'd done to make this woman hate me, but she made it clear I wasn't welcome. A fat cat wound its way around my ankles while his mother completely ignored me.

When Jake returned I let out a breath of relief and hurried after him into the darkness. "I don't think your mum likes me."

"Stepmum," he clarified as lights from a police car spilled into the driveway. Jake laughed when he saw the look on my face. "Don't look so worried—she's rude to everyone." He indicated towards the police car, and I recognised the man who had been talking to McLeod that day on the beach. "And that's my dad."

He went over to say hello, and as he leaned in through

the passenger window I could at last read the tattoo inscribed on his bicep. He had great arms, and it wasn't the name of his ex-girlfriend but actually the word Truth. Interesting.

While we were starting my car and as I drove home, I thought about why this particular word might be so important to him.

Brie was the only one in when I eased the back door open, and I settled down beside her at the counter.

"Letter for you," she said through a mouthful of food and handed me an envelope. My grandmother's familiar writing had been scribbled out and an unknown hand had readdressed it.

I opened it warily, wishing they didn't make me feel so guilty, but I was totally unprepared for what she'd written this time. One sentence, as if she'd known it would be enough.

Have the dreams started?

Chapter Nine

I'm standing on top of a ragged cliff that leans dangerously over the ocean. I can hear the waves surging in, thrashing relentlessly against the rock face. The wind is so strong that the trees surrounding me are almost flattened against the dusty path. It rips at my clothes, and my hair billows around me like a dark cloud. I can smell the dust off the winding track I must have walked up to get here.

Above the thundering roar of the sea, I think I hear something else and spin around. There's nothing there, yet my heart pounds madly against my ribs. The only light is cast by the moon, which is full and bright in the middle of the sky.

Why am I up here? I've never seen this place before. The water below me glints and churns like liquid glass. The sheer drop makes my feet start to tingle, so I inch away from the edge and press my back to the trunk of a tree.

That noise again. Am I really alone up here? I listen again for what I'd thought were distant screams but they have been shredded to pieces and lost in the howling wind.

I shiver. There is something bad about this place, something old and evil.

Below me the ocean writhes impatiently, and now I hear a voice that I know is meant for me. It's coming from beyond the cliffs, and I shudder at the beauty of it. Even though I'm already too close to the edge, I take a step closer. The moon is huge and blinding white. I can't look away and that voice is so lovely.

The wind urges me forward. My arms are no longer at my side—they're stretched out, reaching for the moon. I feel my toes curl over the edge. Little bits of gravel crumble into the sea.

Then I slip.

I'm falling through darkness and I'm screaming, but I'm not the only one. There are others, although I can't see them, and their haunting cries surround me.

It feels like I fall forever. I close my eyes, and the moon is imprinted onto my vision. I plunge into cold water, terrified. This is the end. I'm surely going to drown.

I try to swim but my clothes are weighing me down, taking me closer to an endless, watery sleep. My lungs burn, and stars blossom before me as I struggle to hold my breath. I kick frantically but I'm sinking. I can't hold my breath much longer and the voice that calls to me is disturbingly beautiful.

My limbs are heavy, useless, and I'm painfully tired. I

see my hair float eerily in front of me and imagine dark shapes moving below me. Bodies?

Something brushes against my arm, and I suck in a long stream of water as I open my mouth to scream. The sea surges into my lungs, and in my sleep I gag violently.

Someone is still calling to me.

"Sunlight. Come home."

I woke up gasping for breath. The digits on my alarm clock told me it was almost five in the morning.

Yes, Grandma, I thought to myself, *the dreams have definitely started. But what could you possibly know about that?*

I felt my way down to the kitchen, desperate for a drink. The waning moon was casting weird shadows onto the jetty planks and through the window. I couldn't ignore her letter this time because it had ignited a spark within me that I wouldn't be able to extinguish.

After taking a long swig of water, I put my glass quietly in the sink. My heart was beating quickly and the dream continued to cling to me—I could still feel all that space between me and the ocean as I fell from the cliff.

It seemed like only minutes had passed when the alarm went off. I pulled on yesterday's jeans and a loose jacket, then tried to cover up the dark circles under my eyes, but they came through the foundation like bruises.

Remembering the dream made me press my fingers to

my pounding forehead.

It had felt so real.

I stuffed books into my schoolbag and grabbed a piece of unfinished homework off the desk. No doubt I'd have to stay after the bell to try to catch up. I pulled my long hair into a ponytail and brushed mascara onto my eyelashes. A reflection stared back at me that didn't look like mine.

"Morning," Brie called loudly and I jumped in fright.

"Wow, Sunny, you need to relax."

She went to my wardrobe and pulled down a top, holding it up to herself and posing in the mirror. "Can I borrow this?"

I nodded, not even bothering to check what it was.

"Can you straighten my hair? Just these bits here." She tugged at her fringe and I plugged in the straightener.

She leapt onto my bed, and I tried to forget the dream which kept coming back to me in pieces. Almost instantly I burnt myself on the scorching hot plates and wished I could just go back to bed. I decided then and there I was going to find my grandmother.

"How are things going with Jake?" Brie was fidgeting, which caused her hair to kink in all the wrong places.

"Fine," I said, totally distracted now.

The moment she left I dumped the straightener and turned on my computer. I already had my grandmother's address. She had included it in every letter she'd ever sent me. Now I just needed directions.

If the internet was right, Jane lived in a rest home on

Perry Avenue somewhere north of here. I jotted the instructions onto a piece of paper, shocked that she was so close by. If I left soon, I could still make my afternoon classes and hopefully avoid detention.

I dropped Brie at school and ordered coffee from a café in town. As I sat on a plush red sofa and waited for my cappuccino, I became aware that I was being closely watched. Tilting my head so my hair swung forward to hide me, I peered sideways.

Britta was sitting at a large window seat on the opposite side of the room. Her hands were clasped around a steaming mug, and she had her gaze fixed directly on me. I glanced away, sure that the next time I checked she'd be looking elsewhere, but minutes passed and she didn't move a muscle. I tapped my foot nervously against the tiled floor and jumped when the waitress sat my cup in front of me.

"Here you go, love."

The air was cold when I stepped outside, and icy draughts found their way into my thin coat. I was almost certain Britta would be swivelled in her seat, nose to the glass, watching me cross the road to my car. But what could she find so fascinating?

I drove out of town, on edge from my weird morning and the possibility that I was about to meet my grandmother. I'd never met anyone from my father's side of the family — never planned to until now.

The drive was uneventful, and soon I was pulling into

an empty car park in front of a red-brick building with big, sweeping lawns. I wiped my sweaty palms down the front of my jeans and pushed through the front doors. The lady behind the desk looked like she was starting to nod off and I wondered if it was from all the disinfectant fumes.

"Are you here to see someone, dear?"

I nodded, suddenly unsure if this was a good idea. I peered down the lino-covered corridor. Everything about the place reminded me of a hospital, and I hated hospitals.

I took a deep breath and told myself to be brave. "Jane West."

The lady gave me a genuine smile. "Well, what a lovely surprise! Janie hasn't had a visitor in years."

Sadness tugged at the corners of my mouth. Years? What had my useless father been doing? I felt guiltier than ever, the stack of letters weighing heavily on my conscience.

"Follow me."

We stopped outside a closed door with my grandmother's name on it.

"I'll leave you to it," and then I was left standing alone outside room thirty-one, unsure of what to expect.

I knocked gently before pushing the door open.

A very old woman dozed in a chair beside the window. She had a soft blanket folded over her knees, and a cup of tea looked like it had gone cold on the table next to her. Despite the lack of visitors, a bright bunch of flowers sat in a vase on the windowsill. I let the door click shut and her eyes fluttered open. At first she looked confused as she studied me; then something close to recognition registered on her face.

I stepped further into the room. "Hi, Grandma. I'm Sunny."

Her mouth dropped open slightly, as if she couldn't believe it was really me. When she smiled my heart almost broke.

"Yes, dear, of course you are." Her voice was frail and wavered at every word. "Come and sit down."

I hugged her gently and sat, ready for awkward silences, but surprisingly there were none and I soon regretted every letter I hadn't replied to. I would cry about it later that night.

She told me over and over how beautiful I was, asked about school, my mother, what I liked — and I realised that even though this was the first time we'd met, she'd spent the last seventeen years loving me. Sometimes while I was talking, her chin would drop onto her chest as she tried to evade sleep. I'd pause, wondering if I should leave, but then she'd ask another question.

We went on like this for about an hour, and I forgot entirely why I'd come until a knock on the door interrupted us. Someone brought in a fresh cup of tea and food on a tray.

After the lunch lady left I said, "Grandma, in your last letter you mentioned the dreams. What did you mean?"

She looked at me, clearly confused. Her eyes were dark

like mine, almost the exact same colour. "Did I?"

I nodded, bewildered.

She rested her head against the back of the chair. I could tell she was getting really tired; my unannounced arrival had taken it out of her.

"All the West women dream," she said quietly.

I waited for her to elaborate but she didn't, and I knew it was time to leave. "I have to get going," I told her, standing up.

Above her chair there was a beautiful painting of a turquoise sea. It was a pity she couldn't gaze at it from where she sat, and I scanned the walls for a better place.

My eyes grew wide as I took in the room — properly this time. How had I not noticed before? The walls were crowded with artwork, the ocean featuring in every piece. Some were of the moon on the water at night, others of beaches and hot sunshine.

What did she know that I didn't?

I walked to the door feeling bad for leaving.

"Will you come and see me again, Sunlight?"

"Yes," and she seemed to believe me even though I'd ignored her my whole life.

"I promise."

I'd already decided not to tell anyone about Janie, and the rest of the day passed in a headachy blur.

It was getting dark when I left the library—I'd stayed late again to try to make up for what I'd missed. I was pushing open the heavy front doors, about to step outside, when I saw a light on in the art room. I doubled back and peered through frosted glass.

A small figure was leaning over a canvas, and I could almost feel the concentration oozing out of her. I slipped inside and was hit by turps fumes and the smell of oil paints.

It took Lexie a moment to acknowledge me. "Hey," she said, reluctantly stepping back from the easel and pushing strands of hair off her face.

That's when I glimpsed the painting. It was in thick, dark oils and I leaned in closer for a better look. Within the inky gloom I made out a creature diving down through the black ocean. From the waist up she was human and then her skin melted into scales. Long hair streamed out behind her, and bubbles—dark like poison—escaped her mouth. I couldn't take my eyes off the painting, and Lexie was watching me closely.

"What do you think?" she finally asked.

"Who is she?" I didn't want to sound rude, but I felt as though my life depended on understanding this.

"She's the curse of Procellae Bay."

Was I supposed to know what that meant?

"This town has a lot of history," she assured me as she picked up her paintbrush and mixed more colour.

"You mean the old stories?" I asked and her green eyes

were burning with intensity when she looked up.

"That's exactly what I mean."

I didn't like how she was staring at me, so I stopped asking questions. The dreams had been so similar to her painting. I could still see the girl, swimming beneath the surface, her skin awash with moonlight. But she'd been human ... hadn't she?

How had Lexie put something from my dreams onto canvas? Or more accurately, how was I dreaming of something I knew nothing about?

I'd been so hopeful that Janie could explain things to me, but she hadn't even seemed to remember writing me the letter, and her reply had been vague. *All the West women dream.*

After a couple of lame excuses to Lexie and a hasty exit, I settled back into the cool leather seat of the Mustang, pulling my hands anxiously through my hair and telling myself to calm down. *It's only a painting, you're overreacting.*

But I couldn't calm down. I didn't even bother with assignments that night—Lexie's painting was haunting me worse than the dreams, and I kept picturing my grandmother sitting alone in her room.

I flicked off my light, but as I drifted into what I hoped would be a dreamless sleep I heard it:

"Sunlight."

It had come through my window like the delicate whisper of a wave and I jerked my head off the pillow. "Huh?" I choked.

The waves were lapping at the beach, and the wind rushed across the water. I lay there in the darkness, listening for the voice, but it stayed quiet. Shivering with fear, I hugged my duvet closer to me. This place was doing my head in.

I'm not sure what time I fell asleep again, but it felt late. Almost before my eyes fell shut I could see her swimming at me through the blackness, her sleek body moving through the water towards the surface. The moon shone white, making her skin so pale it was nearly transparent, and this time she turned to face me, staring at me with eyes so familiar at first I thought she was me.

Whoever she was, she wanted to tell me something. I read the panic in her eyes and recognised the fear that darted across her face, but all I could hear was the water — a thick muffled sound that pressed in on my ears. Her eyes were wide and her mouth twisted into speech I couldn't understand. The girl's terror was contagious.

"What?" I asked desperately.

More than anything I wanted to help her, but when I reached outwards my hand passed right through her, blurring her like a water painting, and she was gone.

Chapter Ten

I walked into fourth period late, stumbled to the back of the class and sat beside Amber, who was already trying to mouth something to me. The biology teacher was talking but I couldn't focus on what he was saying because my headache was getting worse and Britta was staring at me from across the room. I was also thinking up an excuse for next period, which happened to be PE. Though maybe it would just be athletics.

The teacher began passing around a huge bucket, and when I saw what was inside I felt my stomach clench. Amber grinned and plunged her hand into the container, pulled out a huge organ that I guessed was a cow heart and slapped it onto the table between us. I tried not to look at it as blood and slime oozed in rivulets towards me. The smell stuck in my nose, and I closed my eyes when the boys next to us started doing something stupid with an intestine.

"Want to do the honours?" Amber held out a scalpel.

I shook my head, hoping I wouldn't have to touch it at

all.

The teacher, who was stalking around the class, eyed me and came over to stand beside my desk.

"To pass this unit you must each have a body part," he said accusingly, placing a quivering blob of something foul in front of me. "Dissect it," he instructed, "and write in detail what function it carries out."

I swallowed hard and reached for the blade he handed me. Amber had put on her gloves and was slicing through the heart, bits of congealed blood splattering the table. My stomach flipped but I forced myself to look at the organ I'd just been assigned.

Before I even made an incision I tasted bile in my mouth and it was all I could do not to vomit everywhere. It was stuffy and hot and I wished the teacher would open a window.

For a moment my eyes slid out of focus and I thought I was going to faint. Instead I slipped with the knife and felt it slice down my wrist. Slumping into my seat, I watched blood bubble from the wound and seep through my white shirt.

Amber let out a dramatic screech. "Sir, quick!" She pulled my arm up high and the whole class turned to look.

"It's nothing," I said quickly, trying to cover it with my sleeve, but I could feel the warm liquid running down my arm.

"You need to see the nurse," Jake said worriedly. I hadn't realised he was sitting behind us.

Taylor scowled at me. "Don't be pathetic! It's just a scratch."

Amber made a rude hand gesture at her and marched me from the room.

In the cool silence of the sick bay my heart slowed down, and I rested my head against the wall while a nurse cleaned the wound. "Almost needs stitching, but not quite," she said as she bandaged it.

"Thanks." I faked a smile and told her I was fine.

At least I had the perfect excuse not to swim now, which was just as well because Mr Jacobs announced we were doing pool relays and I couldn't think of anything I would want to attempt less. As the rest of the class headed to the changing rooms, I approached the teacher.

"No excuses today, miss," he said before I even opened my mouth.

"But, sir, I—"

"Have you got your gear?"

"No, but—"

"Detention," he interrupted.

My arm was starting to throb, my headache was getting worse, and I could see Taylor's evil face gloating at me over his shoulder. I grabbed my bag and strode away from the pool, ignoring my classmates' futile calls.

No one was home, not even Emily. She'd started

waitressing at the local pub and wasn't around much.

I searched through the cupboards and pulled out a bottle of poisonous-smelling spirits. Then I got my guitar and headed for the beach. I wanted to watch the ocean.

Sitting on the sand, leaning against the grassy bank, I took a swig of tequila. It burned down my throat and made me splutter, but it would help to block out the past week.

I stood the bottle haphazardly in the sand, pulled my guitar towards me and strummed at some lazy chords, finding a melody amongst the frets. I kept sipping the ochre-coloured alcohol, closing my eyes occasionally and enjoying the breeze on my face. Hours slipped by without me noticing.

The sun became a ball of liquid fire, turning the ocean a deep, molten orange. It was quickly disappearing and the islands began to blend with the darkening sky.

At some point my breathing had synchronised with the lapping waves, and I fell in and out of sleep. I dreamed that I put my guitar down and went to the edge of the water. That the sea, cool and sweet, swirled around my ankles and then my thighs. That it got so deep I could no longer reach the sand with my toes.

"Sunlight, Sunlight."

Salt on my skin. Salt in my hair. I am floating, weightless …

"Maybe I just should," I said breathily, waking myself up with a start.

"You're not making tequila decisions, are you, Sunny?"

I spun around, surprised to see Jake. He dropped down beside me, and as much as I was glad to see him, I hadn't wanted him to see me like this. It had been a while since I'd resorted to alcohol for its ability to momentarily erase everything, and now it was messing with my head. I looked out once more at the ocean.

"Are you okay?" he asked, eyeing the bottle.

I shrugged. "Is anyone?"

He nodded and lightly rested his hand on top of mine, which was nestled into the sand. The tequila thrummed through me, and I lay down so that the world would stop tilting away from me.

"May I?" He gently eased the guitar off me, tuning it much better than I ever could.

He picked at some pretty chords, finally settling on a song, and I felt as if all my limbs had come loose. When he sang, my blood turned thick and golden like honey. His lyrics were about empty horizons and lonely sunsets — an old song I didn't recognise — and when it finished my mind was quiet.

I propped myself up on my elbows, and Jake pushed my hair away from my face, causing a shudder of delight to run through me. We were so close I couldn't look past his eyes, and this time I didn't want to. They were a stormy blue, as if the very heart of the ocean was being held captive inside him. I wanted to lean into him and breathe in his warm cinnamon skin, but I reminded myself

I was drunk.

"Everyone's afraid of something, Sunny, but ultimately we need to face it so we can move on." His breath was warm on my face, and I reached up to touch his tattoo. He flinched as I traced my finger over the letters.

"What are you afraid of?" I asked, but his face had clouded over and he looked out to sea, his mind clearly on something distant.

I realised too late that it was a very personal question and was about to say so when he looked at me seriously. "Spiders," he answered, and I laughed.

"Anyway, I've got to go." He put my guitar down and stood up, brushing the sand from his jeans before tentatively reaching down and squeezing my shoulder. "Tomorrow will be better," he promised, and I held my breath until he'd broken contact and begun walking away.

"I'll see you at school," I called bravely and he turned to smile.

I let the world fall out from underneath me and slipped into dreamless bliss.

☼

My headache was so bad the next morning that it hurt even to walk. I'd stumbled home in the middle of the night, frozen and disorientated, wanting my bed. The pain in my wrist woke me at dawn and I had just finished showering when Emily accosted me on the landing.

"Oh, my God, look at you," she said gleefully. "You're hung-over!"

"Whatever," I mumbled, and I'd almost stepped past her when she caught sight of my arm and hauled me back in front of her. Apparently bandaged wrists weren't a good look.

"What the hell!" she exclaimed as she peeled back the dressings I'd carefully reapplied.

I felt nauseous just looking at it, and the spiel she'd started to give me was making my head pound harder.

"I slipped in bio, that's all." I twisted free of her grip.

"I'm a terrible sister, aren't I?" she demanded.

I didn't have the energy to get into such a conversation, so even though it was a coffee I wanted more than anything, I told her I was going for a walk. She looked at me suspiciously.

"I'll be back later," I clarified.

The sand was cold underfoot. I walked right to the end of our beach and sat on a big smooth rock that I often looked at from my window. I was in time to watch the sunrise.

I don't know if it was the peaceful quiet, but again I had the fleeting sense that somewhere there was a life much bigger than the one I'd known. Maybe it was meeting my grandmother, or seeing all that space that made me feel as if my very soul was struggling to break free. The horizon was too bright to look at now, the first rays grappling at the top of the world.

I looked down, waiting for the splotches of light to fade from my vision, and found myself staring into a deep rock pool at my feet. Through the clear water I could make out the sandy base. I should do something—anything. I wouldn't let the memory consume me. Maybe it would be a good thing to feel what had once held me so helpless.

I lowered my toes to the surface and quickly pulled them out again. The water was icy cold and enough to get my blood pumping. I watched as the pool rippled and moved. That feeling of being on the edge of something terrifying, but great, was undeniable. My heart beat fast and I trailed my fingers across the surface.

"Sunny?"

Turning quickly, I saw Amber and Lexie making their way towards me. I frowned, wishing the morning had been just mine for a little longer, but raised my arm hesitantly to wave.

Lexie was wearing her usual black—totally inappropriate for such a beautiful day, but I was getting used to it. She was saying something to Amber, who was shaking her head. They paused for a moment to face each other, and I got the impression they were disagreeing on something because after that they approached in stony silence.

"You're alive!" Amber declared as she sat down beside me.

"Huh?"

"Your sister said you'd gone to kill yourself," she replied. I rolled my eyes.

"She's full of it," I reassured them.

Lexie was noticeably quiet beside us, busily arranging her long skirts on the sand. When I looked up, her eyes locked with mine.

"Have you been swimming?" she blurted.

"I don't swim—remember?" I twisted my freshly washed hair defiantly into a bun and stared back at her. The question was innocent enough, yet her tone had unsettled me.

Amber glared at her. The silence that followed was awkward.

"Did Jake find you yesterday?" Amber suddenly asked, and I knew my small, involuntary smile told her too much.

I didn't like that he made me feel this way.

"I'll take that as a yes, so do tell." Her eyes were bright and expectant, but I didn't want to talk about it. I'd never asked to feel these things and now it seemed I didn't have a choice.

I lightly touched the spot where he'd rested his hand on me. "There's nothing to tell."

She let out a sigh. "I can see you've got it bad. Why won't you admit it?"

I shrugged, unsure of what to say. I'd seen relationships fall apart my whole life and weren't you supposed to learn from other people's mistakes? If I could avoid having my heart ripped out, I would.

"Not all of us can be as trusting as you," Lexie said to Amber. Obviously I wasn't the only one who didn't want to be so vulnerable. It was the first thing we seemed to have in common.

Amber shook her head, perplexed. "Being in love puts you on top of the world."

It was here I wanted to point out that it meant a hell of a long way to fall, but instead told her that was the lamest thing I'd ever heard. I dodged the cold water she splashed at me from the rock pool and laughed.

"Seriously, though, maybe Jake is worth the risk," Amber said, and it shocked me that this was in fact what I wanted to hear.

Chapter Eleven

I became restless the minute it got dark. As the night stretched on I considered going for a drive. Mum and Brie had gone to bed hours ago and I'd heard Emily sneak out not long after that. I closed my eyes but didn't try to sleep for fear of dreaming.

My mind wandered to Jake. Everything about him made me want more. Talking to him at school wasn't enough, but if glimpsing him between classes affected me as much as it did, what exactly could I handle? Maybe I felt these things because the idea of it only ever being that—the brief exchange of words and friendly acknowledgement—was more torturous than actually having my heart broken. I thought of his voice as I avoided sleep. Did he think about me in the quiet night hours when everyone else was dreaming?

Tap.

I jumped in fright and peered into the surrounding darkness, but all I could make out were deep shadows. Was it Brie in the next room?

Tap.

I stepped gingerly out of bed and crossed over to the window. In the half-light I could see a tall figure standing beneath the tree outside my room, and I had the craziest notion that my thoughts had drawn him here.

Jake raised his arm again and a tiny pebble pinged off the glass. My heart was going wild as I pushed open the window.

He climbed the tree until we were level.

"Hey." His breath made a pale cloud in the air between us, and the sweet smell of him made me light-headed.

I was suddenly very mindful of how little I was wearing. My flimsy white top showed way too much.

"Are you stalking me?" I asked breathlessly, crossing my arms over my chest and ignoring the smile he hid.

"You wish. I want to show you something."

"Now?" Even though I questioned Jake, I knew I'd follow him anywhere, especially during the early hours of the morning.

"You can only see it at night," he whispered.

"Okay, I'll just get changed."

He smiled and dropped out of sight while I pulled on jeans and quickly tried to fix my hair in the shadowy mirror. I felt absolutely reckless knowing he was out there waiting for me. Was he also addicted to the night? This was much better than venturing out alone.

Twigs caught in my hair as I leapt to the ground. "Where are we going?" I asked. Our lawn was dappled with moonlight, and I tripped on a branch that must have come down in the wind.

"It's a surprise," he said, reaching for my hand to steady me. His long fingers folded over mine, and the contact made my breath rush out in a blazing moment of certainty.

This was right.

☼

Jake led me down the beach to where a little wooden rowing boat rested above the high-tide mark.

"We're going out there?" I asked nervously as he began dragging it to the water's edge.

He stopped to look at me. In the faint light his eyes were silver. "I know you don't like the water, Sunny, but this is the closest thing to magic you'll ever see."

He pushed the boat out until it was floating and I rolled up the bottom of my jeans. I hesitated, looking down at my feet and the waves that reached towards them. The tide swilled in and out, covering the dark sand and washing up handfuls of shells. I didn't want to look like a wimp in front of him but he just stood there patiently, holding the boat still.

I waded tentatively out, startled by how cold the water was and how good it felt. My feet sunk into the sand and I paused again, watching the fog roll in before settling myself onto the wooden seat. Waves slapped against the hull, and Jake jumped in after me, pushing off with his foot and fitting the oars into their rowlocks.

For a while we didn't say anything and the peace settled around us. The oars squeaked in their holders as he pushed them back and forth, and I turned to watch the beach we were quickly pulling away from. I wondered where we were going.

The inky water rippled and parted, the oars slicing almost silently through the surface. I didn't doubt him when he said we were going to witness magic. There was something special about this place, even if I did fear it. I'd felt a breath of it earlier when I'd first touched my fingers to the sea and again just now. Maybe I would have discovered what it was if Amber and Lexie hadn't come by.

Jake finally broke the silence. "Why don't you swim at school?"

Oh.

I usually avoided the truth when it came to this question, and now I didn't know why. Drowning was surely a good enough reason. But possibly it wasn't as simple as that, and excuses were easier.

The pause stretched out between us as I chose how to answer him. I didn't want him to try to understand when I myself couldn't. Besides, I never knew how to word it. If I said I'd drowned, did that mean I should be dead? Had I died?

"It's okay if you don't want to answer that," he said

quietly.

I watched his arms bulge as he pulled back the oars over and over again, his tattoo just visible. Maybe the truth was best.

"I almost drowned when I was a kid."

It sounded so uncomplicated, but maybe my face told him more. Could he see that it had changed me? That in a way it had defined who I was by making me become this so-called miracle child? He was studying me closely, and I knew I looked worried. I hated myself for suddenly needing him to say something that mattered.

He stopped rowing and rested his hands on my knees. "The ocean takes and it gives. Maybe tonight you'll understand what it means to be alive."

Somehow he'd glimpsed the most brittle part of my soul, and I was surprised. All this time I'd given thought to why I hadn't died when maybe I should have been more focused on why I had lived.

He slid me a small smile. "Those aren't lyrics, by the way."

We drifted a little longer, listening to the water sloshing against the boat, and strangely enough I found myself relaxing. He took up the oars again and I lost track of time as we talked. The rowing didn't seem to make him tired.

"Close your eyes, we're nearly there. Don't open them until I say, okay?"

I nodded and waited, unsure what to expect.

"Right, you can look now."

My breath caught in my throat. I'd never in my life seen anything so surreal. All around us the water was glowing, and I was speechless for the second time that night. We were leaving an iridescent trail in our wake, gliding through a narrow gap in the rock and into a bay I'd never seen before.

"What is this stuff?" I whispered, as if somehow I might break the spell, but he just smiled mysteriously.

He took up the oars again and when they hit the water it was an explosion of green light. We were getting closer to a small crescent-shaped beach enclosed by tall cliffs.

"Is that a cottage over there?" I asked, squinting beyond the waves that were luminous and breaking on the sand.

He nodded, and I leaned down to the water to swish my fingers over the surface. It was like a whole galaxy of underwater stars.

"Amazing, isn't it?" he said as he stood up. In one fluid motion he pulled his shirt off over his head and leapt into the ocean.

The water burst into green clouds and then he emerged, grinning. Lights stuck in his hair like fireflies and when he hauled himself back into the boat, beside me, they stayed sprinkled on his skin. I had never seen anything so beautiful—his faultless body outlined against the darkness with some kind of magic clinging to him like he was king of the sea.

I stared deliberately towards the beach in the hope of settling my erratic heart but then he touched me and I gave up trying to control anything. He put his hand on my face, gently turning me to him, and the gesture was so intimate I felt tears come to my eyes.

"Are you afraid I'll break your heart?" he whispered.

"Maybe," I admitted, and for a long minute the cold air spun with silence. "But I think I'm more afraid of not giving you the chance."

He put his arms around me, drawing me close, and I rested my cheek against his neck. I could feel the slow and steady thrum of his pulse and closed my eyes. The wind had picked up, throwing clouds in front of the moon and making the trees behind the cottage creak.

"I'll try not to," he murmured, and it was me who kissed him.

It was so much softer than I expected, and I could taste the salt on his lips. Above us, lightning flickered beyond the clouds, and a spot of rain landed on my cheek. I shuddered as he twisted his fingers through my hair, his other arm still firmly around my waist. He smelled like freshly baked cinnamon buns, even now. I thought of nothing but him. Not the fact that I was floating on the deep ocean or that my dreams had a disturbingly real quality about them.

Jake was my escape, my stardust, my amnesia.

I'm not sure how long we sat there, talking and staring up

into the black sky, but eventually he said we needed to get back.

I watched the dazzling water as he rowed. "Why does it light up?"

"Each light is a tiny kind of plankton, and when disturbed they illuminate. It's called phosphorescence." They left us as we exited the bay.

"Does that place have a name?" I asked.

"The locals call it Angel Bay but you won't find it on any map—they sort of named it themselves." He didn't elaborate and I wondered why he was suddenly frowning. "I can bring you back during the day if you want. It's a nice drive out here. The road goes inland before cutting back out to the coast."

"Do people live there?"

"No. It's been abandoned for a long time."

☼

The next morning I practically floated downstairs to the coffee machine, and I scooped in an extra heap of ground beans for Emily. Today it would be her turn to be hungover. She'd stumbled through the hedge as Jake was kissing me goodnight, and if I hadn't been there to help her I know she wouldn't have made it up the tree and through my window.

As I sat there thinking about Jake and waiting for coffee to brew, I was conscious of movement above me. From the kitchen I could see up onto the landing, and I realised a man was inching out of Mum's bedroom, obviously under strict instructions to remain unseen. Oh, great, another guy. I wondered if he was unemployed or perhaps married. Knowing Mum he could have been both.

He tiptoed down the stairs, pausing at every creak, and was so focused on getting out the door he wouldn't have even seen me sitting in the kitchen if I hadn't spoken up. "Hey, there."

He almost jumped out of his skin, and the first thing I noticed when he turned to me was that he wasn't the usual type. He was older than her by about ten years, and I decided he would have been handsome once. I saw him flick an anxious glance up towards the room he'd just exited, but Mum was nowhere to be seen.

"You scared me half to death," he whispered.

I didn't offer an apology as he made his way out the back door. Emily soon appeared in wrinkled clothes I recognised from the day before, mascara smudged under her eyes. Classy. She swallowed a couple of painkillers and eased herself onto a couch.

"Coffee's almost ready," I told her.

Upstairs I heard Mum turn the shower off and I listened as she clattered about in her room. I could almost see her deciding to leave her hair down and choosing something floaty to wear. I'd witnessed it too many times.

It baffled me that she was still open to love, despite how many failed relationships she'd had. And it was stupid of me to think Jake and I could be anything different, but I refused to dwell on that.

"Isn't it a beautiful day?" Mum gushed as she descended the stairs in a summery dress.

It wasn't just me who noticed she was on cloud nine.

"Do you have another boyfriend?" Emily said bluntly.

Mum blushed bright red. "No!"

"That guy who just left was pretty handsome," I said innocently.

"What?" Emily looked from me to Mum. "Did you actually have a guy up there?"

"He's just a friend I met through work."

We rolled our eyes.

"That's disgusting," Emily grumbled.

"Well, where did you two both sneak in from last night?" Mum demanded. "I heard you clambering through Sunny's window in the early hours!"

"I'm surprised you heard anything at all," Emily muttered.

I went back to the beach, still on a high from my night with Jake. Incredibly, he'd helped me see the ocean through different eyes. For the first time it wasn't just danger I'd seen. The way it had held us on its sparkling, ever-moving surface had indeed made me feel alive.

Everything glinted in the morning sun. I breathed in

the salt air, and my stomach fluttered at the thought of Jake's lips on mine. I was overflowing with energy and felt reckless. I stripped off my jeans and waded into the tide. I wouldn't go in deep, just enough to feel the looseness of the water on my skin.

If I listened closely I thought I could hear the faintest whisper of my name. Maybe it was just the water rushing through the rock crevices behind me. Goose bumps sprang up along my arms. I wasn't sure if it was from the cold or because something was coming back to me, struggling up through layers of a memory I'd only ever half recalled.

"Sunlight."

That voice was so lovely and persuasive, so … familiar. I took a deep breath and let myself remember. It had called to me over and over as a child too, and I'd followed it into such deep water.

Holding on to the memory, I watched my bright red toenails sink into the sand as I waded out further. I stood there for ages, aware of the tide getting higher and the water rising from my thighs to my waist. I could feel the salt seeping through my skin and into my blood.

Before I had time to contemplate it, I dived under and was swallowed up in a burst of cold. I swam down and looked towards the surface. It shimmered way above me like a sheet of corrugated glass, and I could see the rocks I'd been sitting on earlier. How was it possible that I knew how to swim when I'd never actually been taught? I felt invigorated, wild, I wanted to kiss Jake and feel his hard body pressed against mine. Silver bubbles seeped from my lips, upwards and away. I tried to remember why I had been so afraid of drowning.

"You can't drown."

What an unfathomable idea. It took me a moment to realise I should have been more concerned about the voice that had spoken it. I peered through the blue but I was alone. It seemed a while before I needed a breath, and my chest shuddered as I resisted the urge to open my mouth and invite the ocean in. It was so good here, and the salt on my skin was electric.

I shook the thoughts away and swam to the surface.

"Breathe."

Maybe I was more messed up than I knew. I hauled myself reluctantly out of the water and onto the rocks, worried because I knew that hearing voices was a symptom of the unwell.

Chapter Twelve

I woke up before my alarm went off, and groaned. Monday was definitely my least favourite day of the week. I turned on the shower, and steam quickly filled the bathroom.

My wrist was feeling a whole lot better — in fact, the edges of the wound had almost completely knitted back together. It looked weeks old rather than days. Maybe the salt had done it good. I puzzled over it as I got changed, and re-bandaged it merely to avoid questions. Outside, the ocean was sparkling blue and full of secrets. I already longed for the weekend.

Emily was up early too and she made us coffee while I tried to finish the last of another history essay.

"Sunny?" Upstairs, Brie was pounding her fist on my door. Since when did she knock?

"Down here!" I called.

"Sunny! I've got nothing to wear and I need help!"

Unwillingly I pushed my books aside. I didn't want any more detentions, even if the last one had ended well, but I could hear the hysteria in my sister's voice.

"It's okay, I'll go," and for once it was Emily who went to her rescue.

I was just finishing the last sentence when Brie came bounding down the stairs. She was wearing one of Emily's favourite dresses and a huge smile. "Can you believe it?" she whispered in disbelief.

"Not really," I admitted as I slipped the essay into my bag.

"You ready?" she asked.

I nodded, swallowing the last of my coffee and pulling out my timetable. Geography, biology, PE. I bit my lip as I thought about it. "Do you have a bikini I can borrow?"

Brie nodded, surprised, and I watched her leap back up the stairs. She was back a minute later, breathlessly passing me a gorgeous orange bikini I'd never seen before.

"You can have it," she smiled. "It doesn't suit me."

☼

It was hot inside the classroom, and I struggled to understand what the teacher was saying. I felt as though my mind had left my body, and I was just sitting there occupying a space. I was at the beach, walking down to the tide, touching my feet to the water, wading further into the waves.

"Sunlight!"

I was jolted back to reality. "Sir?"

"Are you going to answer the question?"

The class turned to stare at me, and I felt the colour rising in my cheeks. Amber was trying to mutter the question to me behind her hands.

"Detention," he said, smirking as the bell rang. I'd never been in this much trouble at my last school.

Sighing, I headed for my locker in the hope Jake might be there. He wasn't. I swapped books and made my way outside. Blazing sunshine momentarily blinded me. I hiked across the field to where I knew Amber and Lexie would be—hidden from prying eyes behind the brick wall of the courtyard, where Amber could hitch up her skirt and soak up the sun.

I heard them before I saw them.

"But she refuses to swim. Don't you think that's weird?"

As I got closer I could see they had their backs pressed against the warm bricks. Amber shook her head and began fixing bobby pins into her hair.

"Not at all?" Lexie persisted.

"No."

I held back, intrigued by the possibility that it was me they were talking about.

"And as for your painting, she was probably just curious."

Lexie paused as she contemplated this. "No, there was something weird about the way she reacted to it—like she recognised it, almost."

Amber stretched and yawned. "Have you looked at them yourself lately? They're totally intense."

"I'm just saying that if she'd turned up here back in the day, she'd have been taken and trialled. Pale skin, dark eyes ... she fits the criteria."

"Thank God those days are over!" Amber was getting exasperated. I wished I knew what they were talking about.

I waited a while longer but it seemed they were now off the topic. *Well, Lexie, I'll be swimming soon enough.*

☼

"Time trials!" Mr Jacobs clapped his hands together with the kind of enthusiasm that would usually make me sick. "And these will be going towards your end-of-year marks."

Taylor looked over at me smugly. "Ready to flunk?" she said loudly, but I ignored her.

"Well?" she demanded. "What is it you don't want us to see?"

"That's enough," Mr Jacobs said sharply.

"Seriously! I bet she can't even swim!" she said to the class before turning towards the sheds.

A few of the other students looked at me apologetically and Jake was frowning.

What did you ever see in her? I wanted to ask.

"So, what's the excuse today, miss?" the teacher asked

automatically.

"I don't need one," I snapped and headed over to the stands where I pulled off my jeans and slipped out of my T-shirt. I already had my bikini on, having changed earlier in the privacy of the bathrooms. I couldn't think of anything more unbearable than communal changing rooms.

The pool gleamed in the late morning sun and I stood nervously beside it, waiting for my classmates. My heart was beating hard when Taylor appeared.

She was latched on to Jake's arm and talking non-stop, but he wasn't listening to her—he was staring straight at me. I blushed deeply, unable to meet his gaze that swept my body. When Taylor worked out what he was looking at her eyes nearly dropped out of her head. So did Lexie's for that matter.

"You look so much better than her," Amber said loudly as she came to stand beside me. She dropped her voice to a whisper. "But I didn't think you could swim."

"Brie's been teaching me," I lied, shaking my hair free of the elastic and checking surreptitiously that Taylor was aware of Jake still watching me.

"That man of yours can't stop staring," Amber said, laughing.

I stood at the edge of the pool, pushed every worry from my head and dived in like I'd been doing it my whole life. I swam right near the bottom, the concrete brushing against my belly. The chlorine made my skin feel tight but the coolness was refreshing. I didn't surface until I reached the other end and even then I took my time to come back into the air. I could feel everyone's eyes on me, and Taylor just stood there scowling.

"Still think she can't swim?" Amber sneered at her before jumping in after me.

I knew I'd probably made things worse, but for now I didn't care. Time trials were a breeze. I was half a length faster than everyone else. After the bell rang I sat in the sun and towel dried my hair.

"I just can't work you out, Sunny." Jake dropped clumsily down beside me, and my heart leapt at the sound of his voice.

He plucked a daisy from the lawn and twirled it between his fingers before tucking it behind my ear. My body tingled when his hands brushed my cheek, and I took an uneven breath.

"Are you doing anything tonight?" he asked. I shook my head. Even if I'd had tickets to a Led Zeppelin concert I would have said no.

"Great. I'll pick you up at seven."

"Where are we going?" I should have known better than to ask. He told me it was a secret.

I struggled through the rest of the day, impatient to see him, but when I realised he would be on my doorstep in less than an hour, my body felt like it was experiencing a minor heart attack. I tried on five different pairs of jeans and none were good enough. I couldn't believe I'd morphed into the girl who spent too long in front of the mirror.

"Brie?" I called loudly as I plugged in my straightener. "Brie!"

She was also getting ready to go out, but she appeared in my doorway and smiled. "You have a date!" she said instantly, walking over to my wardrobe and flinging it open. "With Jake?"

Just hearing his name made my nerves stretch tighter. I nodded. "I don't even know where we're going. He said it's a surprise."

Brie sighed loudly when she heard that; apparently it made things very difficult.

"It's okay," she said when I frowned. "Go cute and a little dressy, not casual. That way if it's a movie you won't be overdressed but if it's dinner you won't be underdressed." It was sad my little sister had gone on more dates than I had.

"Too ripped, too grey, too tight." She flicked through the options.

Jake picked me up in Charlotte's pink Mini Cooper. For my mother's sake I'd asked him if he had any option other than the bike, and he'd reassured me he would take care of it.

"That's your date?" Emily was in obvious disbelief as they all checked him out through the window.

Mum giggled. "I thought you'd go for someone who …" she trailed off.

"Who what?" I asked a bit too defensively.

"Had a muscle car, or maybe a bike. Your father had a bike," she said wistfully.

Unbelievable.

When Jake stepped out of the car, I got immediate butterflies. He was wearing a thin black tee over a collared shirt, and his hair fell at all the right angles.

"Wow, Sunny!" Mum said, squeezing my hand excitedly. "He is hot!"

"Never use that word, Mum," Emily told her. Brie straightened my leather jacket and steered me outside.

"Don't be back before eleven," they chimed as I walked towards Jake. He was standing there calmly, holding my door open.

"Where's Barbie?" I asked teasingly.

"At home, probably still in hysterics with her friends," he sighed, starting the car.

I flicked through the selection of CDs, but all Charlotte owned were albums of trashy girl bands I'd never listen to. The car crawled through the night, barely reaching the speed limit as we drove inland. We passed quiet woods and empty squares of land before approaching a field bursting with life. A soft glow hovered above soaring white tents and daunting amusement rides.

"Here we are." He pulled into a crowded car park. Fireworks sprayed green stars across the sky, and children stood watching, mouths sticky with candy floss. Jake leaned across me to the glove box, his fingers brushing my knee as he flipped it open. I silently thanked Charlotte for having such a small car.

I watched him extract a silver box and asked where we were. He tilted his head towards me so our faces were just centimetres apart. My heart was throwing itself against my ribs.

"You'll see." He opened the box, patches of light suddenly dancing off the dashboard, and held a sequined mask up to my face. The touch of his cool hands made my vision sway. Was it healthy that another person could do this to me? He pulled me closer to him so he could tie the ribbon at the back of my head and I realised I'd stopped breathing. He swivelled the mirror in my direction.

"Wow. This is beautiful," I told him.

"Yes, you are," he said easily.

I turned to argue but caught my breath. His eyes were bright beneath a black mask that matched my own, and I forgot what I was going to say.

We followed a crooked path towards the crowd. Someone

had strung Chinese lanterns between the old trees and they cast red and orange shadows at our feet. A woman dressed in silk swept by, incense in hand, an elaborate mask concealing one side of her face.

We'd come to a gypsy fair. I stuck close to Jake as we navigated the maze of stalls, afraid I'd get lost in the swarm of people. It seemed most of the locals had shown up.

"This is amazing," I told Jake, but I eyed the rides nervously. A thundering rollercoaster rose above us, and people screamed from the twisting carts. Meanwhile, a fortune teller disguised as a tiger was trying to lure people into her tent, red curls tumbling from behind an orange mask.

Jake steered me over to the stall. "You should have your fortune told."

I shook my head and he laughed at my lack of enthusiasm. A woman in her thirties had just left the tent. She was glowing, her head probably filled with the promise of love.

"Go on," he said, dropping some coins into my hand. "My treat. I'll be over there."

He made his way towards a cart full of cream pies, leaving me alone. I was about to follow him when the fortune teller emerged from behind copious amounts of velvet curtains. She froze when she saw me. Her eyes glittered gold behind her mask and I watched every expression from fear to annoyance pass over her features.

She settled on a smile. "I'm just finishing," she told me, pulling down her sign. I frowned, unsettled by her reaction. Was I being paranoid thinking she didn't want to tell my fortune?

"I want a reading." I surprised myself, as this was now the truth.

"I don't think you do," she said quickly and pushed her way back into the tent.

I looked to where Jake was standing at a brightly painted stall, hurling pies through the air. I ducked under the rope and followed the woman into a candlelit room.

"What's that supposed to mean?" I asked and she jumped, startled.

"Knowing what lies in the future can sometimes be helpful." Her eyes burned fiercely in the dim light. "Other times not."

"I want to know." Even though I'd never believed in any of this hype, I was now intrigued.

"Fine." She didn't look at her crystal ball or examine my palms. Instead she made tea — slowly. I waited uneasily, gazing at her odd collection of inscribed candles while the smell of rosemary tea filled the tent.

She looked at me long and hard before finally speaking. "Your path is a difficult one. It's dangerous actually, how uneducated you are about your own past." She paused, as if considering what she should tell me. "You will be made a terrifying offer — if you could call it that. Be certain that great pleasure is often followed by great loss. Tread carefully." She shuddered slightly.

I waited for her to elaborate but she'd turned her attention back to her fragrant tea.

"What? That's it?"

"Trust me, I wouldn't wish it upon anyone," she said quietly.

Totally unhelpful, but maybe she was just trying to scare me. I brushed past her, ready for our meeting to be over.

"Sunlight—" she said it so quietly I might have imagined it "—if I were you I would get the hell out of this town."

I turned around, stunned. "Excuse me?"

"Sunny?" Jake appeared cradling a giant teddy bear.

The fortune teller smiled at him. "We were just finishing." The firmness in her voice implied it was over, and Jake led me back into the crowd.

"You look very worried, Sunny."

"I am!"

"Remember it's their job to scare people," he assured me after I told him what she'd said. We arrived at a brightly lit Ferris wheel that ascended high into the sky. When Jake said we would be riding it I briefly forgot the fortune teller.

"I don't know. I really hate heights." My toes tingled just looking up at it.

"Maybe this is the terrifying fate you were predicted," he laughed.

I chewed my nails nervously while we waited for the ride to start. What if we plummeted to our deaths due to faulty equipment? And how had that woman known my name?

I couldn't enjoy the view; in fact I closed my eyes and tried not to tremble. As we sat side by side, climbing high into the night, Jake reached for my hand. I didn't have to look to know he was smiling.

"Distract me," I told him. The palms of my hands were starting to sweat and I could feel the ground dropping further and further away. "Let's talk about something."

I felt him lift a handful of hair away from my neck and lean in close.

"What do you want to talk about?" he said softly, his lips brushing my skin. My eyes jolted open at the contact and then I was really trembling. He ran his fingers through my hair, his breath warm against my skin.

I couldn't even begin to form the words in my head let alone speak. The adrenaline already coursing through me had multiplied. Far below us the festival was in full swing but now my mind was completely on Jake. I drew in a frayed breath and kissed him urgently. He smelled like spices and coconut oil, and the combination was dizzying. I held onto him as though he was the only thing stopping me from falling, and he let out a tiny groan. The swooping feeling in my stomach deepened when we reached the highest point and began to descend.

I pulled him to me so that we were no longer sitting and

we lost ourselves in the starry sky.

Chapter Thirteen

That night I dreamt repeatedly of the orange-eyed fortune teller, her chilling words mixing with the hiss of the ocean and making me cold inside. Each time I woke up I'd tell myself it meant nothing, but that didn't settle my frantic heart. I'd move my attention to Jake, try to relive the warmth of our kiss and then fall back into restless sleep.

I woke again at sunrise and threw off the covers. From my window I could see the sun just starting to peek over the islands, splashing them with light. I pulled on my bikini, hurried quietly through the house and let myself outside. Cold sand massaged the soles of my feet and when my toes touched the water I closed my eyes. I let the waves curl around my ankles before wading out and diving in.

I floated beneath the surface and held my breath, wondering how long it would be before I needed to go up for air. The urge to breathe didn't seem necessary — which sounds crazy, I know. The seawater was so full of oxygen it was as though just being amongst it was enough. But eventually I felt light-headed.

"*Breathe.*"

Those words again, and for the second time I considered it. How would it feel to let the ocean rush into my lungs? My hair swirled eerily in front of my face, and as I surfaced I ignored the voice inside my head.

I really was going crazy.

I didn't have any classes with Jake that morning and the hours dragged. While the teacher scribbled copious amounts of writing on the blackboard, I sketched randomly in my notebook and thought of him. The students around me were feverishly taking notes but it seemed lately I couldn't concentrate on anything unless I was with him. I'd fallen hard, despite everything.

Last summer I'd watched as the girls in my year had their hearts broken time and time again and wondered how they could be so naive. Now I was a girl who was obsessed with a boy, waiting for disaster.

The bell rang and I leapt from my seat, already casting my eyes towards the lockers in the hope I'd see him, but Amber was suddenly pulling me from the current of people sweeping down the hallway. I stared at her, startled.

Lexie was at her side, clutching the same book she'd been reading that day at the beach. Her jet-black hair was swept into a teased mess and she was wearing an emerald green dress that touched the floor. I wanted to ask her about the old stories but held back; now wasn't the time.

"We're skipping third period and going to the beach. You have to come," Amber told me eagerly as she towed me to the end of the corridor.

"What's happening?" I was vaguely interested but my mind was elsewhere.

"We're getting tanned is what's happening!" she exclaimed.

I wanted to say no but she started harassing me so much I agreed to go. A group of girls piled into the Mustang and we headed out of town. I hadn't realised half the class was coming until I saw the long convoy of cars in my mirror. We drove for fifteen minutes before Amber excitedly told me to pull over.

When I saw Jake's bike I was glad I'd come. We walked down a bush track that opened out to grassy banks.

"Are you swimming?" Amber asked. I shook my head.

"Will you look after Punky?" She carefully extracted the rat from her sleeve and passed him to me. He sniffed at the air before dashing up my arm and settling on my shoulder. I was getting kind of used to him.

"Thanks." She dragged off her jeans and ran across the warm sand.

I searched for Jake amongst my half-naked classmates.

"Let's race to the island!" someone yelled, and I eyed the small piece of land jutting from the wrinkled sea. The water looked so good but I sat down on the beach, tracing my finger over the scar on my wrist. It was amazing how fast it had healed.

My pulse quickened when I heard Jake's voice. He was over by the rock pools, talking to friends. From the corner of my eye I watched him take his shirt off. How could I not be distracted by someone so perfect?

I quickly pulled my sleeve down when I noticed he was coming over.

"Hey," he said, collapsing next to me. "Not worrying about that fortune teller still, are you?"

I tried not to let it show as the dreams flashed like a video before me. How had she known my name?

I pushed away her creepy prediction.

"No way," I lied, smiling when he slipped his arm around me. We sat in silence for a while, watching our friends swim out into the distance. Jake was drumming his fingers gently against my arm to a tune I'd never know.

I plucked a worn piece of coral from the sand and, keeping my tone light, asked, "What is the curse of Procellae Bay, exactly?"

He turned to face me. "I didn't think you'd be one for fairy tales," he teased and I pushed him down onto the shells. Reaching up, he twisted a long strand of my hair through his fingers. I looked at him expectantly.

"Okay." He shrugged and sat back up. "Some of the people around here say that once, in this very bay, there dwelled a sea god. Imagine that." He rolled his eyes but all

I could think was that if I'd been a god, I would have chosen this patch of ocean too. It was so timeless here.

"Pytheus is so much more than that," a voice said behind me.

I spun around, startled, and Punky pressed himself closer into my neck. Lexie was standing over us, her lip curled slightly as if Jake wasn't worthy of telling such a story. I took a deep breath to help my heart settle but Jake looked merely amused. "Hi, Lexie."

She ignored him and sat facing me, a fierce light shining in her green eyes. I imagined she could see straight into the past.

"Pytheus?" I repeated breathlessly. The word rolled off my tongue as if I'd said it a thousand times before. How was it that the name was more familiar than my worn-out jeans?

"The ocean is his spirit, and the storms and sunsets are his emotions." Lexie leaned in closer to me. "His heartbeat is the very flow of these tides."

Jake started to cut in but she flashed him a death stare better than my own before turning back to me.

"You may not think it now, but this town once prospered. Our people were skilled fishermen and sailors. Hundreds of families lived here and were happy."

I wished she'd get on with it. I'd waited too long to hear the stories about this freaky place.

She carried on, "Pytheus was a shape shifter — "

"Really?" Jake sounded scornful even to me.

145

Lexie disregarded him, barely taking her eyes off me. I could see that she desperately wanted me to believe her.

"Almost two hundred years ago, he took the form of a man and came ashore. He was strikingly handsome with eyes darker than black coral."

Jake gave me a look that said she couldn't have really known that, but I was intrigued all the same.

"He met a local girl," she said, and I knew I was about to be reminded that romance could indeed ruin everything.

"She was elusive and carefree, and more beautiful than anything he'd ever seen. My ancestors say he came ashore every day for an entire month and his heart was painful with love."

I could picture her in my mind now, long-haired and smiling. I wondered if she'd known he was a god. Above us the sky had started to fill with towering white clouds that hid the sun, and a cool breeze blew in off the sea.

"They conceived a daughter together, which posed a problem. Should a mortal raise the half-blood child or was there a chance she would thrive in his watery kingdom? After a bitter argument, Pytheus made her promise to return his child to the ocean. However on the night before the birth, she fled as far inland as she could and hid. This made our god furious. For a day and a night he thrust a storm so ferocious upon the town not everyone survived it. He tore great holes in the nets, drove sailing ships onto the rocks and pulled fishermen to his depths. When the storm subsided, the rain stayed and people began to leave. They moved away from the coast, abandoning everything, and formed nearby settlements that don't exist now. More and more left until just thirteen families remained. The town had been reduced to ruins, and still he lashed the bay with storm after vicious storm. Our people thought that if they could find his daughter, he would restore peace to the area."

"Why didn't your family leave along with everyone else?"

Lexie looked at me as if my question was stupid. "They'd built their lives here and he had been good to them. If anything they owed it to him to find her. She was rightfully his, regardless of whether or not she would have survived."

I took a deep breath, ready to argue, but changed my mind. She was proud of her ancestry and extremely loyal. Whatever I said wasn't going to change what was so deeply ingrained in her.

"So they rebuilt their houses and swore an oath to find her. They wanted to get on with their lives and try to forget the shame that one of their own had caused. They travelled the countryside, searching, hunting ..."

She broke off and I shivered. "But no one found her."

"No," she snarled.

There was a silence then that stretched out to the horizon. I could see the anger in her stance – sense it in the very air around her.

"Some believe his daughter grew to be a radically beautiful sea nymph who, despite having veins that flowed with salt, could possibly survive in both worlds," Lexie said.

I pondered this idea. It was somehow irresistible.

"Without her he was incomplete and his fury insatiable. What an insult that an ocean child would choose to live out her life on land! Storm clouds settled permanently over the town to constantly remind us of our failure."

The weather didn't seem too bad to me. I hadn't been here long but we'd had more sunny days than not.

"Until recently anyway, which changes everything," she said pointedly. "There are things to come. We've seen it in the stars and feel it in our blood."

I wrapped my arms tightly around myself to stop another bout of shivering.

"After all, what the sea wants the sea shall have," she said with finality.

"What would have happened if they'd found her?" I asked nervously and it was Jake who answered.

"If you ask the old families around here they'll all tell you something different. There are so many theories." I could tell he didn't want to get into it.

Lexie nodded. "But it remains undisputed that it would have made everything right. Her precious blood was stolen and the Day of Storms is just a reminder."

At that moment a group of sopping wet students came running up the beach, and Lexie got swiftly to her feet.

"Meet you at the car, Sunny?"

I nodded and turned to face Jake.

"Welcome to crazy town," he laughed, but I was in no position to disrespect these stories; if anything I needed to know more.

"Day of Storms?" I asked, and he told me that every year since the myths began, a hurricane had arrived on the first day of June.

My birthday.

"Some people say it was the date she was born all those years ago."

"It's always on the first?" I asked as casually as I could.

He nodded. "It's purely weather-related. Warm ocean, damp air, converging winds ... you're going to get one mean hurricane, that's just what happens. The timing is coincidental."

I was past trying to kid myself that these were random facts just coinciding with one another, but I didn't know what my birth date could possibly have to do with it. Surely that in itself wasn't enough to make me dream?

"There's a poem written about her on a plaque outside an old stone building. It's not too far from your place, actually. We could check it out sometime if you're interested."

My throat was dry and my palms were sweating. I knew without a doubt it was Pytheus' daughter I was dreaming of. I just didn't know why.

☼

The throb of Jake's bike woke me on Saturday morning. I threw off the blankets and was pulling a top over my head when he appeared at my bedroom door.

"Hey," I said, blushing slightly. He looked even more gorgeous than usual and had a day's worth of stubble on his chin. I bet my hair was a total mess. Why had my sisters let him in without warning me?

"Hey, sleepyhead. Didn't have any crazy ocean dreams?"

I swear my heart nearly stopped. "Huh?"

He looked at me as if I were slightly strange. "Because of all that rubbish Lexie told you earlier in the week."

"Oh." I laughed and shook my head. For once I couldn't remember what I'd dreamt.

"Perfect day for a ride. I thought if you wanted to we could go to Angel Bay."

"Sounds good," I said, even though I had been planning on visiting Janie. Since I'd glimpsed the cottage from the water that night, I'd been wanting to go up there. I could always see my grandmother tomorrow.

"Can we pick up coffee on the way?" I asked.

"Sure." He placed his hand on the small of my back and led me downstairs. It was only early morning, but the day was already warm with sunshine.

"Is the weather really never this nice here?" I asked as I put on the helmet Jake handed me.

"You have no idea. Before you got here a week's worth of sun was unheard of. I think that's why they're all talking about you." As soon as he'd said it he looked uncomfortable.

"Who's talking about me?"

He dodged the question and smiled. "It's just such a coincidence, what with your name and everything."

"Jake, who's talking about me?"

"Britta and her cousins, but who cares? Let's go."

As we headed north I wondered what it was they were saying.

☼

The bay was beautiful and desolate. It was miles from the main road, tucked away and forgotten like a bundle of old love letters.

I climbed off the bike, stretched my legs and walked towards the cottage. It was weather-beaten and wild, backed by creeping vines and overgrown bush. A giant ash tree pushed against the windows, its berries split open and rotting on the ground. Wooden steps led to a sun-soaked deck covered in leaves. I loved it.

Jake was still over at the bike. I climbed the stairs gingerly, but they were surprisingly solid. There was an old wind chime that looked like it would fall apart if anyone touched it, and a couple of empty planter boxes. What had grown there? I walked through crunchy leaves to the front door. The place had a feel of tragedy about it, like it wasn't used to being so unloved.

I wiped a patch of thick salt off the window and peered through the glass. Jake was right, no one had lived here for a really long time. I tried the door handle but it was locked. Did a key even exist any more?

I made my way around the side of the house. Grass had grown over the cobblestones, and a broken statue lay across the path. The back door was locked too.

"You coming?" Jake called and I turned towards him. He was standing on the grassy bank with his hands to his eyes, shielding them from the light. Behind him the beach was a perfect arc of white sand, stretching like a hammock between jagged rocks.

I stole one last look at the yard and jogged over to him.

Chapter Fourteen

Before visiting the rest home this time, I rang ahead so Janie knew to expect me. On the drive up I pondered a question that had come to me in the middle of the night and not left me. It was amazing I hadn't given it a thought until now.

I stopped at a garage and chose a bunch of yellow flowers, still trying to decide if I really wanted to know the answer or not. If I did have siblings on my father's side, surely knowing would only leave me with more loose ends.

The rest-home staff smiled when they saw me, and I hurried down the hallway to Janie's room.

"Hey, Grandma," I called cheerfully, pushing open her door. That deep, sad feeling nearly consumed me when I saw her sitting in the same chair as last time.

"Sunny! I'm so glad you've come—I've been waiting for you," she said as I arranged the flowers in a vase at the sink. "There are things I need to tell you." She was watching me carefully, eyes bright in her crinkled face.

I set the flowers down beside her.

"See those drawers?" She raised an unsteady hand and pointed to the corner of her room. "Pull out what's in there and bring it to me."

I tugged open a roughly made drawer that caught on its rails, and took out a stack of paperwork.

"Grandma, did my father ..." I trailed off, but she seemed to know what I'd been about to ask.

"Have other children? Yes."

I took a deep breath as I passed her the bundle.

"Here, I'll show you." With slow, bent fingers she leafed through sheets of paper and unrolled an ancient family tree. It was badly faded but she knew it by heart and seemed anxious to inform me. "Three half-sisters — see?" She traced her way up through the branches, rattling off names.

More sisters. Did they look like me? Did they even know I existed? I briefly wondered if Mum knew about them.

"... and my two daughters, but they died many years ago."

"I'm sorry,"

"Don't be. I realised not long after I had them that it was inevitable."

What a weird thing to say.

I peered in for a closer look at the branching names. "Are these my cousins?" I asked gently, and another pained look crossed her face.

"Yes. They're gone too."

"What about my sisters?"

"No, they're still young."

How young was young?

Janie pointed right to the top of the page where the tree began. I read the very first name. Juniper. I thought it was pretty.

"Something in our family went very wrong a very long time ago." She looked at me closely as if wondering what I'd believe. My throat had gone dry. "Some say we females are cursed, our destiny entwined so intricately with death we seem unable to live beyond womanhood."

"What happens?"

"The ocean drowns us."

Neither of us spoke for several minutes.

"What about you?" I asked suddenly.

"I came so very close."

I listened intently as she told me about her fifteenth summer.

"Since then I haven't once laid eyes on the sea."

Her eyes fell shut for a moment and I glanced at her collection of paintings. "Do you miss it?" I whispered.

"Every day." She looked tortured just thinking about it. "The salt is in our blood, Sunlight, especially yours."

There was a knock at the door, and the lunch lady bustled in, placing a tray of something steaming on the table beside us. I noticed a line of white pills set out neatly beside a glass of juice.

"They think I'm crazy," she told me when we were alone again, though it was clear to me she wasn't. I wanted to learn more about my ancestry, but from the glassy look she now had in her eyes I could tell she was tired.

"I nearly drowned too, Grandma, when I was little."

She nodded and I was surprised she already knew. "But you didn't."

There was silence for a while as she picked at her meal. "When the moon is full I still dream the ocean dreams," she murmured.

I'd had so many questions for her, but she quickly tired after her lunch came. Instead she handed me all her precious paperwork and said I could keep it. There were photos and letters and a lot of obituaries cut carefully from old newspapers. My own article was amongst them.

I couldn't wait to go through it all, but I arrived home to find Brie waiting anxiously for me in the driveway.

"Sunny!"

"What's happened?" My heart rate had already quickened unpleasantly.

"I've messed up. There's an assignment due tomorrow that I haven't even started! Sam said I can borrow her books—"

"You need a ride," I interrupted. Nodding, she handed me a piece of paper with her friend's address scribbled on it.

And so the rest of my Sunday consisted of me playing taxi driver and helping Brie write up her report.

☼

It wasn't until Monday that I discovered her—or more accurately, Brie did.

We were running late for school as usual. I was trying to assemble books, homework and coffee while Brie was plastering on makeup using my hand-held mirror that I thought I'd lost during the move. She was perched on the back of a chair because the table was barely visible beneath piles of our textbooks and assignments.

Somehow, between applying mascara and eating, she was managing to flick through the stack of photos Janie had given me.

"So this is your dad's side of the family?" she asked with interest. "Where did you get all of this stuff?"

I replied with a vague answer that seemed to satisfy her. I was kicking myself for leaving it there. It was stupid, but I felt very protective about the whole thing, especially when I hadn't even had a chance to look at any of it myself.

"Wow. These are seriously old photos! Look at this one."

I was too busy and knew she wasn't really asking for my attention. How had I lost my phone in the last two minutes?

"Crazy to think you're somehow related to all these people."

Not really.

She started talking non-stop, so I wasn't surprised when she choked on her cornflakes, spraying a fine mist of milk out in front of her. I slapped her on the back and began wiping clean Janie's irreplaceable photos.

"Come on, we have to get going," I told her as she gasped for air.

"Look." She thrust a photo in front of me.

I plucked a cornflake from one corner and focused on the picture. The room went very quiet. I was aware of the fridge humming and the coffee machine winding down.

I let out my breath. "Oh … my … God."

"I know!" Brie said excitedly over my shoulder. "She looks just like you!"

Here was the sad girl who came to me in dreamland. I can't explain how eerie it was to discover she was real.

"Who's that?" Emily asked, appearing at my side.

Brie shrugged because I was still unable to respond.

"Weird," Emily commented. "She even has that same sulky look you pull off so well."

Thanks a lot. I started getting that light, swimmy feeling behind my eyes.

"Sunny, are you okay?" Brie was staring at me.

I slid the photo into my pocket.

"Sunny? We're late."

Damn. I threw back my coffee and we ran to the Mustang.

☼

I couldn't pay attention to any of my morning classes. I'd finally found the girl who connected my dream world to my waking one. When no one was looking I'd sneak glances at the photo. I don't know how many times I did this before discovering her name had been written on the back.

Evelyn.

The bell rang and I went outside for fresh air and quiet, but I wasn't alone for long.

"Did you meet up with Jake in the weekend?" Amber asked as she pulled the sleeping rat from her sleeve and placed him on the grass. He squinted in the morning sun and shook himself, clearly disgruntled.

I nodded and her eyes lit up, eager for details, but I didn't feel like talking. The photo was burning a hole in my back pocket.

I watched Punky scamper into the roots of a nearby pine tree. "Aren't you worried that one day he won't come back?"

"He will always come back," she said confidently, "and don't change the subject."

"We rode up to Angel Bay. It's so beautiful there."

I didn't get the response I'd thought I would. Lexie choked on the diet Coke she was drinking, and Ginger — one of Amber's friends from the year below us — stopped making a daisy chain to stare at me in awe.

"Lexie, leave it," Amber said warningly.

"But that's a sacred place!" she hissed.

"You're brave!" Ginger said as she linked another daisy into her chain.

"Huh?"

"I mean, I know it all happened a really long time ago but still, the place totally freaks me out." She shuddered.

"Jake should have known better!" Lexie gasped, struggling to get her breath. She slammed her empty can down on the grass, and I watched as she unfurled her fingers from the crumpled aluminium.

"What are you talking about?" I demanded.

"No one goes there!" Her green eyes were wide in her pale face. I hadn't thought it possible for her to become any whiter.

"Lexie, come on!" Amber pleaded.

"Why doesn't anyone go there?" I asked, ignoring Amber, who had thrown herself down amongst the pine needles.

"Because that's where they were pushed," Ginger said softly.

"Where who were pushed?" Fear niggled at the inside of my stomach.

"The girls."

I wasn't following.

"Seeing as none of you seem capable of explaining it, I will," Amber snapped, rolling onto her stomach to face me. "It all started when the so-called curse was first spawned—and let me just point out now that the only thing this nightmarish fairy tale has ever done is cause trouble. Anyway, there were a group of freaky locals—"

"My ancestors, you mean," Lexie reminded her fiercely.

"Who made a promise to a sea god." She curled her fingers into quotation marks mid-air and Lexie scowled. I already knew this part of it.

Amber continued, "They swore to find his half-god daughter, but this proved to be much harder than they'd first thought. They became desperate and dangerous. A council was formed and girls from all over began to be trialled."

"Trialled?"

"Historic texts describe baths as the preferred method," Lexie answered.

"Supposedly there was, like, this dungeon with stone baths set deep into the floors," Ginger told me. "And girls were kept locked down there for days, waiting."

"Only until the full moon," Lexie clarified.

I could almost see it now, a group of terrified, innocent girls trapped in the dark with no hope of escape.

She carried on, "They were chained to the bottom of the baths. Then someone would open the taps, and the girls were observed by an elder."

"Elder? Don't you mean a filthy, loathsome murderer?" Amber was angry. I was starting to wonder why these two were even friends.

"They sound like witch trials." I tried not to sound too disgusted in the hope Lexie would proceed with her story.

Appearing thoughtful, she nodded. Hadn't I overheard

her the other day saying I would have been a suitable candidate for trialling?

Lexie had her eyes fixed on me. "Some believed the girl would start speaking in strange tongues. Others said as soon as the water touched her she would morph into a creature so terrifying they would be blinded."

"But they all just … drowned?" I asked tentatively.

"Yes," Amber snapped before Lexie had a chance to defend anyone. "No one survived the trials, and the bodies were taken up to Angel Bay where they were thrown from the cliffs as a sacrifice."

"Why didn't their families do something to stop it?" I asked.

"At first no one knew what the trials involved, and they wanted their daughters proven innocent. They didn't realise there was no favourable outcome. When girls started disappearing, more and more families left town out of fear." Amber sounded sad now. "Some didn't get a trial at all. Locals often took matters into their own hands. There were cases where girls were taken straight to the cliffs and pushed off alive." She scooped Punky up and stroked his nose. "It wasn't the fall that killed them, but the impossible task of swimming ashore."

"But then how would they know if they'd found her?" I queried.

Amber shrugged. "I suppose the weather would have improved."

We were quiet as the morbid story settled around us. A

single cicada screeched from a nearby tree.

"On particularly still nights, it's said the spirits of the girls still walk the beach," Ginger whispered into the grass.

"That's horrible," I said.

"They were bad times, Sunlight," Lexie said simply, as if that explanation was enough. Her green eyes burned through me. "But like I said, there are great things to come. Pytheus is very, very pleased about something and there's only one thing that could be."

Chapter Fifteen

This depressing new piece of information cast a shadow on my weekend spent with Jake. I'd fallen in love with Angel Bay, not expecting it to have such a dark past. I still desperately wanted to know who had lived there. Had they played a role in what had gone on? I knew there would be records somewhere on this town's strange history, and a few days later I set off to the school library in the hopes of uncovering them.

I didn't make it down the corridor. Taylor was standing near my locker, waiting for Jake, and when she looked at me I braced myself for trouble. She wore a short black dress that showed all her curves, and a smile borrowed from the devil.

Jake appeared in the crowded corridor.

"There you are," she cooed, closing in on him. He didn't know I stood behind them, and for a second she looked past him and straight at me. Her eyes glittered through smoky makeup.

"My dad's throwing a party next month and he wanted

me to invite you." Her voice was sweeter than her candy scented lip balm. I saw him tense up and knew it was the very last place he would want to go.

She leaned into him so that he had maximum view of her cleavage and then pressed a slip of paper into his hand. I wanted to march over there and stab her with one of her heels but I refrained.

"So you'll be there? He needs numbers by the middle of next week," she said loudly.

I knew he wouldn't agree — from what I could gather he was sick to death of her.

Then I heard him sigh. "Yeah, I suppose so."

My breath caught in my throat and she glanced at me before flinging herself at him. "Great!" Why had he said yes?

He carried on down the hall, still unaware that I'd witnessed her gross display of promiscuity. Taylor and I locked eyes as she sauntered towards me, her faithful friends in tow. I wanted to say something but was determined not to give her the satisfaction of knowing she'd gotten under my skin. She breezed past me, thrusting her shoulder into mine, and I dropped everything on the floor.

"Oops, sorry," she said, giggling as papers fluttered to the ground. I gathered everything up after she left, taking deep, even breaths. My blood was loud in my ears like waves on a rough day and I strode out to my car, abandoning it all. I'd come back when I felt calm.

I pulled into our driveway, fuming, and wrenched open the back door. Emily was on the couch, painting her toenails. She looked up at me in surprise. "Bad day?"

I nodded and paced restlessly in front of the table. Part of me wanted to sit down and go through every single photo; the other part wanted to burn it all, afraid of what I might find. *Something in our family went very wrong a very long time ago,* I remembered my grandmother saying.

I heard my phone ringing from the depths of my bag and ignored it. Maybe Jake had noticed I wasn't in PE.

"I'm going for a walk."

Emily just nodded as she concentrated on painting her little toe.

The beach was deserted. Even though the tide was out, my footsteps were the only ones that marked the sand. A huge crab scuttled into the waves as I kicked off my shoes and waded around the rocks. My jeans were soaked by the time I reached the little beach, but here I was safe from inquisitive eyes. Unless someone climbed the rocks and walked right out to the end, I was hidden. There weren't any fishing boats out today either, just a tiny dot of a cruise liner on the horizon.

I settled onto hot shells and drew in the sand with a piece of driftwood. Taylor was just insecure and playing games. Could Jake not see that? Perhaps I'd stay here the whole afternoon and unwind.

I stood up, checked I was still alone, and stripped down to my underwear. The sea was warm and green, and I walked straight in. It washed around me like a delicious memory. The fear that had gripped me for so long was gone and I dived under, turning a somersault before carving my way deeper. I pictured the dark-haired girl swimming up to meet me. Evelyn. I had a name for her now.

My hair drifted behind me like a stream of fish and the water made my skin look green. It was so quiet that even my thoughts deserted me.

I swam right to the bottom, trailing my fingers through sandy valleys the tide had created. The air was a long way above me and it occurred to me after several minutes that I should have needed it, but I didn't seem to.

I mused over this as the water stirred the ocean bed. Once I'd looked at sand under a microscope and marvelled at the chunks of glass it seemed to consist of. I imagined I could hear the tinkling collision of it now, the crash of colourful pieces a song in my head. Then I heard something else.

"Breathe."

That voice again, so lucid and real in this underwater place. A ripple of delight ran through me at the mere idea of it, and that alone was terrifying. I peered into the distance, towards the black rocks and swaying weed, but that was all I saw. Had it really just been in my head?

Regardless of where it came from, that one word stuck in my mind — not because I ever thought it would work but because the notion was too beautiful to ignore. I knew if I opened my mouth and lungs the ocean would rush in to drown me, so why was I still playing with the idea of it?

I swam slowly along the sea floor, letting my belly scrape the sand, and my eyes adjusted to the dimmer light. When my lungs started to hurt I headed for the glittering surface. It didn't take long to reach, but still I couldn't bring myself to break through, even when I was so short of oxygen.

"Breathe."

I had to know. Only when I'd coughed and spluttered my way back to shore would I be able to kick myself for being such a dreamer and push the thought away. Perhaps I was much more disturbed than anyone knew.

I needed air. I was starting to feel dizzy from lack of it. Something in me battled, as if either option wasn't quite right. At least I was near the surface if it didn't work.

If? Don't you mean when? You are crazy, Sunny, I told myself.

It was hard to actually open my mouth and take in water. I gagged as it surged into my airways, my body immediately rejecting it. The cold that spread through my chest was overwhelming and the pain scarily familiar.

In hurried strokes I tried to surface, but I was getting sucked out to sea. There was nothing I could do about it. An invisible current pushed me down into shadowy darkness, and thick tendrils of weed brushed my feet and slid over my thighs.

Terror coursed through me. I was drowning—and the worst part was that I'd chosen it. My frenzied attempts to swim only made me more tired and the pressure in my lungs was so intense I wondered if they might be about to burst. The skin of the ocean was high above me now, gleaming and untouchable. There was no longer air in my lungs. I'd watched the last of the bubbles escape like life rafts towards the surface. My chest was excruciatingly full but I only drew in more water.

Maybe this had been my fate all along. Why had I ever thought it could possibly work?

Lights were starting to explode around me and I slipped, barely conscious, through the quiet water. I closed my eyes, letting the currents pull me closer to the bottom.

"Come home."

As I lost consciousness I was aware of the ocean being sucked down into my lungs, and then there was peace.

Chapter Sixteen

Everything was dark when oxygen began re-entering my bloodstream. I was resting on the sandy floor—so far down I could only just make out the surface. My chest ached as if I'd run a marathon.

I lay there listening to my heart, which was beating slowly but surely. That meant I was alive, right?

I'm not sure how long it took before my eyes started to focus, adjusting to the faint light. The ocean filled my airways, slipping in and out of me as easily as air. I could feel the salt mixing with my blood, glittering in my veins as I remembered the dreams. Is this what Evelyn had been trying to tell me? I could smell the salt and the seaweed, feel the currents that danced past me and sense the dark shapes of islands that rose into the air.

"Welcome home."

I drew in a shaky mouthful of ocean and completely freaked out.

☼

I pulled myself to the surface and pushed through to the air. At first I couldn't breathe at all. I gasped and choked as the pressure threatened to sink me again but then the sea poured from my mouth.

Drawing in a painful breath, I looked to shore. It was much further away than I'd expected and my muscles cramped with every stroke. Eventually I stumbled from the sea and collapsed on the beach. My chest heaved as I took breath after breath of dry air and my hands shook while I dressed. The wind blew in from the south, cold and harsh.

I clambered around the rocks, my whole body aching, and avoided the tide which was creeping higher. The sight of our house made me almost cry in relief and I hurried home, hoping Mum would still be at work. I heaved open the door, ignored Emily's look of alarm and took the stairs as fast as I could, though my limbs were heavy like I had weights attached to me.

"Your shirt's inside out," she called, but I barely heard her.

I dropped my shoes, and sand spilled onto the floorboards. What had happened? Swiping frantically at my wet hair plastering my face, I peered into the mirror. My eyes were crazed like a creature from the wild — pupils huge and dilated. I reached up to touch my cold skin, just to make sure I was still connected to the person staring back at me.

When my phone rang I jumped in fright. Amber's name

flashed across the screen and I considered telling her for about a split second.

Of course I couldn't tell her. Maybe I could talk to Miriam …

What was I thinking? I couldn't tell anyone. *Hey, Miriam,* I imagined myself saying. *How are you? By the way, today I drowned again, yet here I am!* I let out a hysterical laugh.

"Sunny?"

I spun around and Emily was standing in my doorway.

"What's the matter with you?" she gasped and it scared me how she saw, so obviously, that something in me had changed.

☼

I didn't dream that night, but I didn't sleep either. What happened earlier must have been a mistake, something dredged up from my imagination.

It just wasn't possible …

But even as I tried to deny it, I couldn't help remembering the feeling of the ocean as it pushed the air out and filled my lungs. The salt still tingled in my blood, dancing like an aqua current. I was good at denying things I didn't want to accept. I could place them in the darkest corner of my brain and shut the door, only this was different. It was more than a mere thought or memory — it was more real than I could ever explain because something inside me had become very alive.

What the hell is wrong with me?

I tried to will away the panic simmering just millimetres beneath my unstable reasoning. The tide was out but I could hear the water curling low around the jetty posts as if it had been magnified. When the tide turned I wondered if it was reaching for me. Sleepless hours passed. I listened to the waves washing in, smoothing out the sand and wiping everything clean. My pulse finally slowed.

And another thought managed to penetrate my brain. In just over two weeks the moon would be full, and I wanted to be there with the locals when it rose.

School was irrelevant. I went, but I barely remembered getting there. I had dark circles under my eyes and it hurt to breathe. The teacher set us a new assignment and afterwards I couldn't even recall which subject it was for. Lack of sleep was part of it, but only a small part. In the days leading up to the full moon, Jake kept asking me where my mind was.

It was far, far away. I was thinking about the ocean, and Evelyn—the girl from my dreams who looked just like me. The girl I had a photo of, who I was probably related to …

I could still feel the sea, woven through my blood like silver threads, even though it had been almost two weeks since I'd swum. And I was constantly aware of the ripening moon. When the day finally came it was all I could focus on. In my mind I saw it, huge and round in the sky, pushing the waves past the high-tide mark. I pictured diving off the rocks at the end of our beach and swimming down into darker water. I'd feel its weight press around me and bathe in pale moonlight.

Suddenly I was conscious of the hard desk I sat at and the teacher, who seemed to be bringing the lesson to a close. I raised my head from the desk and glanced at the students around me. Only Amber was looking at me weirdly. Had I fallen asleep? Was it me I had imagined diving deep into the darkness, or Evelyn? I felt my breathing become shallow, and a lightness filled my head that made me need to steady myself against the desk.

Get it together, Sunny, you're losing it.

I wasn't the only one though. Lexie, along with half the class, was totally unfocused. No one else seemed to notice them, or maybe they were just used to it, but I found their frustration unsettling. The whole town seemed to be wired differently. My classmates could barely keep still, their eyes bright and wandering through every lesson. When the bell rang I was first out the door. Fifth period would be a waste of time. I walked unnoticed to the Mustang and went home to wait for the moon to rise.

I made sure I wasn't the first one there. When it started

getting dark I slunk down to the beach and stood near the back of the crowd. I'd pulled my hood up so Lexie wouldn't recognise me and angled my face away from her. She was near the front with all her friends, and I didn't want them to see me.

I looked out over the bitter, cold waves and shuddered. I'd spent the last two weeks obsessing over what had happened and still hadn't come up with a theory I was happy with. It had been terrifying, knowing I was about to drown again. Did I drown? I hadn't felt that alive since ... well, I couldn't even remember. I drew my attention back to the locals. Their anticipation was palpable but for what I wasn't sure. I doubted anything ever happened.

It was eerily quiet. Children huddled close to their parents' sides, wide-eyed and solemn. The elderly were already facing out to sea, heads bowed in respect, and then through the crowd swept the man I'd seen from the jetty that first moon. He wore heavy boots and a cloak that skimmed the sand. I had the sudden urgency to leave but didn't want to draw attention to myself, so I pulled my hood down further and hid my face in shadow.

When he spoke, his voice was quiet but it held such authority no one could have possibly missed a word. The air was still and charged with expectation. I wasn't sure if I imagined it but the sea seemed to grow, the waves crashing a little harder on the beach. He spoke of the past, and the underlying anger I heard made me tremble. It was starting to cool down and I stamped my feet on the sand to try to warm up. The family next to me turned and glared.

I focused on watching the moon rise. It floated up over the islands like a huge pale balloon and lit a path across the ocean.

The man spoke for a little longer, then faced us.

"Light your candles," he instructed and I decided to leave. This age-old tradition seemed so pointless. It was obviously getting them nowhere.

"Don't you have one, dear?" An old woman with quaking hands passed me one of hers and I forced a smile while she lit it.

I didn't expect to feel the jolt at my fingers when I placed my candle on the water, nor the yearning that filled me. How good would it feel to walk straight in and let the ocean close around me?

The locals were chatting now, pocketing their matches and spare candles as they got ready to leave. Maybe I could dive in unnoticed. I looked longingly at the horizon, which is why I saw it before anyone else — how it rose from the surface of the water like a ghost, silent and powerful.

Fear shot through me but all I could do was watch in shock as the wave continued to grow. The tide swirled over my shoes, soaking through to my socks, and still I didn't move. Moonlight flickered along its watery spine, and the panic breaking out behind me meant others had now most definitely seen it.

"What are you doing, girl?" someone gasped as they seized my wrist and tugged me up the beach. The wave was surging inland and I continued to watch, mesmerised. The woman gripping my arm looked at me as if I might be crazy. "Run!" she screamed and her terror finally penetrated my brain.

I stumbled after her, shoes heavy with water, the sand swallowing my every step. I was breathless by the time we made it to the grassy banks but kept running. It wasn't until we reached the hill that I turned back to face the bay. I collapsed onto the ground, out of breath, as the wave covered the beach and then the lawn we'd only just crossed.

It stopped metres from us, depositing a huge pile of driftwood and seaweed at our feet. And somehow, miraculously, a candle was still alight, the tiny wick blazing from amongst a tangle of kelp. Everyone was speechless for a split second before all speaking at once.

"Pytheus!" a woman exclaimed, and I found myself scanning the horizon for any signs of the sea god.

"It's an omen!" another whispered. I shivered, suddenly aware of how cold I was. The overhead sky had turned a dark, clear blue; it was time to go home.

As I pushed my way through the jostling crowd I bumped into Lexie. It took a moment for her to process who she was seeing and her green eyes widened in surprise.

"What are you doing here?" she asked over the noise of the locals, and my heart beat hard as I tried to stay composed.

"Just thought I'd check it out," I said with a shrug, already knowing this would intrigue her. "Sorry, I've got to go," and I jogged across the sodden grass towards home—away from the candle that, in my heart, I knew was mine.

☼

I sat alone at the kitchen table that night and pulled my family tree towards me. I found Evelyn right near the top and traced my fingers over the faded lettering.

Only child of Juniper, father's name not stated.

I studied the other names on there before warily hunting out the corresponding obituaries. There were so many.

Eventually I drifted upstairs.

I was still awake when the moon reached the highest part of the sky, and I watched the sea reflect onto my ceiling, rippled and patched in the shadowed light. I imagined I was resting beneath the ocean's surface, bubbles bursting around me. What would happen if I chose to float there forever? Maybe I had—all those years ago—before the lifeguard pulled me to shore.

Sleep continued to evade me. I pushed open my window as far as it would go and leaned out. The smell of the beach hit me, and suddenly I was letting myself out the back door. It felt good lying on the sand. Was there really ever a woman who fell in love with a sea god? Was I related to a beautiful sea nymph who caused the town to fall?

Thoughts slid into dreams, and Evelyn was again swimming to me through moonlit water. Her skin was smooth and paler than milk, and now I could see her for what she was. Her flat stomach melted into scales as it had in Lexie's painting, and when I looked closer I saw her features—so similar to mine, though her eyes weren't quite so wide set and her cheekbones were a little higher.

She came to a stop in front of me, treading water slowly, and our identical black hair drifted out in front of us. For long, drawn-out seconds she held my gaze. I tried to ask her what she wanted, but we seemed to be in a silent film where no one could speak. The water swirled around us like a soft piece of music, and the moon was high above us in the middle of the sky.

Then she was reaching her hand out to me, passing me a string of beautiful pearls, white like the moon.

The scene changed. We were close to shore, watching the beach. Waiting. Finally the townspeople appeared, green eyed and angry. She turned to face me. Iridescent tears seeped through her lashes, mixing with the ocean, and she disappeared soon after.

I woke up crying.

Chapter Seventeen

They went all out wild that weekend—not that I saw them doing it this time. I heard from Jake that they set the public toilets on fire and burned couches on the street. If everyone knew who was doing it, why weren't they stopped?

But I had more pressing matters to think about. The locals had seemed so sure that finding the daughter of Pytheus would solve everything, but I didn't think that was the case. If my dreams were showing the past, then Evelyn *had* returned to the ocean, yet everyone was still certain the bay was cursed. Is this what she was trying to tell me?

At night I listened to the tides and stared up at my ceiling. I was dreading school on Monday, certain that Lexie would want to know why I was on the beach with them at the full moon. As I expected, the topic was pounced on the minute I entered class.

Lexie was sitting straight-backed at her desk and watching the door, anticipating my arrival. Her stunning green eyes willed me into a seat between her and Amber. I took a deep breath, wishing she hadn't seen me at the beach. Her friends were all seated near the back of the room, no doubt discussing in depth what had happened. Amber was hurriedly trying to finish what looked like an English essay, her blonde hair falling forward to reveal bright streaks of blue.

"Love your hair!" I said and she looked up pleased.

"I did it myself. It's not too obvious, is it?"

The teacher cast her eyes in our direction and frowned. Oblivious, Amber began telling me about some guy she'd met in a band. Lexie cleared her throat loudly. We turned to face her, and she was staring at us exasperatedly.

"What?" Amber asked.

"You'll never believe what happened at the full moon," she said quickly, but Amber held up her hands to silence her.

"I've already heard—it's all they can talk about." She jerked her head towards the group of chalk-faced students in the back row.

Lexie didn't let our lack of enthusiasm dampen her spirit; instead she turned to me. "What did you think? Nothing like that has ever happened before."

I shrugged, keeping my expression vague, but she held my gaze with such intense curiosity my heart started to pound.

"Tell me you don't actually believe that junk," Amber said, now looking at me too.

"I don't."

She nodded, satisfied, but Lexie was getting frustrated. "You don't think what happened was strange?" she persisted, and I shook my head.

"I don't believe for a second there was anything supernatural about it, if that's what you mean. Currents, wind … those are your likely answers." I began searching through my bag, hoping she'd take a hint.

"Well, everyone's saying she's back!" Lexie flashed Amber a meaningful look but she was focused on her essay.

"I don't believe any of it either," she muttered and that got Lexie really mad.

I could tell she was about to go off on a major tangent, so I interrupted. "If the old stories are true, wouldn't the daughter of Pytheus have died over a hundred years ago?"

"Yes, but it's believed she had a child—one who's quite possibly carried her blood right through to now."

Good guess.

Lexie was looking at me closely, eyes glittering with a dangerous excitement. "The moon brings back to the ocean what it rightfully owns—remember that," and without another word she stalked off to where her friends were whispering animatedly to one another.

☼

I couldn't seem to get away from them that day. From my locker I could see a group of pale students huddled near

182

the end of the hallway. They were muttering darkly and I hoped no one would learn the fun little fact that the Day of Storms coincided with my birthday. It wouldn't be good. I was trying to listen in on their conversation when Jake came up and slipped his arm around me. I jumped, startled.

"Whoa, just me."

I'd calmed down since the episode with Taylor and had decided not to make a big deal out of it. I hauled a stack of books from my locker.

"Are you doing anything this weekend?" I asked casually, unable to resist.

Maybe he heard something in my tone because for a second he frowned, his blue eyes suddenly troubled. "I have to make an appearance at Taylor's on Sunday," and as if on cue she rounded the corner. Her heels clicked menacingly on the wooden floor and she flashed me a look brimming with hatred. If he noticed, he didn't let on.

"Have to?" I asked, but the look on his face told me not to push it.

"I don't want trouble," was all he said.

It was hardly an explanation.

On Friday Jake and I piled duvets and pillows on the back seat of the Mustang and drove up to Angel Bay. How long had it been since anyone had slept in the abandoned little cottage? Thinking about it gave me a strange feeling.

I was relieved to be away from school where Taylor seemed to be everywhere, and even though it was the weekend of her party, I tried not to let it get to me. I'd slept badly the night before, asking myself over and over why Jake had agreed to go, and woken up still confused.

We parked beneath the ash tree, and I couldn't help but wonder if he'd ever brought her here. I sighed, annoyed that she was in my thoughts.

After we'd lugged our bedding up onto the deck, Jake picked the lock. I was nervous about getting caught, but as true as Ginger's word, we were alone. This was a forgotten place.

Jake laughed when I checked behind me for the third time.

"You scared?" he teased, pulling me into a one-armed hug while continuing to jiggle the door knob.

I turned to face the sea. It was calm as always, sheltered by the ragged cliffs that had apparently been a site of sacrifice. A shiver ran through me as I scanned the grassy slopes leading upwards. Where exactly had those girls been taken?

A lonely gull wheeled circles overhead, letting out a cry that echoed back to us. Behind me I heard the lock finally click, and Jake eased the door open. Stale air pushed out past us.

A heavy oak table stood in front of an empty fireplace, and a rug was stretched out in the middle of the room.

Through a window that looked over the back path, I could see a tangle of green garden and some overturned pot plants growing at weird angles.

We spoke gently as we moved through the rooms, and even that seemed too loud. Had children ever climbed trees here and run wild through the yard? Had a man and woman sipped coffee on the deck, watching the sun rise over the sea? I wanted to know who had walked out the door and locked it for the last time. It sounds odd, but it felt like the house missed them. I could almost hear the voices of the family who had been here.

There were three bedrooms—two with sea views and one that looked out over the garden. They were mainly empty, but beneath one window sat an old set of drawers. I trailed my fingers over the cold wood. Who had they belonged to and why had they been left to decay? Termites had burrowed into the delicately carved surface, leaving little piles of wood shavings on the ground. I slid open the drawers, hoping for a clue about whoever had lived here, but they were bare. I pushed them shut and when one jammed I knelt down to see what was stopping it. A book had fallen to the floor. Reaching in past cobwebs that brushed my skin, I grasped it in my hand. It seemed to be some kind of diary written in an old cursive style I couldn't make out. I flipped through the crinkled pages, disappointed. It may as well have been in a foreign language.

☼

We set up in the lounge beneath the window. I spread out bedding while Jake piled food onto the table.

I liked how the sunbeams looked when they shone through the salty windows and how in places the floorboards no longer met properly. I was certain, had the bay's history not existed, that a million-dollar mansion would have long ago replaced this cottage, and the idea was sad. They would have cleared away the driftwood littering the beach, cut down the messy ash tree and thrown dinner parties that filled the bay with noise.

Jake came and rested his hands on my shoulders, putting a stop to my thoughts.

"Let's go swimming."

I knew it was probably a bad idea and he picked up on my uncertainty. I hadn't been in the sea since I'd achieved the impossible, and just thinking about it made me edgy.

"Or we could go for a walk," he suggested, but I'd already looked out to where the water was glassy calm. The tide was so high you could have dived right in from the bank, and it was a hot afternoon.

"A swim sounds good," I told him, and when I slipped my T-shirt off over my head he didn't look away. Adrenaline was already pumping through me as I wriggled out of my jeans.

Jake let out his breath. I wondered what he'd done with Taylor but I pushed the thought away. It didn't matter.

☼

The water was warm from washing over hot sand and it got deep suddenly. I closed my eyes and breathed in the salt. *Home.*

"Are you all right, Sunny?"

I forced my eyes open to look at him. The sun hit my face and I was temporarily blinded. I think he looked confused.

"Yeah, why?"

He shook his head, but still he watched me as if he'd seen something unsettling. I pushed him playfully and he reached for me, smiling now.

"You don't seem that afraid," he told me as I waded out further, but I barely heard him.

Slipping beneath the surface, I relaxed as water closed around me. My worries disappeared, drifting away on a southbound current. I wanted to dive down until I touched the bottom of the world — let the ocean in and push the air out. Light filtered down at me and patterns danced upon my skin. I could float here forever.

"What's stopping you?"

I peered through the water, sure I'd see something, but all I saw was a school of fish disappearing beyond thick weed. If I wasn't getting short of oxygen I would have followed them.

"Is it that useless boy up there?"

I looked upwards.

Was this all in my head? Suddenly, far above me, I was aware of a great disturbance. The ocean split open and then Jake was taking hold of my arm, hauling me to the surface.

"What's wrong?" I asked, irritated, squinting at the brightness.

"Are you kidding?" he gasped, pushing my hair away from my eyes. His hands were shaking. "You were down for nearly two minutes!"

Really? He was staring at me, waiting for an explanation, but I didn't know what to say.

This had been a bad idea. I began making my way to shore.

"Sunny?"

"I'm cold," I called, relieved when my feet hit the sand.

"Well, wait up." He pulled himself through the water and stood beside me.

The ocean urged me not to leave, curling around my ankles like a persistent cat.

"You don't need him."

Jake wrapped his arms around me and asked if I was okay. The waves hissed behind us as we walked up the beach.

☼

When the bay filled up with darkness, and Jake's breathing turned to gentle snores, I only became less tired. I couldn't forget what Ginger had said about this place, and I kept imagining lonely souls wandering along the beach.

From my bed on the floor I watched the ocean; just looking at it made my skin thirsty. Our brief afternoon swim had left me craving more.

"Come, Sunlight."

I closed my eyes, contemplating the idea again. It would be easy to walk across the shells and fall quietly beneath the surface.

"Don't you want to feel the turning tide?"

The truth was I already could. I'd felt the water slipping down the beach, further and further until it could go no more. For a moment everything had gone slack. Then, as if it were in my very veins, it began to flood back in. The sea called to me like a sweet song.

"It's so good tonight."

I pulled the pillow tight over my ears, ignoring every instinct within, and dreams got the better of me.

The water looks dark and cold beneath an angry sky. I only recognise the town by the shape of the beach that hugs the edges of Procellae Bay. None of the houses that are there now exist, not even the jetty. The whole place looks bare, empty.

Further inland are streets flanked by big brick houses that I'm familiar with. I seem to drift above the town in this bubble that is my dream. I know I'm dreaming this time. Everything is soft and blurred like a water-stained photo.

People bustle through the darkening streets, their voices urgent and footsteps hurried. The clock tower strikes seven and they drain away like water from a bath. In under a minute the town is deserted. Curtains are being pulled shut, doors locked and I watch in wonder.

For a moment there is nothing except a straggly dog that sifts through a pile of rubbish in the hope of finding dinner. Then from shadowy doorways men silently appear, their hoods pulled down over chilling green eyes. They scan the street for signs of life and sweep from their houses like bats flying into the night. Even though I've never seen them before, a deep instinct warns me they are dangerous. *Stay away, stay away, stay away.*

I notice a woman peering out from behind thick curtains, worry scribbled across her features. She stares down the road, her lips shaping impatient prayers.

Movement near the trees grabs my attention. A smiling girl runs from the forest, her dress torn and a baby goat in her arms. When she sees the empty street, all colour leaves her face and she shrinks back into the shadows of trees. She has heard what happens if you're out past curfew.

Just three houses along, the girl's mother crosses her heart and pushes herself up from the window. She eases the door open a crack and glances down the badly lit pavements. The last of the men have disappeared around a bend and she throws her door open, anxiously beckoning her daughter. The girl bounds from her hiding place, the goat cradled carefully in her skinny arms.

Even I don't see where the two figures appear from. They close in on the child, and her mother lets out a sob. "Please!" she cries as the girl trips and falls onto the road. "Please, it's not her you're after."

She is right but they ignore her.

"Get up!" one of them demands roughly.

The girl moves slowly and reluctantly. Her hands are grazed but still she clutches the tiny goat to her chest, smearing its fur with her blood.

"Quickly!" he snaps, and the other one hauls her to her feet.

"You're hurting me!" She squirms beneath his grip.

"Stay still, girl." His fist is closed around her forearm so tightly I can see it turning white.

"What is this filth?" he spits when he sees the goat.

She clutches it tighter. "I found him, sir. He was stuck in the river."

There is no compassion in his eyes when he knocks it to the ground and shoos it back towards the forest.

"No!" she screams and her mother rushes for her, fear flashing on her face. The man pushes her away as if she were a fly.

"Please! She's not the one you want!"

"She is of age, and the rumours can't be ignored." His voice is hard.

"She went swimming once, she's just a child!"

"The girl's coming with us." He says it with such authority, such finality.

Their captive struggles frantically against them, and I see her teeth sink into one man's arm.

"Lottie, no!"

"Brat!" he snarls. With that they leave, dragging the sobbing girl behind them.

Terror-stricken neighbours watch from their windows, and the woman collapses to the ground—her terrible wailing still ringing in my ears when I wake.

Chapter Eighteen

Sunday had me restless. It was the day of Taylor's party, and I was feeling bitter to say the least. The Mustang had a full tank of petrol that wanted to be used and I couldn't sit still.

I decided to head across town and find the historic building Jake had told me about. The poem he'd mentioned intrigued me, and maybe I'd drive past Taylor's on the way home. No, that would class me as a total loser.

Amber gave me a rough set of directions to the site, and I was backing out of the driveway when Brie came hurtling towards me. Before I even had a chance to slow down, she flung open the door and climbed in beside me. I was unfocused but she didn't seem to notice and happily told me about a role in the school play she wanted to audition for. I couldn't think of many things worse than being on stage in front of a crowd.

It didn't take long to get there. We drove through the winding streets, then along an uneven road where trees grew tall on either side of us. Since moving here I hadn't ventured far from the sea, and now—with the trees all around—I felt slightly claustrophobic. I'd become used to the vast space over the ocean with all that blue leading out towards forever. It made me think of how poor Janie must feel, always resisting what she wanted most.

The building was hidden amongst a grove of ash trees on the edge of a field. If I hadn't known what I was looking for I probably wouldn't have seen it.

We drove a bumpy, overgrown path towards it, and I left the car idling with Brie in it.

"Won't be long," I promised.

She was watching me curiously, unsure of why exactly I had wanted to come out here. I'd told her it would help with an assignment on local history. I hated lying to her, but it was better than trying to explain why I really wanted to come.

I could hear it now. *Oh, I'm just starting to wonder whether a sea god called Pytheus really does exist.*

It was cold when I entered the woods. Trees towered above me, and I stumbled over roots that jutted from the path. Standing before the stone structure, I shuddered. Bars covered what would have been windows, and moss clung to everything. I forced myself to step closer.

The plaque, which was fixed to the mossy door, was dull and so pitted with age I could barely read the words. I rubbed my sleeve over them to try to see through some of the grime.

Girl with stolen sea blood
Elusive, dark, wild
Cause of curse and heartache
Cold ocean child

Pale-skinned creature
You are what we seek
Beauty, lies, deception
Such sins we should not speak

It is in the bay we'll find her
Tempted by your silken waters
The moon it draws her to the deep
We'll find your daughter
Our promise to keep

I practically fled back to the car. The place had freaked me out, no doubt about it. On the drive home I considered the verse. Had the locals really thought Evelyn's destiny was their choice?

Too many questions presented themselves to me, and I got distracted when Taylor's car came screaming around the corner towards us. Lace and denim spewed from the windows. I glimpsed thin girls with glazed eyes crammed into the back seat. Jake didn't belong in their world and it depressed me knowing he was there without me. I was bound to hear all about it at school tomorrow.

I took a deep breath and went over the poem again and

again in my head.

☼

Monday morning started off clear and full of sun. I got through my first two classes before Taylor made me the angriest I'd ever been, and then, as if to match my mood, the sky filled up with black storm clouds and the smell of rain.

She'd been loitering beside the drinking fountain in the corridor, surrounded by friends, and I wondered what could possibly be going on in the land of lip gloss and fake tan. I had the feeling I was about to find out whether I wanted to or not.

They had their heads bent together and were whispering loudly, setting the scene and creating insecurity from thin air. I knew more about girl world than they realised.

When I approached my locker they fell silent. The air was thick with anticipation, and their eyes were on me as I eased the door open. My breath caught in my throat.

Taped to the inside wall was a photo. How did they even know my combination?

I exhaled slowly and plucked it from the steel. It was of Taylor and Jake at her dad's party. She wore a strapless white dress and he had his arm around her, his hand resting neatly on her waist. She was staring directly into the lens at me like she'd planned this before it was even taken.

Anger turned my insides hot. I was aware of footsteps closing in behind me and slammed the door shut.

"Don't you think we look good together?"

I spun around and she was just centimetres from my face. It took all my willpower not to hit her. Her clones giggled from across the hallway.

"I told you, Sunny," she said sadly. "People like Jake don't belong with people like you." She snatched the photo from my hand and I felt something inside me snap.

The sunbeams that had been filtering in through the high windows were fading. We faced each other like jungle cats, silent and glaring. Her eyes glittered under the hallway lights but mine were looking straight through her. I could see the ocean, dark and rough, even though I was miles away in the confinement of school. I could even smell the salt.

Thunder rumbled like a warning in the distance, and Taylor was suddenly distracted. Her eyes darted to the windows as if to check that the weather really had changed so quickly. A look of uncertainty crossed her features. Outside, the pressure was building. I felt the storm collecting over the town.

The double doors at the end of the corridor burst open and a crowd of students pushed their way inside, shaking drops of water from their hair and brushing rain off their jackets. A few of them paused when they sensed something between us. High school drama—there's nothing like it.

I could hear the rain tipping down outside, and now the windows were dark with clouds.

Taylor turned back to face me, all confidence restored. "He'll never love you."

A gust of wind tugged at the posters on the walls and rattled the long line of locker doors. Down at the beach the waves crashed angrily against the sand, the wind pushing them up past the high-tide mark. I wasn't focusing on words to spit back at her; all my attention was on the storm.

"Sunny?" Jake was walking towards us through the still darkening corridor. Drops of rain glistened on his skin, and as he shrugged off his jacket he looked at me. Instead of closing the space between us he kept his distance.

Taylor stepped back innocently and hid the picture behind her.

"Taylor?"

Just hearing him say her name was enough for my blood to boil over. He kept flicking me worried glances as neither of us spoke, and I hoped he wouldn't notice my stormy eyes. The ocean was dark inside me.

Rain lashed against the windows, and the wind was so strong it was affecting the power lines outside our school. The lights flickered.

Taylor and I locked eyes. She wouldn't dare say anything in front of Jake in case it made her look bad. I could feel the intensity of her stare boring into me but she had no idea what I could see. I saw dark waves rising into the air, a storm so powerful that it could flatten her in an instant.

Eventually she pulled the photo back in front of her and folded it up, sliding it into the strap of her singlet.

"What's that?" Jake asked, but we both ignored him. The storm was wheeling in my head and it made me dizzy.

"See you round, Sunlight," she said, and then the lights shut off completely.

"Sunny?" Jake was caught amongst the students who were now in a hurry to get to class.

While everyone's eyes adjusted I slunk from the hall, ignoring Jake's voice as he searched for me in the dim light. I could barely hear him anyway. The ocean was too loud in my ears.

I walked along the beach. The sea was black and choppy but the rain had stopped on the drive out. A cool wind whipped damp hair into my eyes, and I gave up trying to push it away.

I felt exactly how the water looked — dark and angry. My phone was ringing from somewhere in my bag but I let it go to voicemail. I stood on the sand at the far end of the beach and watched the ocean as it slowly settled.

"Sunlight."

The voice came from far away — so distant I could have

been dreaming. I pictured myself clambering awkwardly around the rocks and diving into the delicious cold.

I gave a little sigh. It was dangerous, I knew that. Goose bumps sprinkled my arms, and I pulled my jacket tighter around me.

The sea continued to whisper my name in soft, alluring syllables. *"Sun ... light,"* it breathed.

Climbing over slippery rocks, I peered into the glassy waves and thought back to when it had last filled my lungs. Had it taken long to make the transition from air to water? Had it been seconds or minutes before I'd drifted weightlessly to the seabed? I'd never felt such agony — as if there were scorpions stinging at the inside of my chest — but there I'd been free and breathing in another world. Nothing had ever made me feel more alive.

I sucked in a huge mouthful of air, as if just thinking about it made me short of breath. The waves sloshed against the rocks, spray leaping up to soak my jeans. Did I really have to drown again, just to feel alive?

I eased myself carefully around the outcrop of rock and out of view. I didn't think anyone saw me undress and dive in.

Chapter Nineteen

Deep inside the ocean it is very still. After I drown there is a moment of nothingness. My thoughts are dormant, lost things, like specks of salt amongst the sand. It lasts until I feel the broken shells beneath me and remember who I am.

My name is Sunlight. My heart is beating. I'm alive.

It could have been five seconds, or five minutes, I didn't know. I sucked in a long jet of water and waited for the pain to fade. It had been equally as bad this time, maybe worse. I took another slow breath to try to overcome the pain and told myself I'd be okay. Salt seeped through my skin, instantly giving me what I'd come for — the sense of waking up.

Floating there, I was aware only of the tides and my heartbeat, which could have been the same thing. No Taylor, no questions, no worries.

I pushed myself off the sandy floor and swam to where kelp swayed thick in front of me. I pressed through it, the greasy fronds sliding over my legs.

On the other side I came to a huge drop-off leading

down into darker water. I kept swimming, savouring the quiet and letting it relax every cell in my body. A school of fish flitted past, my presence unnatural to them. I was a strange, pale life form existing somewhere I shouldn't; only somehow, insanely enough, I felt as if I were becoming a part of this sunken world and it made me calm.

☼

With lazy strokes I pulled myself nearer to the surface, preparing for my first breath of air. I hesitated, listening for the bodiless voice I often heard. Nothing.

I broke through the skin and took a ragged breath. My lungs felt too full and the pressure was intense but then the sea gushed out and the air swirled in, hot and painful. I coughed and hacked all the way to shore, then staggered up the beach. Flopping down, I struggled to control my breathing. It was quick and irregular, verging on hyperventilation. I tried to relax. Every breath hurt, and I hoped the water hadn't damaged anything.

From the corner of my eye, I caught movement near the end of the beach. Something dark was peeling itself off the rocks. With a sense of unease I wondered how long the man had been there. Surely anyone would just assume I was taking an afternoon swim. But what had he seen?

And no one swims in this weather, a little voice told me. It was right. The ocean was still grey like the sky.

I was doing up the buttons on my shirt when he began making his way towards me. My fear swelled. To get home I'd have to walk right past him, and I was more than uncomfortable with the idea. I eyed the rocky cliff, still breathing in gasps. If it came down to it, I could probably climb up to the grassy ledge and escape through the trees. My only other option was retreating to the sea, but that would be a definite giveaway.

The man was closing in fast; it was time to move. I ran for the cliffs—lungs heaving. Staring up at the near-vertical rock wall made me swear loudly. This was dangerous and I hated heights.

Finding footholds in the cliff was hard but I started pulling myself up, away from him.

"Hey, you there!"

My knee knocked into the rock and I felt a dribble of blood start. He was right beneath me, staring hungrily upwards. My heart did a double beat as I remembered back to the hooded figures from my dream. He had the same pale skin and too-green eyes, like Lexie and her freaky cousins at our school. No, I was being paranoid.

"I just want to talk to you—ask you a few questions!"

Paranoid or not, it didn't change the fact that he scared me. I worked faster, focusing only on where to put my hands next. When I looked again he had started climbing, and there was another dark figure rounding the corner.

My hands were soft from the water, and the rock ground off layers of skin, but I kept going. Dragging in breath after painful breath, the steely taste of exhaustion soon tainted my mouth. I felt like a hunted animal. What would he do if he reached me?

Eventually I felt grass beneath my hands and with my last bit of strength, I pulled myself up onto the ledge. I winced at the sensation that shot through my leg. There was a hole in my jeans and a dark red stain where I had hurt myself. I'd worry about it later. I wanted to lie there beneath the trees and rest, but my pursuer wasn't far behind.

Broken twigs stabbed at the soles of my feet, and spiny branches pulled holes in my shirt. I was disorientated but pressed on. The path I took was far from well worn. Eventually it veered to the left and led down into a shallow valley. I paused, listening for the crash of footsteps, but my breathing was so loud it was the only thing I heard.

After scanning the bushes behind me, I slumped onto the pungent-smelling earth. I'd arrived in a clearing surrounded by mossy boulders and as my heart slowed I flinched at the smallest of sounds. I hung my head in my hands, dizzy from exertion. I desperately needed a drink. There were scratches up my arms and I rubbed away specks of drying blood.

Half an hour passed before I decided it was safe to make my way home. When I stood, my knee ached, and I limped slowly through the trees towards our house.

☼

I didn't bother getting up for school the next morning, and Brie had to catch a ride in with one of her friends.

My whole body hurt when I sat up around midday. I took a potent cup of coffee with me to the jetty and dangled my feet into the sea. The salt seemed to soak through my skin and ease away some of the aches. If I looked closely I could almost see the giant bruise on my knee fading.

I cast my eyes towards the rocks at the end of the beach. Was that a person crouching there? I'd just convinced myself I was imagining it when a man stood up. Someone really was there, watching. Would he tell others what he'd seen yesterday?

"There you are."

I jumped at the sound of Jake's voice. Why wasn't he at school? I hadn't even had time to think about what I was going to say to him.

Lowering himself down beside me, he ran his fingers gently over the remains of my bruise. "What happened?" He sounded genuinely worried, and once again I told myself that he did care. It was Taylor causing the problems, not him.

He turned to face me, trying to meet my gaze, but I looked away. My heart hammered as he ran his fingers over my skin.

"I tripped," I murmured, trying to forget how terrifying

205

it had been getting chased up that cliff. I could see it from here—alarmingly high and with bone-shattering rocks spread out beneath it.

He put his hands on my face, gently tilting me towards him. Uncertainty had filled his blue eyes, and as he twisted a strand of hair behind my ears I shuddered.

"You ran out yesterday. I couldn't find you."

"I know. Taylor was ..." I trailed off, not sure what to say. That she showed me a picture of them together at the party? It sounded pathetic. He was here, wasn't that enough?

At the mention of her name he looked confused, his forehead wrinkling into half moons. It was obvious he didn't realise how spiteful she was being. The waves grew a little darker, as if mirroring my frustration.

"Are you over her?" I asked.

"I was never really into her." He wrapped me in a hug, and the ocean settled with my heart.

The moon was almost full again when I next saw my grandmother. I felt bad knowing she spent so much time alone in her little room, but that wasn't the reason I wanted to see her. I genuinely liked being in her company.

Walking into reception now, I barely noticed the piney smell of cheap disinfectant. The lady behind the desk warned me that Janie was having an off day.

My heart sank. "Is she sick?"

"Sometimes she's not ... entirely with us. She gets confused and speaks of senseless things."

"Full moon tomorrow," a passing cleaner added. "Never helps any of them."

I hesitated outside Janie's door before entering. Would she even recognise me?

She was fast asleep, her purple blanket clutched tightly in her hands, and under her breath I caught words amongst mostly incoherent speech. Words about oceans and old stories — things I knew she had knowledge of that I was yet to hear. Did she too dream of Evelyn?

"Hey, Grandma," I said softly, feeling bad when she woke with a start. I saw her trying to remember me before slipping back into troubled sleep. Hopefully tomorrow when she saw the fresh bunch of roses I'd brought, she'd realise I'd been to see her.

I made it back in time for my afternoon classes. When the three o'clock bell rang, Jake asked me if I wanted to see a movie, but I still had detentions owing and had to say no.

Britta and her aberrant friends were also staying late. She had turned up this morning looking other-worldly in an eighteenth-century gown, and I'd mentally prepared myself for the full moon madness.

They were wound up and angry, their criminal

activities for the night probably already planned out. It was no surprise they had all ended up here.

Being around them made me uneasy. For the last few weeks I'd been waiting for the stories to start—of how someone had seen a girl emerging from the ocean—but so far whoever had seen me was keeping quiet.

Britta breezed into detention late, her corset laced so tightly it was a miracle she could even breathe. Her skirts brushed my chair as she chose the seat directly behind me. I suppressed a shiver.

"Hey, pale-skinned creature."

I could feel her green gaze on the back of my neck but ignored her. She was out of control. I scribbled down my lines, anxious to leave.

"Are you the one we seek?" she whispered, and I composed myself before turning to face her.

"I don't even believe such a person exists."

She tilted her head to one side as she considered me. Was she just messing around or was she being serious?

"You would say that." Her tone was soft but it made my skin crawl. She leant forward, her eyes lingering on my face. When she brushed her fingers across my cheek I was too shocked to move.

"Beauty, lies, deception."

"I'm not—" but she interrupted me, her voice now colder than ice.

"Such sins we should not speak."

Chapter Twenty

"Assignments, everyone!" our history teacher announced the next morning, causing me to hesitate in the doorway. What assignment?

The students were handing in thick stacks of paper, and I wondered if I could slink back out undetected. Maybe I could pull an all-nighter and slip it in tomorrow morning. I'd been so distracted lately ...

At that moment the teacher caught my eye, so I reluctantly made my way to the back of the room. There were a lot of empty seats, and most of Lexie's friends were AWOL. I wondered what they'd done last night that would warrant them missing school.

I'd watched the full moon ceremony from my bedroom window and only gone to bed when I could no longer see the candles burning out at sea.

At sunrise I'd risen for a swim. I could smell the salt that still coated my skin and feel the dull ache in my lungs. I yawned behind my folder.

"Last week's essays are marked. You can collect them at

the end."

It was a struggle to stay focused, and when the teacher mentioned exams I felt sick. I barely knew what topics we'd covered, let alone dates and names, but they were still months away ... I switched off after five minutes, turning my attention outdoors to where I had a clear view of the field.

Jake and his friends were striding across the green, late for their next lesson. He was becoming tanned from all the sun, and I wished we were back at Angel Bay. To my disgust, Taylor was also watching. She arranged herself suggestively on her chair as they passed the window, and a few of his friends definitely noticed her — one of them looking twice at her long, bare legs. Did they think he'd made the wrong decision choosing me?

"Sunny, would you like to start the discussion?" The teacher was staring at me through narrowed eyes.

I shook my head slightly.

"Didn't think so. Come and sit up the front, please."

The hour didn't improve. He handed me my essay, and I groaned when I saw the F he'd written in thick red pen.

"I know you can do better, Sunlight. Where's your assignment? I don't see it here," he said, quickly sifting through the stack on his desk.

"I haven't done it. I've been really busy." Possibly the worst excuse I'd ever come up with.

"Detention," he told me bluntly.

"What is up with you?" Amber asked as we spilled into

the hallway.

I muttered another lame excuse.

"Hey, I turn eighteen soon," she said brightly. "My dad isn't really into parties, so every year Lexie's mum lets us throw one. It's always a big deal—everyone comes. We're going to start planning it tonight. You should help us."

☼

We met at Lexie's just as it was getting dark. The air was still and charged with static, which put me on edge. There was a storm coming.

I clutched Amber's hand-drawn map as I passed the rows of mournful houses. She'd told me Lexie's family had been here forever so it shouldn't have been a surprise that number four was the oldest on the street. It was at least three stories high and a fresh branch of ash had been cut from their tree and nailed to the door. My muscles were tight with nervous energy. The thought of turning around and going home was tempting.

Before I had even knocked, the panelled front door swung open and I was greeted by Lexie's mother. She had dark hair, and eyes the colour of mashed peas. "You must be Sunny. The girls are upstairs. Second storey, fifth room on the left."

Fifth? How many were there?

She handed me a tray of sugary biscuits and pointed in the direction of the stairs. I climbed the wooden staircase

211

and entered a hallway. Lining the walls were oil paintings set in heavy frames. The people depicted could only have been Lexie's ancestors, with their delicate features and green eyes so brilliant in colourless faces. It was weird to think they might have lived in this very house, walked the same dark passage that I was now … A cat ran out in front of me, and I let out a startled cry.

"Sunny?" Amber poked her head out of an ornately carved doorway.

"Hey," I said, relieved to see her.

But if I was nervous before, it was nothing compared to how I felt when I walked into Lexie's room. Covering her walls in a patchwork of black and white were pictures of the same creature I'd seen her painting that day at school. Canvas after canvas had been tacked unevenly to the wallpaper, only half of them finished. In some places she had sketched directly onto her walls — rough images of the same girl diving down through moonlit water. As if I needed a reminder at a time like this.

"Don't worry, it creeps me out too," Amber said with a shudder.

Lexie was stretched out on a luxurious four-poster bed, stroking Amber's rat with the tip of her finger. She watched me carefully as I scanned the walls.

"Nice decor," I told her.

"We're just printing the invites now. See what you think," Amber said, handing me a sheet of paper still warm from the machine, which was whirring busily in the corner.

"The party's on a Sunday?" I asked, surprised.

Lexie nodded and Amber shrugged, as if it were as good a day as any to get wild.

While they wrote invitations in curly black writing and downloaded extensive amounts of music, I tried not to stare at the walls. One of the paintings looked scarily similar to me, and I wondered if Lexie had created it before or after we'd met.

I didn't want to be there.

"Where's your bathroom?" I asked, and Lexie gave me an elaborate set of directions. When I reached the hallway, I ducked into the nearest room and rang Jake, speaking softly so no one would hear.

"Can you pick me up? I'm at Lexie's."

"Am I your getaway driver?"

"Something like that," I admitted guiltily before making my way back to the bedroom.

"Did you find it okay?" Lexie asked.

"Yeah."

When I heard the unmistakable roar of Jake's bike I feigned surprise, peering inquisitively through the curtains. His lights brightened the driveway, and I watched his dark silhouette walk to the front door.

"Who's here?" Lexie asked and I was about to answer when Amber passed me her iPod.

"Sunny, can you load all this music for me?"

"It's Jake," I told them.

Amber looked at me. "Huh? I thought you were helping us tonight."

I could see she was put out.

"I didn't know he was coming over," I lied. "I'll do the music next week, okay?"

I picked up my bag, despite her reluctance to agree, and practically fled from the house. I couldn't get away from those creepy paintings quick enough.

"Thank you," I said breathlessly as Jake pulled me into a leathery hug.

"I missed you," he murmured. It had only been hours since I'd seen him, and I smiled. He swept me off the ground and onto his bike.

I had no idea where we were going. There wasn't much to do here but it didn't matter; with him I had butterflies regardless.

We sped past silent houses, the wind tearing at our clothes and scattering my worry. It had started to rain by the time we parked and I could smell the road, warm and dusty.

I followed him through a narrow alleyway, our footsteps loud and echoic, until we reached a huge old building made from terracotta-coloured bricks. It was deteriorating in places and one of the turrets had crumbled in on itself. At some point someone had organised for scaffolding to go up, presumably with the intention of having the place repaired, but the steelwork was rusty now, bolted to the side of the building like a parasite.

Thunder rumbled overhead and I knew we were about to get soaked.

Jake looked up towards the empty rooms, then back at me daringly.

"No way," I told him as lightning reflected off the dark glass, illuminating us.

His eyes were bright for the split second that I saw them, and I knew the night made him reckless, like it often did me. A deafening clap of thunder shook the ground and reverberated through me. The energy of it took my breath away, and Jake kissed me when I was least expecting it, slow and deep.

He pulled back way sooner than I would have liked and grasped the metal railing. "Come on."

I didn't hesitate this time. We climbed the scaffolding like a jungle gym, pulling ourselves higher and occasionally using the window eaves as footing. It seemed we were headed for the top floor and I refused to look down. My heart was beating hard from exertion and adrenaline. The wind picked up, whistling around the sides of the ancient building and urging me on faster. I felt drops of rain splatter my cheek, and more through the thin denim of my jeans.

"Here we are," Jake said, pulling me up to a rickety pair of makeshift stairs and hoisting up a window. We slipped inside just as the skies opened.

From what I could gather between flashes of lightning, the room was circular with a high, domed ceiling. It was mainly bare and Jake led me over to a bay window full of rugs and cushions. There were candles on the ledge and he pulled a lighter from his pocket.

"What is this place?" I asked, watching as he lit them.

"It used to be a post office way back in the day. My grandfather said the homing pigeons came and went from this window."

I looked down at the streets, so dark and empty. It was hard to believe this town had once been a busy point of trade.

"Some friends and I found it years ago. We used to come up here to smoke and tell ghost stories."

We stayed there for hours, lying amongst the cushions while the wind howled and rain battered the windows. Jake traced his fingers across my back as we talked, and I wished it could be like this always.

Chapter Twenty-One

By the end of May all anyone could talk about was the Day of Storms. Some families were organising places to stay out of town, and those who lived close to the beach were stacking sandbags against their houses in an attempt to hold their lives in place. Like Jake, a few of the locals believed it was entirely weather-related but the majority were still convinced there was something much more sinister at work.

I had purposefully kept my birthdate quiet because of this, and it worked in my favour — I'd always found the whole birthday thing embarrassing anyway. Regardless of what people thought the cause to be, everyone agreed the Day of Storms would definitely arrive.

When June eventually rolled around, the whole place was like a ghost town.

I lay in bed, watching the minutes on my clock inch closer

to midnight. In ten minutes I would be eighteen.

The promised storm everyone had been preparing for didn't seem to be happening — if anything it was especially calm in the bay. Through a gap in the curtains I could make out the sky, which was clear and strewn with stars.

Even though I'd been busy with my family all day, I wasn't tired. We'd taped big crosses to the windows and rolled up carpets, and now I wondered if it had all been in vain. To be honest, I was a little disappointed. It would have been exciting, almost, to watch all that power and destruction.

I stared out at the stars, trying not to look directly at them or they would disappear. Where was the storm? The locals had been certain it would arrive, ravishing everything in its path as it took control. They said the tide would rise high enough to flood the streets and invade the houses.

I farewelled my seventeen-year-old self and counted down.

When midnight ticked over I was peering through the darkness at my reflection in the mirror, as though half expecting to see some kind of change, when it started. A feeling more than anything — a sense of such restlessness that my heart started to beat inconsistently in my chest.

Ignoring it, I pulled my sheets tightly around me and willed sleep to come, but my hands were sweating and I couldn't stay still. Something outside had changed.

I kicked back the heavy blankets and crossed over to

my open window. The curtains had come to life. A cold breeze rushed inside, plucking at my thin T-shirt and delivering on its sigh the smell of ocean. I inhaled deeply. Suddenly my little room suffocated me. I wanted to be down at the beach, breathing in the salty night air and feeling the cold water slither over my feet.

Opening the window as far as it would go, I leaned out. When I saw the ocean I almost reeled backwards.

It was angry. There was no other way to describe it. The sea had been like crushed velvet before — navy blue and gently wrinkled by the wind — but now it was ugly and dark, blacker than spilt ink, and the surface had transformed into liquid hills. This was no ordinary storm brewing. I could feel the nature of it deep within my being.

The locals had been right after all, and maybe it was stupid of me to be unafraid of what was coming. But instead I found myself overwhelmed by someone else's fury, an ancient emotion almost as old as the bay itself. I could feel the energy about to be vented by this storm — so undiluted that the passion was becoming my own. The sea pitched and rolled. The tide came in too quickly. Wind streamed into my room, knocking over a vase and scattering the floor with papers. I imagined it was urging me to do something.

"Pytheus?" I whispered it into the darkness, and the wind roared louder.

I pushed myself away from the window and headed for the stairs.

☼

Outside, the wind was gusting so hard I had to struggle against it, and the jetty groaned as it tried to keep up with the bucking ocean. It tilted one way, then another, and I stumbled with every step.

The waves had grown even darker and so big that I was crazy to be outdoors, but the storm had gotten inside my head.

When I knelt down and lowered my palms to the cool water, I wasn't prepared for the rush of energy that ripped through me — so intense it stole my breath. Anger and power surged through my veins. This was *my* storm.

I rose unsteadily, arms outstretched as if I could gather it to me, but the emotion was too much, the sea too big to be inside me. An uncontrolled cry left my throat, and lightning slashed through the sky. A brilliant tempest danced at my fingertips. I wanted waves — huge waves that would rise up and swallow the town until everything was beneath the ocean. I felt it respond, saw the waves on either side of me grow taller and race for the mainland.

"See what we can create together?"

My concentration shattered and I dropped my arms. The storm was back on its own course, gathering power.

"Pythcus?"

Nothing came back to me but the roaring of the ocean in my ears. I wasn't sure what had just happened, but I was exhausted — almost too tired to notice how still the jetty had become. Water swirled peacefully around the posts, and the wind didn't touch our house, yet just beyond us the storm was raging.

The bay was being punished as they had said it would be. Alarming noises had me visualising windows breaking and floorboards being ripped up. Was this my fault?

"Join me, Sunlight."

That voice again.

It was tempting — all that power was exhilarating — but I turned my back on the storm and hurried along the jetty towards our house.

"It is your destiny."

I pressed my hands over my ears and bolted inside, locking the door behind me even though I knew it was unnecessary. The house was quiet. Everyone was fast asleep, completely unaware of the havoc overwhelming the town.

I fell into a restless sleep sometime after three and woke to Brie throwing herself down beside me and wishing me happy birthday. She flicked my radio on at the wall. Her eyes were unusually bright and I noticed she had sand all over her jeans.

I wriggled out from underneath her and sat up. My head was pounding and I felt confused.

"You won't believe this!" she said excitedly as she tried

to find the local station. "They were right about the storm."

The storm! Sunshine was streaming into the room like it hadn't even happened.

"Here, listen to this." She held the aerial upright.

"And last night the worst storm in decades has touched down on Procellae Bay, leaving the little town in mayhem. Families have been left with no choice but to leave their seaside homes and take refuge in the new community hall. Aid workers are being flown in and are expected to arrive around midday to assist with the clean up. A relief fund has been set up for anyone wanting to make donations. I'll have that number for you right after the break."

I massaged my temples.

"You want to come for a walk? All the houses along from us have been torn apart! Ours is the only one it didn't touch—we're so lucky."

Panic rose in my chest. *No, I couldn't have caused this.*

I pulled on loose jeans and stared out the window, waiting for my hands to stop shaking. The house closest to ours was leaning precariously to one side, the front windows jagged and broken. All along the beach, people were searching through rubble for lost things. Even if Brie couldn't see it, I knew how bad this looked. How was it possible for our house to go untouched when we'd been right in the middle of the chaos?

All day I worried, nausea hitting me in waves.

Mum took us out to get lunch but the café was knee-deep with water.

"We are so lucky," she kept muttering as we walked through the damaged streets. "I don't understand how the storm missed us! Have you seen the Petersons' house?"

Brie nodded energetically. "It's so weird!" she agreed.

The roads were thick with muddy silt the tide had carried in, and men were busy shovelling it aside so cars could get through. A couple of times I thought I heard whispers about curses and sea gods but I couldn't have been sure.

Back at home I leafed anxiously through Janie's paperwork. There was only one other picture of Evelyn. It was a painting, done solely in dark ink. She was standing beside Juniper, a beautiful woman with pale curls and a wide, laughing mouth. I brushed my fingers across their faces. Mother and daughter shared no resemblance, but Evelyn could have been my twin. The only real difference was that she looked about eight months pregnant. Was that why she appeared so troubled? I'd have given anything to hear her story.

Behind them lay a stretch of beach, and the water glittered — even in black and white.

I shut my eyes before forcing them back open. They were leaning against wooden railing, sunlight bouncing from their hair. The picture cut the bay in half but I would recognise those jagged cliffs anywhere. They were standing on the deck of Angel Cottage. With shaking hands I read what someone had written on the back: *home sweet home.*

My keys were in my fist before I'd put down the painting.

☼

I walked straight past the cottage, unable to face it, and jogged across hot sand. The water was so still. *A perfect canvas.*

Last night's episode rushed before me, and I squeezed my eyes shut until I saw zigzags. The storm had been invigorating.

What is wrong with you? You destroyed people's homes, you could have killed someone!

If there was ever a doubt in my mind that I had some role in this whole thing, it was gone now. What a coincidence we'd moved back to the very town where it had all begun.

But had I really controlled the weather last night? I needed to know.

My heart was in my throat when I turned to make sure I was still alone. The cottage was silent and watchful. It was hard to believe Evelyn had lived there.

Thinking back to the storm, I wondered where to begin. Should I light a candle? Say a few words? No. A ritual would be pointless.

I shook my mind free of everything and let my eyes fall shut. I wanted waves that surged up the beach, past the shells and driftwood that marked high tide. Past the sea's boundaries.

When I opened my eyes, the ocean was as calm as it was before. Okay, try again. I wanted wind that rolled the surface into waves and rustled the leaves on the ash tree, but not even a breath of air ventured into the bay. It was frustrating because I knew something big had happened and I wasn't about to give up on it. I'd try once more.

I erased my mind, my emotions, my very being. My arms hung heavy and useless while I abandoned myself and imagined I was the ocean. The change I felt was gradual.

It started in my blood. Tiny electric pulses matched the rhythm of my heart until it felt as though the very ocean was swirling under my skin. I formed my lips into the shape of a kiss, blew a stream of air out into the bay and smiled. The water was no longer flat. Waves rippled the surface before rushing in towards me, the wind urging them higher. Behind the cottage, trees swayed gently and delight filled me. Cool seawater curled around my ankles, and I heard Him the moment it touched my skin.

"Feeble attempt."

My mind went dark.

I saw waves rising up like mountains, and buildings crumbling around me. Anger that had come from nowhere suddenly coursed through me. The sun hid behind thick cloud, and the waves grew taller.

"See what we can create together?"

Turbulent water sucked at my legs, inviting me to

venture out further.

"Feel it."

When I held my palms out in front of me, there was a heaviness that was hard to explain. I shook my hands to rid myself of it and I swear shards of light blazed at my fingertips.

"You can do better than this. Use your emotions!"

Without warning, unwanted memories resurfaced. I was a child again, crying at the school gates as I said goodbye to my friends.

We're leaving because Mum's got another boyfriend! Emily told them, squeezing my hand and pulling me towards the car. Fast-forward a few years to the night that same boyfriend we'd uprooted our whole lives for got taken away after committing assault. I was twelve, helpless and scared as hell—watching red and blue lights flickering in our driveway. Mum dabbed at her bloodied lip and told us everything was fine. Then I was fifteen. Angry and frustrated. The world looked different and I didn't seem to belong.

And now, Taylor, smirking at me over her shoulder, trying to ruin the best thing I'd ever had.

The emotion took me over. Black waves crashed through my destructive thoughts and I called the storm. "Waves!" I screamed, and they rose up like walls around me.

"Yes," he urged me on.

"Wind!" I fought against gales that threatened to push

me deeper. The storm was draining me of energy and drawing power from my most painful memories. I was up to my waist in water when I came to my senses. The sea churned, dark and raging around me. I struggled back to shore, broke into the cottage and watched the storm grow.

☼

The house felt different now. It was weird knowing whatever I touched, Evelyn had too. I traced her footsteps into rooms that held thousands of memories I'd never be a part of. This place was a direct link to my past — a chapter in a story so extraordinary only a few people on earth believed it.

I walked shakily down the hallway and stood at the window, still feeling as if all my energy had been stolen. Aged curtains fell apart in my hands. Staring out to sea at the walls of rock surrounding the bay, I imagined Evelyn doing the same — looking at this exact scene. For a moment I lost myself.

Would I ever find out what had happened here? I was so close to my history yet knew nothing. It was frustrating. There wasn't a clue to suggest anything about how she and Juniper might have lived.

Scanning the room, my gaze landed on the deteriorating set of drawers. They had been empty, apart from the diary.

The diary!

Why hadn't I thought of it sooner?

I took one last look at the room and locked the house behind me.

☼

I drove home too quickly, desperate now for the book I'd cast aside weeks ago. Suppose it had been Evelyn's or her mother's? Was there a chance it had been written by the very woman who'd mixed salt into our bloodlines, leaving us cursed and despised?

After closing my door I stared hopelessly at the mess before me. It could have ended up anywhere. I emptied drawers, pulled up the rug and frantically rummaged through piles of unread schoolbooks.

"Sunny?" Mum's footsteps stopped outside my room.

I swore inwardly as I stood up and crossed over to my door. "Yeah?" I yelled, throwing it open.

"There's a friend here to see you."

I smelled her lip gloss before I saw her. Taylor was standing innocently behind Mum, her hair freshly bleached. Typical. Even when the town was in disaster mode she looked perfect.

"Happy birthday," she said sweetly, as though we were the greatest of friends, and I was momentarily speechless. How had she found out?

"Thanks, Mum," I managed to choke.

I listened to her footsteps fade down the hall and crossed my arms. "What do you want?"

"So it is your birthday. Isn't that interesting?" She was looking at me intently, her eyes full of questions. "What do your friends think about that?"

I didn't answer. Wherever this was going, I knew it wasn't anywhere good.

"Ah," she said softly. "That's what I thought. It's also interesting that your house is unscathed when every home on this beach has been reduced to rubble — even the Petersons' which is just over the fence."

"What do you want?" I repeated and she stared at me, searching my face. We were so close I could see the little gold flakes in her eyes and feel her breath on my cheek.

"Maybe this sad excuse for a town really is cursed," she said and I laughed in her face. Her confidence flickered for a second and she stepped back.

"You really believe that centuries ago some god cursed this town, just because the weather here is bad? I thought even you were smarter than that." I twisted my thin silver ring round and round my finger.

"It doesn't matter whether I believe it or not. Other people do, and when they realise your birthday is the Day of Storms, your life won't be worth living." Her eyes danced with blackmail.

"Millions of people around the world share this birthdate," I said scornfully.

"Whatever. They don't live here."

"Has manipulating others always been your hobby?"

"I'll keep quiet if you stay away from Jake." She raked

her blonde hair away from her expectant face.

"Are you serious?" I spat.

"It's your choice."

"Get out of my house." I felt the ocean outside stir.

☼

My heart was pounding hard when I turned back to the mess in my room. She could make accusations but no one could actually prove anything, could they?

The book was resting in a pile of clothes under my bed, and I reached for it like it was the most precious thing in the world. Inside the cover was a message.

I read the words aloud. "To beautiful Evelyn on your seventeenth birthday."

I ran my fingers over the date at the top of the page—the same as today, only about a hundred and seventy years prior.

Letting my eyes close, I fell back into the pillows. It was hard to believe I was holding the actual diary of my ancestor. Even though I could feel exhaustion creeping into my bones, I lifted the cover of the little leather book.

Evelyn's writing was all loops and curls but I eventually got the hang of it, finding it easier to skim over the words rather than focus on individual letters. I started piecing together the broken sentences. She was running—for reasons she hadn't written, perhaps in fear of prying eyes—from a judgmental society.

Tramp, harlot, devil's child, what other names will I hear whispered from the church pews every Sunday? These women who call themselves godly are so blinded. In their eyes I'm a sinner, a ruined girl – but I loved him! How could something so perfect be considered evil? It doesn't make sense to me. Of course we had plans to marry, and such beautiful plans they were, too. Did it really matter in which order we chose to do things? What we had was so right. Like the moonlight on my skin, like my own heartbeat. But nothing matters now. He's gone.

I flipped forward a couple of entries and lost myself in the tricky writing.

Chapter Twenty-Two

School was cancelled that week due to flooding. It rained for days, but that didn't stop the locals combing the beach from morning till night, gathering up the few belongings the tide gave back. Brie was right there with them, helping clean up. I watched from my window as our neighbours pulled items from the waves, piling them above the high-tide mark. Every time they came near our house they would stare up at it in confusion, and I'd duck behind my curtains so they wouldn't see me.

At night when they finally dragged their weary bodies home, I snuck down to the jetty and played with the water.

I would still my mind and focus inward. That's when I could feel it — the hum of energy like bees in a hive. If I just sat there patiently it would grow and grow until I felt as though a live current was streaming beneath my skin. I'd never felt as real as I did in those moments. Everything I thought I knew about myself fell away. I'd found my way back to the core of my being and liked it there.

I could become the ocean. I'd twist the water with my

mind, ruffle the surface like frills on a wedding cake and pull the waves as high as I liked, but then all it took to lose control was a single drop of salt to touch my skin.

"Destroy," he would tell me, and resisting him was harder than trying not to blink.

It was so easy to drag the clouds overhead, as easy as wiping up spilt coffee. I would gather them into the bay like faithful dogs, and then struggle with the battle raging inside me. He would fill my mind with fear and anger, only to feed off my emotions. I ripped the surface into waves and sent the wind screeching towards town. I was angry at the locals for being so selfish. Their ancestors had thought they had the right to send Evelyn back to the ocean. I still didn't know what had actually happened, but these people certainly weren't going to dictate what I did. How naive of them. I could destroy them in a heartbeat.

"Let's do it," he'd whisper, and then I'd catch myself.

I would shake away the terrible thought and try to take back the gathering storm, but Pytheus wouldn't let me. He would make it grow, throw lightning out of the sky and release rain over the sleeping houses.

☼

The following Monday we returned to school—me with shadows under my eyes and that light, spacey feeling that accompanies true exhaustion. I let myself drift with the current of students through the corridor, too tired to push through them to my locker.

Jake's face expressed concern as he pulled me aside. "Are you okay?" His eyes lingered on my tangled hair.

"Yeah," I yawned.

"Are you having trouble sleeping?"

The truth was I'd evaded sleep with countless cups of coffee the night before, wading through the diary and all Janie's paperwork. Evelyn's journey to Procellae Bay had been perilous, and her bravery—although she herself hadn't seen it—was enviable. She'd departed in the silence of night, leaving a letter she knew her mother wouldn't find for months. It was cruel but it would guarantee her plenty of time.

There were many cold nights on the road, but a hopeful thought prevailed—maybe when she reached the bay her mother almost refused to speak of, the father she had never met would welcome her with open arms. If only she'd known it was the last place on earth she should be going.

I'd flicked through at least half her entries after that, scanning the pages for anything that might give me answers. How she described seeing the ocean for the first time had given me a panicky feeling. It was too familiar, and I'd shoved the diary under my pillow before turning off the light.

Remembering what she'd written, I shuddered and turned my attention back to Jake. Behind him stood Lexie's friends, talking just loudly enough for me to hear them.

They were discussing the storm.

And then Taylor was upon us, clad in a dress so short it would have made any guy stare. Jake, I noticed, was still waiting for me to answer. I couldn't remember what he'd asked but I nodded and he seemed satisfied.

"So," she gushed in conversational tones while she stood too close to Jake, "what did you get Sunny for her birthday?"

I could have strangled her right there in the school corridor. He looked at me with surprise, his eyebrows knitting together over his beautiful eyes, and asked me if it was today.

"Oh, she didn't tell you?" Taylor feigned horror like that of a pro actor. "It was on the first," and then she disappeared into the crowded hallway, deliciously pleased at the bombshell she'd just dropped.

"Like I'd admit to my birthdate in this crazy town!" I didn't mean to sound so vicious, but I felt scared.

He let out a chuckle. "I find the coincidence amusing."

"Well, that's just great," I muttered.

"I'm still getting you a present," he told me as he sauntered off down the corridor.

When I turned, the group of pale students were staring openly at me, their green eyes wide and unblinking.

"What?" I growled, and stalked off when no one responded.

☼

I was aware of the rumours starting up after that. From corners of the school came whispers, and the shadowy students who trusted in the old stories watched me as I passed. Their unsettling green eyes lingered on me far too long, their expressions laced with accusation.

Lexie in particular became obsessed with me, watching my every move and dissecting each sentence that left my mouth.

Despite this, I kept returning to the sea. I could hardly stay away and didn't want to. For so long I'd felt detached, as if the very particles that held me together were coming undone, and somehow the sea had fixed that.

Maybe if I'd never tasted the salt I would still be avoiding it, but I'd experienced the high and it was now my cocaine. Every day by half past three, my clothes lay in a heap on the sand and I'd begun my swim out to the Hidden Islands. The sky turning pink was my cue to leave. I had exactly half an hour to get back, shower and act as though I'd been doing homework as Mum came through the door. I looked forward to those swims more than anything, even more than seeing Jake.

"You want to grab dinner tonight?" he asked hopefully as he dropped me home one afternoon.

It was tempting, until I looked past him to where the ocean was so blue.

"Sorry, I need to write my English essay." Technically that wasn't a lie. I needed to do a lot of things, like visit Janie. It had been a while and I hoped she didn't think I'd forgotten her.

Disappointment clouded his features, but he leaned forward to kiss me. "Good girl." He pulled away, smiling again.

The roar of his bike echoed down our street. I didn't even make it to the house. Dumping my folder beside the path, I ran to the far end of our beach.

There was no prolonging it these days. I dived, pushing out the air in jets of bubbles, watching them fly skywards in whirls of silvery blue. Closing my eyes, I drew in salty mouthfuls of water and braced myself for the initial hurt.

There was still that tiny bit of doubt in my mind. What if one day it didn't work and my heart stopped beating?

Seawater flooded my lungs, the familiar pressure erupting inside me. In an attempt to ease the raw feeling in my nose, I inhaled deeply—though nothing I did ever made the change quicker or easier. Every time, I promised myself this drowning would be the last, but such thoughts were fleeting—the increasing pain too distracting.

I rode it out, drawing one lungful after another, trying to quicken the transition from air to ocean. As I slipped from consciousness, the fire in my lungs eased.

Aqua, lilac, indigo—I fell into a dream of impossible colours. Lights danced before my eyes, and for a moment I was drifting through an underwater carnival.

I woke to big space and blue light, the beauty of it masking the pain still stabbing away at my chest. As I massaged aching ribs, salt penetrated the pores of my skin, entering my bloodstream and bringing me to life. I dismissed the promise I'd made repeatedly to myself—the agony now forgotten.

It was peaceful here, and quiet. So beautifully quiet. Nothing mattered. I'd turned Jake down and had a ridiculous backlog of homework piling up, but it was okay.

The carpet of broken shells lifted and fell with the rolling ocean—a sequence so soothing it could have put me to sleep. My breathing slowed to match its rhythm, and I realised after all this time that I'd found myself.

☼

As always now, I surfaced carefully.

I swam upwards, close to the rocks that would hide me from anyone on the beach. Though there was no reason anyone should be there—it was starting to get dark.

I broke the surface and took a small breath. It was so painful I had to reach for the rock in front of me and hold on. Fronds of seaweed slid beneath my fingers, and when I peered towards the shore, my vision blurred. Had my sight been clearer underwater? I felt certain no one was there but scanned the length of sand again.

Damn. Yes there was, and they were close, too.

I ducked back under. Was it the same person who had chased me up the cliffs? Had they been waiting for me? I pushed off from the rock and headed for home, holding my breath this time. My lungs were too sore to fill with water again so soon.

Once I'd reached the shelter of the jetty, I hauled myself up the barnacle-encrusted ladder and slunk inside the house. From my room, I watched the figure walking along the rocks I'd just hidden behind. He crouched down and peered into the water. I swore under my breath. Was there a possibility he'd followed me along the beach earlier? Had he seen me strip down to my underwear and stash my clothes under a bank before wading out and disappearing for an impossible amount of time? The night was setting in quickly and I soon struggled to make him out.

"Sunny?"

I stepped back from the glass as Mum eased my door open.

"Dinner's almost ready. David's coming over in half an hour and I want you girls to meet him."

It took all my willpower not to roll my eyes. I had no faith he'd be any different from the others.

"Okay, I'll be down soon."

She left and I returned to my window, but everything had blended into the night. I'd go back for my clothes in the morning.

Mum cooked an amazing dinner, and David said all the

right things. He even brought flowers, which I thought was sweet. No one but me saw Emily pretending to gag. Brie sat beside her on the couch, watching the evening unfold through analytical eyes. I really hoped this man was worthy of Mum's attention.

The night consisted of seriously boring work conversations. From what I could gather, David worked in real-estate, and the sections he was trying to sell were the same ones he had listed ten years ago. This came as no surprise to me. The town didn't exactly sell itself. I was stacking plates into the dishwasher, readying myself for bed, when David said the first interesting thing I'd heard all night. He'd pulled my family tree towards him, tracing his finger through the years of generations.

It made me very uncomfortable, but I stayed quiet for Mum's sake. I'd only intervene if he touched the photos.

"You're related to Jane West?" he asked slowly, and I had to hold my tongue. *No, actually, it's just a joke — someone put her name there for fun,* I imagined saying. I wanted to grab the bundle of family history and run. It was none of his business! But what did he know about Janie?

Mum placed her hand on David's waist and peered over his shoulder. I looked away.

"That's Sunny's grandmother," she answered, and my mouth suddenly went dry. *Shut up,* I felt like yelling. *Shut up, shut up, shut up!* The less everyone knew, the better. There was already so much suspicion.

"Is she in the area?" he asked and Mum shook her head,

though she didn't look certain.

"I'm sure she owns land somewhere around here," he muttered, scratching his head.

That got my attention. Was there a chance Angel Bay was still in the family? I'd assumed it had changed hands multiple times since Juniper and Evelyn lived there. The possibility made me indescribably happy.

"The name is common enough. It's probably not her," Mum said as she dismissed the idea and wiped down the table.

I finished loading the dishwasher, casually gathered up Janie's paperwork and left the room.

Chapter Twenty-Three

Whoever had chased me up the cliffs and been waiting for me on the beach the other night had started to talk, because suddenly all of Lexie's friends knew, their whispers like the drone of insects in my head.

"Someone's seen her twice now!" Lexie announced as we stood at our lockers that morning.

I was honestly surprised it had taken this long to get out.

"Seen who?" I asked offhandedly, even though I'd overheard them gossiping at morning tea. *Someone saw a girl walk straight out of the ocean! She took off, running ...* They'd been huddled together in the courtyard, their green eyes so wide it looked like they were in a constant state of shock.

I turned to Lexie.

"The girl who has this town cursed," she said slowly, as though she were explaining it to a small child.

Amber, who was trying to entice her rat out from behind a stack of books, sighed in exasperation, causing him to recoil back into the depths of her locker. "When is this madness going to end?"

I thought it was a rhetorical question but Lexie answered anyway. "Much sooner than you think."

I didn't like the sound of that, not one little bit.

☼

Within minutes of the lunch bell ringing, I was pulling away from school and driving the now familiar stretch of road to the rest home. I stopped in at the supermarket to pick up a dozen yellow roses and a selection of fruit.

The receptionist at the rest home beamed when she saw me.

"How is she today?" I asked, hurriedly signing in.

"Better. She'll be happy you've come." I felt bad for leaving it so long.

"Sunlight!" Janie exclaimed the moment she saw me. "I'm so glad you're here." She looked tired, and I wondered if she'd had a night full of dreams. There was no mention of my last visit.

I gave her a hug and asked if she wanted some fruit. She nodded, and I began cutting a melon into bite-sized wedges.

Suddenly I remembered what I'd been meaning to ask her. "Is the land at Angel Bay yours?"

"Yes." She was smiling but her eyes were sad. "I inherited it from my mother. It's been in the family a long time. I lived there until I was fifteen." She sighed despondently, then quickly looked back at me as though something had just occurred to her. "Have you been there?"

"Yes. I think I'm about the only one who goes up that way now. It's abandoned and beautiful."

Tears filled her eyes. "I often think of that place. I spent so many hours in those gardens. I bet they're not even there now."

"They are," I assured her. "They're just wilder. The daisies are a tangle on the path." And then the idea came to me. "I could take you out there!" I said excitedly, but her eyes grew wide, and she pressed herself further into her chair.

"N-no," she stammered. "The ocean. I can't."

So instead I described to her the salt-coated windows and the angel statue covered in moss. She told me the ash tree had been planted by her grandmother.

"The key to the front door is somewhere in here," she said suddenly. Beside her was a small oak dresser I'd never noticed, and she reached down to open one of the drawers. Excitement hummed through me as we searched for it amongst a mess of books, lists and letters.

"Here it is. Will you take it and air the place out for me?" she pleaded, and I promised I would.

"You're a good girl, Sunlight. Do you know it was me who picked out your name?"

That was the very moment I stopped hating it.

"Really?" Why hadn't Mum told me that whenever I'd complained to her about it?

"Oh, yes. I lived in the caravan for three weeks after you were born, helping your mother out. I knew my useless son wouldn't be any help."

I bit my lip, but we didn't dwell on the subject of my father.

"The moment I saw you, I knew you would be the one to end the darkness."

My heart beat quickly. The territory we were now getting into made me afraid, yet I was desperate to understand. I rubbed my thumb over the key to keep my hands busy.

"Remember how I told you something went wrong right at the start of our lineage?" She spoke slowly, as if afraid I wouldn't believe her.

I could breathe underwater. At this point I'd believe anything.

"Pytheus," I whispered and she leaned in close to me.

"We are cursed, forever drawn to the ocean because of the salt in our veins. We can't resist it and we can't survive it, but there was a prophecy. One day a daughter would be born who would have the strength to lift the curse. You're the one we've all been waiting for."

I shuddered. "How do you know that?"

"I can smell the salt in your skin. You drown over and over and still you are here, but living in both worlds has never been an option, my darling."

I didn't really understand. So far it hadn't been a problem.

"You leave the air more and more?" she asked, sensing my confusion. "When the moon is round you can barely resist him luring you to the deep? Sometimes you question why you bother returning to land at all."

For a moment there was silence and I suddenly felt anxious. "I'm in control."

She shook her head sadly. "We never have been. It's just a matter of whether or not we can survive it, and you can. Your earth ties are weakening. Can't you feel that?"

I was dangerously unfocused on the drive home, at one point so distracted that my car crossed the centre line, causing me to swerve violently to avoid an oncoming vehicle.

Although Janie hadn't said it directly, I knew what she'd meant—to lift the curse, I had to choose ocean. Leaving my family and Jake behind was a terrible thought, but beneath the waves these things didn't seem so important. I realised what a risky game I was playing.

I swung into the school car park and waited for Brie. A group of laughing girls came running down the path and she burst from amongst them, carefree and smiling. It was nice having her beside me on the ride home. She told me her friends wanted to raise money for the people whose homes had been damaged in the storm.

"I thought we could have a cupcake stall. What do you think, Sunny? Is that a good idea?"

Swallowing my guilt, I nodded. "It sure is."

She smiled broadly. "We could make chocolate and vanilla ones. Ooh, and raspberry! I want to decorate them all differently. I'll look through Mum's recipe books tonight."

Pulling into our driveway, we had a clear view of the beach, and what I saw made my breath catch in my throat. A group of tall, darkly dressed figures were pacing up and down the water's edge. The sight gave me chills. It was like they had stepped straight out of my dream and onto the beach. As we walked inside I tried to glimpse their faces, wondering if I would recognise anyone, but they were hooded and turned towards the sea.

I sat restlessly at my window, unable to concentrate on the reading we'd been given for English. Outside, the light was fading. Usually at this time I'd be swimming back from the Hidden Islands, gliding home on the incoming tide and feeling content. I silently cursed those interfering locals.

Even though my conversation with Janie had been disturbing, it wasn't enough to keep me out of the sea. But her words continued to run through my head. *Living in both worlds has never been an option.*

I told myself this wasn't true and turned my attention back to the search party. How long did they plan to stay?

Tapping my foot impatiently, I willed them to leave. I'd be swimming in the dark at this rate.

As night crept in, the group dispersed. I watched them wander up the grassy slopes towards town. When their trail of glowing lanterns grew dim, I cast my textbook aside and reached for my bikini. It was still wet but I didn't care and went to draw the curtains.

"What the hell," I muttered. Others were arriving, and in the darkness they appeared more sinister. Had they really assigned people to watch overnight?

The bikini slipped from my hands. What was I going to do now?

"Call a storm."

I honestly couldn't tell you if they were my thoughts or his. Biting my lip, I pondered the idea. My palms already tingled with anticipation. Knowing I could take the weather in my hands and twist it whichever way I chose gave me a rush of something frightening, but I wanted them gone. On a wild night, who in their right mind would linger?

The ocean was still and dark in the dying light. Was it even possible to manipulate the weather from here?

It took an eternity for the locals to reach the beach's furthermost point.

I closed my eyes but found it hard to focus. Not only was I plagued by Janie's unsettling information, thoughts of school and how Lexie now looked at me crammed my head. If she'd been suspicious before, she was almost condemning me now.

Concentrate.

I wanted rain—cold and wet—to splash from the heavens and send whoever was down there running. Who were they to get in the way of what I wanted? They may have scared Evelyn, but times had changed. Like caged cats they paced.

The rain didn't come. Minutes passed, and I grew increasingly frustrated.

Try harder.

Lifting the latch on my window, I flung it open. A cold breeze swept off the sea, carrying the smell of salt right into my room. It was like someone had flicked a switch on in my brain.

To have rain you must have clouds.

My own logic made me smile. I knew exactly what to do, my focus so absolute it was almost too easy now. Drawing clouds into the bay was second nature, and the sky grew heavy with them.

For waves, you need wind.

Breezes grew to gusts that funnelled through the channel and tore at the ocean. My efforts were not going unnoticed by the group who had suddenly turned seaward. Did they suspect anything unusual about the storm I had brewing? The sky above took on a slight tinge of green as my energy filled the bay. I heaved the surface into waves that crashed against the sand, and smiled as rain fell.

They were leaving. As their lights disappeared over the hill, my squall eased slightly, but I brimmed with recklessness, far from satisfied. I pulled the waves higher and turned my energy into lightning that seemed to flicker from the very core of my body. Thunder crashed so loudly overhead I jumped, startled.

Suddenly my door swung open, and I leapt up guiltily. Brie stood there, confusion growing in her sweet face as she scanned the room.

"What the hell is going on in here?" Emily pushed past her, a look of disbelief in her eyes.

Pulling my attention away from the storm, I glanced around my room. It was mayhem. Ripped posters hung from the walls, and an old vase Mum had given me lay in pieces. I reached past torn curtains and tugged the window shut, trying to get my head around what had happened.

"You're going to be in so much trouble," Emily told me.

"It's not my fault!" Another lie. "The wind blew in before I could shut the window. It's wild out there."

"The wind?" she said scornfully. "Don't blame that on the tantrum you've just had." She sauntered out, and I turned to Brie.

"Tantrum?"

I didn't like the way she was looking at me.

"We heard you ..."

"Heard me what?"

"It sounded like you were literally tearing your room

apart."

Books were strewn across the floor, some with their pages torn loose, and I gathered them up with trembling hands, avoiding Brie's inquisitive gaze. Rain pelted our roof. The thought of a swim no longer appealed to me.

Later that night, as I put my room back together, I noticed scorch marks on the floorboards where I'd been standing earlier.

I ran my hands over the smooth, blackened wood and covered it with a rug.

☼

The men returned at sunrise and maintained a twenty-four hour vigil. I didn't swim for a week—it was too big a risk.

During the day they remained heavily cloaked, making it impossible for me to see their faces. But come nightfall they shrugged off their hoods. Initially I could only make out their silhouettes, visible in the lanterns' soft light. Several nights passed before moonlight began revealing them. They stalked the beach relentlessly. It wasn't until the moon grew fat in the sky that I was able to see them properly. I didn't recognise anyone, but their pale features told me enough.

I couldn't resist any longer. The moon was perfectly round and almost as beautiful as the ocean. I'd just be really careful.

I pulled on my bikini, tiptoed across our shadowy front

lawn and snuck down to the jetty. Dozens of candles flickered at the water's edge. The crowd made me uneasy, but I knew the sturdy posts hid me well enough. I silently disappeared beneath the surface.

It must have been deep, because I was still drifting through the darkness when I came to. Usually I woke upon a blanket of shells.

I let myself fall—it was really all I could do. Until the salt worked its magic I was helplessly vulnerable, but it never took long. The change was incredible, like being injected with undiluted bliss.

Inhaling deeply, I smiled. There were jellyfish in the water around me, glowing like little pink clouds. I pulled myself towards the skin and lay just below the surface. The moon looked undefined through the water, its edges blurring like a bad photo. As I floated on my back I was lulled into a peaceful trance. The darkness became a blanket, the moon my night light. This world of mine was perfect.

My eyes closed. I wouldn't sleep—I'd just rest for a while.

I woke to chaos.

Chapter Twenty-Four

Sharp shells bit into my skin as hands dragged me roughly from the shallows. Blinding sunbeams pierced through salt-induced dreams; it must be morning.

"Oh, God!" A distressed woman with masses of blonde curls fumbled with my wrist. "Sweetie." She slapped me lightly on the face.

I took a breath and the sea poured painfully out of me. It was worse than ever this time. Realising I was alive, she let out a hysterical wail. I sat up, disorientated, and winced at the stabbing sensation somewhere just below my ribs. Why was I here? After drawing in another agonising breath, I pulled myself up to dryer sand.

"Oh, thank God," she cried. "I thought you were dead!"

Ropes of sopping hair fell in my eyes as I scanned the length of beach. This was bad. Where were those freaks who had been keeping watch the night before?

"You must have fallen off one of the boats." She sounded unsure, her gaze sweeping the bay. A lone fishing vessel was lowering its huge nets into the water.

"Yes ... I work on that one there ... with my dad," I lied, water dribbling from the corner of my mouth. "I remember falling in."

"Here, have my coat. I'll just call you an ambulance. Oh, sweetheart, I really thought you had drowned, just floating there so lifeless." She shuddered and pulled an expensive phone from her pocket.

"Oh, you don't need to—I'm okay." I tried to peer around her, worried we'd be seen, but she was blocking my view of the beach now.

She shook her head and started dialling.

"Really, you don't need to call anyone. See that house just there?" I pointed to a badly damaged shack with fishing rods leaning against it, knowing it had been abandoned since the storm. "I live there with my mum."

She looked doubtful, and I swayed as though currents still rocked me. In the distance I spied a pair of dark figures walking over the hill.

"I'm fine," I told the woman hurriedly, and thanked her for 'saving my life'.

I stumbled towards the little house, hoping it was unlocked. When the handle turned, relief filled me, and I slipped inside.

The whole place reeked of fish, which only made me feel more unsteady. Beer cans and discarded nets littered the room. I swept piles of junk off a seat and collapsed onto it, trying not to think about what could have happened.

That woman knew my story wasn't right, but I didn't care. Through a gap in the curtains I watched her stare out at the fishing boat. I shivered as the cloaked men brushed past her.

She wasn't one of them, which was all that mattered.

☼

I couldn't stay still that day. It made me unsettled every time I thought about how wrong my morning could have gone. History and English were the last things I wanted to think about, and the hours dragged.

Jake was waiting for me outside my second class, but Taylor practically pushed me aside, demanding that they needed to talk. He didn't look in the least bit surprised and reluctantly led her back into the empty classroom.

"I'll see you in a bit, Sunny."

What could they possibly need to talk about?

The bell rang to signal the start of PE and it was exactly what I needed. When the teacher announced we would start training for cross-country, the students hauled themselves unwillingly from the stands. But I was already tying up my laces and stretching. I ran fast, my trainers pounding the dirt. At first my lungs hurt — badly — but as I covered more ground, I felt myself unwinding.

"Take it easy, West!" the teacher yelled from the sidelines. "You'll burn out!"

I didn't. I ran lap after lap, pushing on relentlessly,

trying to burn up the restless energy that had been thrumming through me since my sleep in the sea. After PE I staggered into a shower and slumped against the wall. Hot water burned my already hot skin. What I really needed was a swim.

As I sat outside and towel-dried my hair, a group of athletic-looking kids eyed me from the stands. They told me I should join track.

☼

"So what did Taylor want to talk about?" I uncapped a bottle of water and looked at Jake. He'd barely said a word in the last half hour.

"It's complicated." He stared out across the field, but his rigid posture told me he was seeing something much more complex than the game of football being played.

"What is?" I pressed.

His reluctance to talk made me desperate to know what had gone on between them, but who was I to get involved? Of course they knew things about each other I didn't.

The tense silence was suddenly broken by the shrill ringing of his phone. I just had time to see her name appear on his screen before he turned it off. The way he gripped it, I was sure it would break.

He turned to look at me, the blue in his eyes unreadable. "I honestly wish I'd never met her."

I spent the rest of the day worrying. He wasn't prepared

to talk, which left me guessing. For someone with an overactive imagination, that could only be a bad thing.

☼

Taylor began demanding more and more of Jake's attention.

I think what bothered me most was not understanding why he felt so compelled to give it. The week before, he'd spent an entire day fixing her car while she no doubt pranced around in tiny, revealing clothes.

She was using whatever had happened between them to wedge us apart, and I couldn't seem to stop her. Every time his phone rang I assumed it was her, and whenever she walked past me I felt small. I hated her perfect blonde hair and the way she looked at him. I hated knowing that he had kissed her the same way he kissed me.

When life became too complicated I would escape to the ocean and forget everything. It might have seemed like I was avoiding real life ... hell, that's exactly what I was doing.

Had it not been for the searching eyes of the superstitious, I could have gotten my fix during the day when the water was bursting with light. Now I relied on the cover of nightfall. To my surprise I discovered I actually preferred this. I thought the great depths and its creatures would scare me, but they didn't. I now longed for the very thing that had once made up my nightmares.

I'd wait until a deep quietness fell over the house before leaving my room. And only when the glowing lanterns hovered at a safe distance would I tiptoe along the jetty and disappear below the surface.

It was like waking up after a long sleep. The water lifted my hair, filled my nose, and the salt … it was beautiful.

While underwater, it really didn't matter that I wasn't going to pass this year at school, or that my boyfriend was still tied to his ex. I hated that these were my very first thoughts each time I resurfaced.

So as not to avoid life entirely, I'd promise myself I wouldn't be gone longer than an hour, but more often than not I stayed until the sun started to rise, casting its white rays through the water and puncturing the darkness. I'd swim right out to an island, walk its beaches and settle on cold sand to watch the sun trip over the edge of the world.

On days following a night in the ocean I could barely keep still. I started running before school in an attempt to unwind. I'd lace up my trainers and head out, pushing myself hard because it seemed about the only way to burn off all my energy. I'd fall into the shower — hot, sweaty, and somewhat more composed.

It also distracted me from thinking about Jake. He still wouldn't confide in me, and I wanted to ask him why he felt he couldn't, but then I'd have to take a long look at myself. I told him virtually nothing about what was going on in my life, so why should he?

But the day before, I'd heard a conversation between him and Taylor when they thought they'd been alone, and it was eating away at me.

"Let's get back together, Jake."

I'd watched as he firmly unwound her arms from around his neck.

"You know the only reason I keep our little secret is because I love you," she pouted.

He looked furious but kept his voice steady. "What do you want, Taylor?"

"You."

Her words had spun possible scenarios in my head all afternoon, and it was this kind of stress that pushed me to the ocean night after night. My skin became clear — not a single spot blemished my face — and my hair grew at an unnatural rate. It hung thick and dark, almost reaching my lower back. People noticed small changes in me, and I became good at telling stories to explain away the unbelievable truth.

Good at lying. It didn't sit right with me.

"What did you do in the weekend?" Amber would ask.

Oh, I spent Saturday night exploring a reef, and Sunday mapping out underwater ridges crisscrossing our bay. Did you know that the coral declared extinct last September grows in abundance on the left side of the smallest island?

"Brie and I went clothes shopping."

She and Lexie would nod, then fill me in on the latest party plans. It was all they ever discussed, and I found myself wishing my biggest problem was what colour streamers I should be buying.

☼

That weekend I escaped to the cottage. I longed for cleaner water and empty beaches. On the drive up I thought about Evelyn. The night before, I'd made myself reopen her diary, knowing I couldn't ignore it forever. Some of what it contained scared me, but I'd also learnt how she'd come to inherit the land at Angel Bay.

The cottage once belonged to an old woman. Marlene had spent her days planting flowers and painting shutters until her fingers became too bent with arthritis to tend even the simplest tasks. Weeds sprang up everywhere, and the property grew tired with her. She needed help but had no one to ask, having outlived all her friends and most of her family too. Being alone in the world hadn't worried Marlene, but she'd become upset by the neglect her precious flowers suffered. She decided to find a gardener and considered asking a handsome young man from her church.

A pregnant teenager was the last person she had expected to bring home.

According to the diary, Marlene had been eyeing up possible candidates one Sunday when she overheard

Evelyn pleading with the Reverend. Her fraught plea for help had fallen on deaf ears, and his eyes lingered on her swollen belly before he began to disapprove loudly. Marlene interrupted, telling Evelyn if she brought her flowers back to life she could have a room in return. She later told Evelyn that getting under the Reverend's skin had been a bonus.

And so they put their meeting down to fate. Marlene hadn't realised just how lonely she'd been, and it turned out Evelyn could work magic in the garden.

I'd read through her next few entries too, searching for clues amongst what she'd written about her evidently broken heart. From what I could gather, her lover fell victim to a tragic accident, destroying her dreams of marriage.

The ocean is absolutely breathtaking. I never tire of watching storms out at sea, she'd written. *There is something so beautiful about saltwater on my skin.*

I pulled off the main road and into the driveway at Angel Bay.

It amazed me that Evelyn had written most of her story from this very cottage.

Down on the beach I sighed contentedly. Being away from the locals in all their black attire was a welcome relief. Amber laughed at how ridiculous the whole thing was, but their presence bothered me more than I would admit.

Here I was safe. I basked in the warm water, aware of stingrays doing the same nearby. My chest rose and fell. How was it possible for me to breathe water? Was my anatomy somehow different?

Pytheus stayed quiet until I swam to the surface, preparing for air.

"*Stay,*" he urged. So tempting, but I couldn't. He told me I didn't need my life up there—that he could give me everything I had ever dreamed of and more. My skin shone bright in the green light.

"*Stay, Sunlight,*" his voice whispered through the currents, full of promises and so alluring that I stopped breathing.

"*You belong here.*"

I wanted to ask what would happen to my earth life, but it seemed he could read my thoughts.

"*What life?*"

And I forgot everything. Land, Jake, everyone I cared for. Nothing mattered but this—the currents running through my hair, the arc of white sand covered by high tide, the hypnotic sway of leathery kelp. I closed my eyes, smiling as the ocean rippled over me.

"*You never have to leave.*"

Light slipped away, and I thought of nothing.

☼

When my memories came spiralling back, the bay was draped in darkness. Inhaling sharply, I pulled myself skyward. My first logical thought was of Jake.

Jake! I couldn't picture his face, and horror filled me as I struggled to surface. It felt as if watery ropes had attached themselves to my ankles, anchoring me to the seabed. Finally breaking free, I took a panicky breath of air and headed for shore. I pulled on my clothes and stumbled to the Mustang, still unable to conjure up an image of his face. All I could see was ocean.

"I can give you everything."

"No!" I screamed. "No, you can't!"

Saltwater dripped from my hair, leaving dark patches across my shirt, and my hands shook with the cold. I let out a distressed sob. What if I couldn't remember where he lived?

I peeled out onto the main road and sped in the direction of home, passing my street without a second thought. When Jake answered the doorbell I practically threw myself at him. Only later did I realise how unnerving that moment must have been for him — finding me on his doorstep so late at night, face frightened and hair sopping wet.

"What's wrong?" he asked urgently as he untangled me from around him, searching my face for an answer.

I tried telling myself to be calm, but my chest was tight with anxiety and there was too much air. *Too much air! What the hell is that supposed to mean?* I pondered the thought, momentarily side-tracked.

"Sunny, what's happened?"

"Can I stay with you tonight?" I couldn't stand the thought of being alone. Besides, our house was too close to the sea, and the lack of control I seemed to have scared me. My grandmother was right.

He led me silently down the hall, ignoring his stepmother who called out gruffly, and pulled me gently into his room. I slipped out of my clothes and climbed under the blankets. In the dim light I watched him undress, aware of what I was about to let happen. *Are you being reckless?* asked my inner voice, which I chose not to answer. I needed this distraction. His arms bulged when he tugged off his shirt, and I shivered with anticipation.

Chapter Twenty-Five

"Sunny!" Mum's stare, ice-blue and indignant, met me the minute I arrived home.

"Yeah?"

"Where have you been?" she demanded, voice shaking slightly.

Uh-oh. I hadn't even thought to call her. After leaving the ocean last night, all I'd wanted was Jake. She looked tired like she'd been up all night and Brie was watching nervously.

Guilt crept up on me. "Sorry. I fell asleep at Amber's."

She took a step closer, a combination of annoyance and sadness growing on her face. "I rang her father at midnight when I was going out of my mind with worry. Where were you, really? I want the truth."

The truth was I hadn't actually spent much time with Amber at all lately. It was partly to do with her attachment to Lexie but mostly to do with my general detachment from everyday life. They tried to include me as they planned what outfits and decorations to buy for the party, but my heart wasn't in it.

"I stayed at Jake's."

Emily had appeared, and at this sentence her eyes lit up, but I focused mine on Mum. Her expression had hardened.

"Is he the reason you're failing school?"

I shrank back when I heard the unfamiliar sharpness in her voice. "What? No!"

"I talked to your principal just last week on the phone. He told me about the detentions, and the classes you've missed."

There was an uneasy silence between us, which I wasn't used to. All I wanted was to go upstairs and shower.

"I would hate to think a boy was behind all of this."

That got me really mad, and a storm licked at the outskirts of my subconscious. "Just because you choose losers doesn't mean I will."

The words were out before I could take them back, and her pretty eyes widened. "What?"

"You heard."

Fat tears wobbled at her lashes, and I left before I had to see them fall.

☼

Under the pummelling jets of hot water, I stood and cried. Failing school was the least of my problems, but Mum didn't know that. Steam filled the bathroom with clouds and worked the salt from my skin. My whole body shook as I struggled to contain my emotions. Being with Jake last night had done something strange to my heart.

When had life gotten so complicated?

Eventually I turned off the shower and wrapped my hair in a towel. Guilt niggled away in the pit of my stomach. I'd have to apologise to Mum, even though what I'd said was basically a harsh version of the truth.

I would probably never meet my dad — not that it really bothered me. He was just another one of her bad choices. Emily had cut all contact with her father the summer she turned thirteen, and as for Brie's, we didn't even know his name. They were just three in a long line of no-hopers.

Emily was sitting on my floor, waiting for me amongst a ridiculous mess of clothes and shoes. If she had come to gloat I'd be quick to tell her where to go.

Instead she wanted to know about my night with Jake. I guess the look of confusion on my face told her everything and she hugged me tight. We sat cross-legged on my bedroom floor and talked through it like I'd never thought we could.

Mum didn't speak to me all day. The silence between us was so awkward I had to leave.

I pulled on my running shoes and headed towards the end of town. It was a relief to be alone. Someone had told me about a track through the forest, which sounded like a pretty good place to go while my heart was so ocean drawn.

The beach was virtually deserted, and I ran past dark figures that paced the water's edge. They contaminated what would have been a perfect afternoon. No wonder the beach was empty of sandcastle cities and the bustle of families packing up for the day.

My feet pounded a steady rhythm on the path, and my breathing was effortless from weeks of running. I found the track easily enough. It wound through tall trees, up the side of a mountain. Half my blood may have been ocean, but what about the other half? Surely I had some control over my destiny ...

Earthy scents of moss and rotting leaves quickly overwhelmed me, and I suddenly struggled for breath. My blood felt starved, even in this oxygen-rich forest. Were my earth ties really weakening?

I was dripping with sweat when I reached the top, and I let myself collapse on the ground. My mind instantly reverted back to Jake. I sighed audibly. Already I could feel something had changed within me.

Being with him had turned out to be more complex than I'd ever imagined, but in a beautiful kind of way. Just thinking about it made me light-headed—his warm skin against mine, and my vulnerable heart caught somewhere beneath it. The intimacy had shocked me, and I'd found a place better than reality, even if it was temporary. I placed my hand over my racing heart, closed my eyes and fell into the hurricane that was my emotions.

☼

I didn't want to go home. As I sat on the beach, shadows grew long, and the seawater turned green from the sinking sun.

Teens with armloads of alcohol now crowded the waterfront. A band was due to start in an hour, and I watched a bunch of black-teed musicians lazily assembling a gazebo. I briefly wondered what Amber was doing; usually she would have texted me, but my phone hadn't received a message all day. I missed her yet could no longer relate to her ordinary life, which probably made me appear indifferent.

The moon, not quite full, peeked out from behind the islands. It was sitting directly above us when the guitarist wound up with a final fast-paced solo.

Once the lights in our house had been turned off, I slunk to the end of our jetty and lay with my cheek pressed to weather-worn boards. While underwater yesterday, I'd somehow forgotten everything. It was enough to keep me on land tonight. What if it got to the point where this secret took complete control of me?

Closing my eyes, I listened to the crash of waves breaking against the jetty. They reverberated through me, drawing me into their mesmerising rhythm until I was no longer just a girl lying out in the cold night. I became part of the sea, floating on tides that were being pulled by a white moon.

I sat up, still caught in the dream-like trance the ocean seemed to hold over me, and reached down to dark water. In the wobbly reflection I saw my pale face. For a shocking moment I imagined it could have been Evelyn staring up at me from beneath the surface, and my heart jolted.

I slashed my fingers through the image and darted inside.

Chapter Twenty-Six

After school the next day I swung by the huge library in town, pausing before a set of wide marble stairs. Apparently the building had been here as long as anyone could remember, and I wondered if my foremothers had also gazed upon its great stone pillars and complicated archways. A cold wind started to blow, scattering leaves and tossing them into the air.

I hurried up to the front door and pushed my way into a spacious foyer. The librarian barely glanced at me as I stepped past her into the maze of aisles.

Following little polished plaques and well-placed arrows, I was directed to a section that promised information on local history. If my family name was documented anywhere, surely I'd find it here. The shelves were packed tight with old books, and I trailed my finger across their spines, reading the titles. I wrestled a hopeful-looking one off the shelf and let out a cry when green eyes filled its space.

Britta was staring at me hungrily through the shelves

that separated us. "What is it you want to know, Sunlight?"

It took a moment for me to compose myself, and she didn't wait for an answer.

"I know everything there is to know about this town— its families, its history, its deepest, darkest secrets." Her eyes narrowed as she considered me. "Though perhaps there are things you know too—sacred knowledge that is only passed between mothers and daughters."

"Or perhaps I know nothing and I'm here trying to figure out why you're so certain Evelyn—" I quickly stopped myself, but already the hunger in her eyes burnt greener. My palms grew clammy beneath the leather-bound book I held.

She was beside me in an instant. "Who's Evelyn?" Her intensity made me take a step backwards. "Is she the one who haunts your dreams so badly you call out in the night?"

"Excuse me?" I choked, and she merely shrugged.

"You sleep with your windows open, and sound carries easily on that beach at night."

My heart twisted with fear. "You are totally insane," I whispered as images of them watching our house filled my head.

A distraction in the form of a beautiful woman came gliding over to us. As if woven from smoke, her grey dress swirled, and clouds of red hair framed an elegant face. Why had she stopped in front of us? I marvelled when tiny orange-winged butterflies took flight within her irises. Maybe I was the one going insane.

It took a moment to realise she was smiling at me, and an even longer moment to realise I'd seen this woman before.

"Sorry I took so long, Sunlight." Her breath smelt like rivers and wild flowers. "Are you ready to go, or am I interrupting?" She juggled a stack of books to her other arm and gave me a meaningful look. A diversion. Britta was casting uncertain glances between the fortune teller and me.

"No, that's okay, I'm ready. Just let me get this book out," I replied tentatively.

She nodded easily, her orange eyes now seemingly normal. I didn't dare ask myself if this day could get any weirder as we pushed out of the library into gusting winds.

I was hoping for advice and reassurance, but all traces of her smile were lost when she turned to face me. "I told you not to stay because of people like her."

With that she walked away, leaving the unmistakable scent of earth in her wake, and me too shocked to follow.

While I spent hours wading through Evelyn's sad diary entries, I knew Britta would be trying to track down my family tree. In my haste to escape her the day before, I'd chosen a totally unhelpful library book—another local author's far-fetched interpretation of the curse.

I'd get distracted from my reading every now and then, by thoughts of green-eyed residents peering through our windows. I imagined their breath misting the glass as they plotted my downfall.

I bolted the windows and pulled my curtains shut, scowling at the sight of them patrolling the beach. How dare they? I felt the familiar tingle of rage come to life inside me, and I took a deep breath.

"Easy, Sunny," I muttered, blinking away visions of striking them down with lightning. I settled back onto my bed and reopened the library book, though I already knew most of this.

"Once upon a time, a beautiful woman ..."

More like unsuspecting, I thought bitterly as I read through the legend yet again. I skipped a couple of pages, unfocused.

"She and every daughter who follows will remain cursed, as shall we."

The storm was rising from the pit of my stomach, gathering just beyond the bay ... waiting. I tried to will it away, but knowing I could pull my anger out of the sky in great electric currents was intoxicating—the power hard to ignore.

I leafed furiously through the bundle of papers Janie had given me, pausing only when I smelled smoke. At first I thought it was Emily sneaking a cigarette before bed.

When I realised it was actually coming from the paperwork—the edges scorched and curling beneath my touch—I was stunned. Dropping it all, I examined my hands. Apart from the fact I was shaking with pent up anger and energy, they didn't look any different.

Again I told myself to calm down and gingerly sought out the painting of Evelyn and her mother at Angel Bay.

It was the only picture I had of Juniper, and she was stunning. If innocence and purity had a face it was certainly hers.

"I bet Pytheus tricked you," I whispered, moving my gaze to Evelyn. She was also beautiful—in a dark, unusual way—and suddenly I was all too aware of her blood running through me. Our salt blood. I understood why I dreamt of her, why I wept for her, why I felt for her.

Turning back to the stained pages of the library book, I read on. *By right she is his.*

I hurled it across the room, and thunder growled in the distance. We'd never stood a chance. Fuelled by rage, I rushed to the jetty. It was already raining and I watched with satisfaction as the locals reluctantly made their way home.

Tonight I would make sure I was in control. I could create and destroy; it was exhilarating, like a sweet kiss on salty lips. Maybe once I was done here, I would run to Jake's.

Wind swept into the bay, stroking my flushed skin. Stretching my arms out like wings, I urged the waves high.

It happened even faster this time. Within minutes I held a destructive force in the palm of my hands.

"Do it."

The jetty lurched as I thrust the storm from my fingertips. Rain pelted down in icy sheets, chilling me to the core, but I stayed with my chaos, pushing it harder. Lightning staggered out of the sky, and what it illuminated made my breath catch in my throat.

To the left of the islands a small boat was being tossed as easily as if it were a piece of paper. It was dangerously close to the hidden reef, and guilt quickly clawed its way into my stomach. I dropped my arms to my side, urged the storm to die down — to go back out to sea — but Pytheus picked up where I'd left off. The waves swelled and crashed harder against the rocks, spitting foam high into the air.

"No!"

"Yes."

I wanted to run away, aware this whole thing was much bigger than me, but made myself stay. Dark waves grew blacker, and strong winds wilder, before the boat hit the rocks. I pictured its hull splintering into jagged pieces and knew the ocean would already be filling it.

"Look what you've done!" he said gleefully.

I frantically undressed and dived off the jetty, curling in agony as the cold water entered my airways. I was determined not to pass out. There were moments when my mind went blank and I would drift helplessly towards the deep, but eventually the pain passed and I made for the islands. My muscles cramped from the cold water, making my journey slow.

I knew I was nearing the wreck when I tasted diesel. I dived deeper than I ever had, my ears popping painfully. The blackness was so absolute I'd be lucky to find anyone, but I had to try. This was my fault, though the guilt would have to wait; I needed to focus my attention on finding whoever might be down here.

The boat lay ruined on the ocean floor, and I slipped inside, tearing my flesh against the broken planks.

Ignoring the pain that spread across my torso, I searched with urgency. The eerie stillness within the cabin was overwhelming. Was I too late?

Back and forth I swam, terrified I'd take hold of a lifeless limb at any moment. Defeated, I headed slowly upwards, my heart heavy with failure.

☼

I found him as I neared the surface, spiralling slowly downwards to rest beside his boat.

Letting out what would have been a grateful cry had I not been underwater, I dragged the unresponsive body alongside me. We burst into dry air, which burned as I gulped my first breath. It took all my strength to overcome the searing pain and concentrate on him. His head rolled forward and I slapped his ashen face.

"Hey," I said, trembling, trying to rouse him. His eyelids appeared to flicker, but in the darkness I may have imagined it.

Battling with the fire still licking at my lungs, I swam us to shore, struggling to keep him afloat. Relief and exhaustion hit me when my feet touched the sand, and I hauled him from the waves onto wet shells.

He was young—I could tell that much. His skin felt smooth as I tilted his chin and pressed my cold lips to his. Desperately trying to remember how many compressions per minute I was supposed to do, I blew air into his lungs. Water gurgled loudly inside him. Were my attempts at revival pointless? I was shaking with cold and began to cry hysterically.

"Wake up!" I shook him as hard as I could, pounded on his chest in frustration and watched dumbfounded when water spilled from his mouth. He took a ragged gasp and sat up.

I guessed he wouldn't have been any older than me. I was brimming with too many emotions to even consider there was a chance he might recognise me from school.

"Who are y-you?" he stammered, shivering.

I ignored him, unsure of what answer to give and suddenly mindful of how little I was wearing. Self-consciously angling my body away from him, I fretted over what to do. If I left him here overnight he'd surely freeze to death. His teeth were already chattering uncontrollably. My shoulders sagged from fatigue. Had I been alone, I would have crawled up to the safety of the trees and rested a while.

As I weighed up my options, I heard the distant rumble of engines, and a boat rounded the point. I shrank back from its sweeping searchlight.

"They must have heard my mayday," the boy said, standing to get their attention. I turned my face away so he couldn't see me.

"You're hurt," he told me worriedly when the light touched near us. A deep gash lay across my ribs, blood oozing from serrated edges.

"I'm okay," I said doubtfully. The light swept closer, revealing the little beach, and I was back in the water before they had a chance to see me.

"Where are you going?" he called. I didn't answer him.

The ocean was considerably calmer now, all traces of a storm gone. Even so, it took ages to reach the jetty. Pytheus took advantage of my exhaustion by attempting to stop me leaving. He told me I belonged to him. It took all of my remaining energy to wrench free from his grasp and pull myself onto the jetty.

Chapter Twenty-Seven

"Sunny! Time for school," Brie sang as she knocked on my door and headed for the stairs.

I rolled over and winced at the shooting pain in my side. Carefully I lifted up my top. The gash had healed a lot in the night—been reduced to a graze—but a painful bruise flowered across my ribs. I splashed it with water and cleared away the dried blood, hoping I hadn't done any internal damage. A minute in the sea would work wonders, but I didn't have time for a shower, let alone a swim, so I twisted my hair into salty curls and brushed mascara over thick eyelashes.

Mum eyed me as I moved slowly about the kitchen, but she didn't say a word. When I put my hand gently on her arm she flinched.

"I'm sorry." My voice shook slightly. "I shouldn't have said it."

She picked up her bag, unable to meet my eyes. "I'm late for work."

I swallowed the lump in my throat and pulled out my

timetable. Once again I'd be coming up with lies to get out of PE.

My excuse was a migraine; the teacher gave me a detention.

"Just add it to the stack," I muttered wearily, trying not to limp as I headed for the stands.

While sitting there I worked myself into a state of panic. I'd taken a huge risk by revealing myself to someone, but it was my own fault for chancing another storm. Even though the boy hadn't actually seen what I could do, how could I possibly explain why I was out at sea in the middle of a storm, or why I'd returned to it? Hopefully nothing would come of it, and people would put his story down to delusional babble. It was the very last kind of news that needed to get out in a town as superstitious as this one.

Jake asked me if I was okay, but I was so deep in thought I barely spoke to him. Would the boy recognise me? It had been dark — really dark — and my hair had been wet. I was clutching at straws.

Later, as I whiled away hours of detention, I convinced myself it would all be okay. But I was wrong.

The next morning, Lexie arrived clutching a crumpled newspaper.

"If this isn't the proof you've been waiting for then I don't know what is," she announced, her irises so green I looked twice. Amber stole the rustling pages off her, narrowing her eyes doubtfully.

"Did you see anything, Sunny?" Lexie demanded. "I

mean, that island is literally in front of your house."

I didn't like what she was implying.

"Let me see that," I said, peering over Amber's shoulder.

Wow, I'd made front page. A big headline read *Sailor Claims Mermaid Saved His Life.*

Amber looked sceptical as she skimmed the article. "It says right here that the boy suffered a traumatic experience, which in turn can result in a false recollection of events."

Lexie snatched it back. "You're wrong this time," she said confidently.

"Lexie, lack of oxygen to the brain causes hallucinations. When we were kids and my brother tried to strangle me, I swear to God I saw my mother, but she died when I was born. It's nothing."

I was shocked by what Amber had just shared, but Lexie still managed to distract me by thrusting her finger at a dark photograph near the bottom of the page. "Then explain this."

Amber and I leaned in close. Surely they couldn't have got a photo? My heart hammered.

You could make out the beach and tall trees, lit up by the camera's flash. The guy I'd resuscitated was standing there, his arms raised in a whirlwind blur as he flagged his rescuers down, and in the shallows a hazy figure, merely a shadow in the badly lit night, diving beneath murky waves.

"That is kind of weird," Amber muttered as she pulled it nearer. At least I was totally unrecognisable.

"Who the hell had a camera?" I never meant to say it aloud, and Lexie looked at me so quickly I'm surprised she didn't get whiplash.

"People are watching now, Sunny. These storms aren't normal, not even for here. The only reason he got picked up was because of our patrol boat."

Patrol boat? This secret was getting harder and harder to keep.

"Maybe there was water on the lens," I suggested, and Amber nodded.

"Yeah, probably just a trick of the light."

"Well, if it's anyone at this school he'll soon be able to identify them," Lexie said sourly as she stormed off.

"He goes to this school?" I sounded a little breathless, but Amber didn't seem to notice.

"Levi's in the year below us."

That week I saw copies of the article everywhere I went. Shopkeepers pored over it, and kids pressed their noses against windows where the photo was displayed. I couldn't get away from it.

While I dreaded the day Levi returned to school, everyone else awaited it with great enthusiasm. When he set foot off the bus on Monday, a flock of followers bombarded him with questions. Every time I glimpsed him, which seemed to be often, I felt sick with remorse. Someone had nearly died because of me.

It should have been enough to keep me from the ocean, but selfishly that wasn't the case.

I still craved it, and now just the thought of a storm sent ripples of excitement through me. Sometimes at night, when I lay soundlessly beneath the surface, all I wanted was to reach up and pull the patrol boats under, dragging them into the shadowy depths below me where they would lie forever. These thoughts made me start to hate myself. How could I think such dark things?

On Wednesday I visited Janie and told her she was wrong to have named me after something so warm and bright.

It is only light that can banish darkness, she'd said, and I was thinking about her reply the next day when Jake found me sitting in the shade of a pine tree.

"Sunny, if you're feeling weird about what happened, let's talk about it." He looked concerned, and I realised I'd barely spoken to him since I'd turned up at his like a maniac and given myself to him in a moment of desperate passion.

"What? No, it was great." I shoved my books, including Evelyn's diary, back into my bag.

"Okay," he said a little unsurely as he tucked my hair behind my ears. I was shocked at the warmth of his fingers, surprised how suddenly my emotions seemed to

284

come back to me.

I sucked in a deep breath. "But Taylor will ruin us."

This time he didn't turn away from me. He clasped my knees with both hands and groaned. "I know she's hard to deal with, and I'm sorry." He genuinely looked it.

"Why are you still trying to keep her happy?"

"Something happened last year."

"Something?"

He sighed, his shoulders slumping forward. "Taylor and I ended up in the wrong place at the wrong time."

I frowned. What could have happened that was so bad?

It was like he read my mind, because he said, "Trust me, it's bad."

He paused and I fidgeted—part of me expecting him to clam up again—but to my surprise he started speaking, quickly, as if suddenly desperate to be rid of his secret.

"She phoned me at two in the morning needing a lift from up north. Taylor always needs something."

I nodded in agreement.

"That call was the last straw. I planned to tell her it was over on the drive home—for real this time. But she'd drunk a bottle of vodka and was wasted; I couldn't do it. The return trip took ages because we stopped so many times for her to be sick."

"Did you take your bike?" I asked incredulously, trying to picture this. He shook his head.

"My stepmum's car. I couldn't risk her getting vomit on the seats, so we ended up in an overgrown rest area, waiting for her to stop throwing up."

"Lucky you."

He grimaced slightly. "I'd almost fallen asleep when the lights from a car blinded me. A little white Honda pulled in across the road, and the last person I expected to see getting out was Sergeant McLeod." His expression darkened. "We watched him haul something large from the boot, and I ignored Taylor when she asked me what it could be."

As he spoke, the night that so obviously troubled him unfolded before my eyes. The bell rang, but we stayed put. I don't think Jake even heard it. In the distance I saw Amber and Lexie making their way to class.

"It was my turn to feel sick," he admitted. "Nothing about the situation felt right, you know? I was glad the trees hid us. McLeod seemed extremely agitated, then relieved when another car showed up. I couldn't believe who the driver was, and Taylor just stared at me." Jake's hands were clenched so tightly his knuckles had turned white.

"Who was it?" I whispered.

"My father," he said gruffly, and then turned quickly to make sure we were out of earshot. A group of students hurried past, and he lowered his voice. "I wanted to hear what they were saying so wound down the windows. Dad was walking towards the sergeant, asking what the hell was going on, when he tripped over what was on the ground. He flicked on his torch, which is why I saw ... it."

"It?" I asked tentatively.

"The body. I can't describe how disturbing it was to see someone just lying there, lifeless."

I felt my eyes widen in shock. This wasn't what I had been expecting to hear. Jake absentmindedly took my hand in his and continued, "It was impossible to think straight, and I missed some of what they were saying. I remember McLeod insisting he hadn't killed the girl ... and believing him. My father told him he didn't want anything to do with it. He looked really shaken."

I swore softly.

"I told you it was bad," Jake said, his blue eyes piercing as he scrutinised my face. "I dream about it often."

Images and questions began to crowd my mind, but I stayed quiet and he rushed on.

"From where I sat, I couldn't see injuries or blood, just a young person in a soaking wet dress—like she'd been left out in the rain. I told Taylor to stay where she was and crept to the edge of the trees for a better look."

Jake gripped my hand tighter. My heart hammered.

"I recognised the girl straight away. She hadn't been in town long—maybe six months—but I'd seen her around school a bit. And her face on the news every day that week. Seventeen and vanished; could have been anywhere, they said. The sergeant dragged her to the driver's side of the Honda, sat her in the seat and shut the door. He begged my father for help. They stood there for a while, staring at each other in the darkness. They'd always been close—almost as close as brothers." He sighed and looked down at his hands. "I knew Dad wouldn't say no. Something passed between them, and together they pushed the car to the edge of the cliff."

I let out the breath I'd been holding, and Jake shot me a look.

"Yeah. I can still see the stones crumbling and falling as the tyres teetered over the edge, and how the car just dropped towards the sea. No one said anything. It was horrible. The next morning, Claire Maine was pronounced dead in a car crash."

Now I understood. His father's future rested in the palms of a manipulative teenage girl. I would want to protect my father too, if I had one who loved me.

Jake pushed his fingers to his temples, massaging them deeply. "If it hadn't been for Taylor I never would have witnessed a damn thing. Dad was stupid to get involved, and sometimes I hate him for it. He should have taken the whole case to his senior."

"Taylor's father," I sighed, and he nodded.

Which was how she was controlling him. Surely there was a way to take that power away from her?

It wasn't until later that I started thinking. Why would a cop try to cover up a death unless he had something to do with it?

My thoughts had me restless, but it was too early for a swim. Besides, the patrol boats had further complicated things. According to Lexie, they'd recently been fitted with state-of-the-art marine radars, making it even harder for me to remain undetected.

I reached for my running shoes instead.

I'd only planned on going to the end of the road and around the block, but I hadn't even broken into a sweat so kept going. I was halfway up the old mountain track when I stopped to catch my breath. After a couple of minutes, I wound back down through the maze of tall trees. I felt good now; I was breathing hard, and my back was slick with sweat. Hopefully tonight I'd sleep well.

I ran through the deserted streets towards home, my shoes pounding out a steady rhythm on the road.

Suddenly, from somewhere to my left, I became aware of movement in the long shadows. I paused to see what was there, and even though I could have sworn I'd seen something, now I wasn't sure. I carried on, wishing the streetlights weren't so useless. I shouldn't have come out this late, but I'd had too much energy to stay indoors. Maybe now I would be able to sit still long enough to write an essay without driving myself crazy.

What was that?

I spun around again, strands of long hair whipping my hot face, but there was nothing there. It had only been the slightest of sounds, a scuff against the asphalt. Probably just a dog.

Or the footsteps of someone who has been quietly hunting you for the best part of an hour.

I was determined not to let my imagination scare me

and pressed on. More than anything, I wanted to end the run with a delicious swim …

That noise again.

I stopped dead in my tracks, turning slowly. Was that a shadow sliding into the alleyway? My breathing was loud in the quiet street, and my heart did a double beat. Rain began to fall soundlessly onto the road, and I pushed back my sweaty fringe, peering into the darkness. I couldn't see anything, but as I ran faster I was certain of movement behind me.

Glancing over my shoulder, I gasped. A figure dressed in black was sweeping down the street towards me, his hood pulled up to conceal his face. Not looking where I was going, I tripped and fell hard. He was upon me before I knew what was happening. With rough hands he dragged me to my feet, and though I tried to squirm away he held me tight.

"What do you want?" I spat, but my voice cracked with panic, and his scowling mouth twisted into a sneer.

"I knew it was you the minute I saw you."

My breathing was ragged and my mouth dry. "I don't know what—" I started, but he shook me so hard it left me winded.

"Yes, you do," he snarled. I wrenched myself from his grasp.

He made a lunge for me, but I took a step back.

"You're the damn girl I chased up the cliffs." He must have seen the fear that skipped across my features, because he chuckled.

"Prove it," I challenged.

He flew at me, but I was too quick. His face was contorted with such hatred that I felt a shiver of terror rip through me.

I tore down the street, gritty water soaking into my trainers and splashing up my legs. The rain came down harder. I turned into a narrow alley that led away from home. I wouldn't lead him back there.

His footsteps were muffled by the ever-falling rain, but I knew he was close behind. Wet hair plastered my face, and my singlet clung to me, drenched right through. Even though I'd been running for over an hour, I was starting to feel the cold. An icy wind chilled me to my core as I ran down streets I'd never seen before. Adrenaline spurred me on, but I wasn't sure how much longer I could outrun him.

At one point he made a swipe for me. I felt him grab a handful of my shirt in his fist, but I pushed myself forward, heard it rip and kept going. I wanted to call out but my voice had dried up, and I didn't know if the people in these old houses would even help me. Maybe they'd help him ...

Rounding a corner, I ducked behind a couple of bins that had been left on the curb, and pushed them into his path as hard as I could. Without hesitating to check if it had deterred him I kept running. He cursed and yelled as tins and bottles clattered out onto the road, and I sprinted ahead. Already I could hear him back on his feet, pursuing me, but it had given me the distance between us that I needed.

After following a confusing labyrinth of streets, I came to a tall, unkempt hedge. I squeezed through it, collapsing into a field on the other side, and realised I was lost.

Shivering beneath the dripping hedge, I gradually became certain of the correct direction to walk in. Surely cutting across the field and turning right would lead me to the sea, but then I felt doubtful. Since when had I ever had a good sense of direction? Even with a map in front of me I was useless.

Finally I decided to trust my instinct—there was no way I was spending the night in a wet field. Wind whistled through nearby woods, and I decided it would be better to walk in the safety of its shadows rather than venture into the open. My pursuer was still out there somewhere. I slunk along the hedge line until trees towered overhead, and it was with great reluctance that I stepped into darkness. As I stood there waiting for my eyes to adjust, rain dropped silently from the branches, sometimes landing in my hair and sliding down my neck. When a big brown owl flitted in front of me, I stifled a scream. I was jumpy. Keeping to the edge of the woods, I started making my way home, but voices soon stopped me dead in my tracks.

I peered between swaying tree trunks and held my breath, shocked. Up ahead was the old stone building and the plaque etched with that strange poem Britta had quoted. I'd come quite a way.

Light flickered beyond the empty windows, and I crouched low in thickets of wet bracken. Thoughts chased themselves around my head, the predominant one telling me to hurry up and go home, but curiosity had always been my weak point.

Creeping into the grove, I ducked behind a tree. What was going on here? I took a steadying breath and looked past moss-covered bark to the window. What I saw made my heart stutter.

Despite how late it was getting, despite the rain and wind that blew through the building and tore at their clothes, a meeting was in place. Thirteen people sat around a table that was illuminated by the flames of thick white candles. Hours of burning had reduced the wax to misshapen mounds within glass lanterns.

I inched forward. Black hoods were pulled up against the cold, casting shadows across sallow faces. I couldn't see their features; nor could I make out what they were saying through the howling wind. The man at the head of the table tilted his face towards the light, and with a shudder I knew he was the one who stood on the beach when the moon was full, leading the locals through their worship. His eyes were hypnotic, a dazzling shade of green that held me transfixed.

Dread gripped me for the second time that night, and I felt like throwing up. Evelyn had feared these families. I wondered if her memories of them somehow lived within my subconscious.

The wind died down enough for me to hear probably all I needed to. "So it's only a matter of time," he assured them. "Lyle claims he's seen her, and our children have given us a name. Sunlight West."

I flinched. The night had just gone from bad to worse.

They rose from their seats like leather-winged bats, and I fled, weaving through the trees. I tore across fields and roads and eventually came out on a street I knew. When I caught sight of the sea glimmering in the distance, a huge amount of relief overcame me.

A full moon hung over the islands, shattering dark water with light, and a crowd of locals had gathered on the beach.

I turned the shower onto full blast and peeled off my wet clothes. Steam spilled into the bathroom, and I leaned against the basin until I'd stopped shaking. Surely the locals knew it was illegal to kill someone ... Stepping under streams of hot water, I let it burn into my skin.

"Dead isn't what they want," I whispered as I slid my finger across misted glass. Claire's name seemed to have inserted itself into my mind. If a car crash hadn't killed her, what had?

Fearful thoughts pushed aside any rational solutions I came up with, so I gave up trying not to be afraid. I had the call of Pytheus in my head and a town full of people who would hunt until they found me. I could run inland, as Juniper had, but her decisions hadn't helped any of us.

I wrapped my hair in a towel and retrieved my phone. There was a message from Jake and several missed calls from Amber. I think I was supposed to have been helping with last-minute party arrangements. The night had ended up being much more eventful.

Settling into bed with Evelyn's diary, I flicked on the lamp. Dramatic shadows sprang up around my room, and I jumped at the sight of Mum passing my doorway.

"Are you all right?" she called as she made her way to bed.

"Yes," I lied, leafing through to the next entry, glad it was about something other than her crushed heart.

It's rained every day since I've been here, and the stories about this place are disturbing. I don't understand how anyone could believe something so far-fetched.

The townsfolk say they're cursed, and that one girl is to blame for all their misery. I don't leave the house much because of this. Marlene insists it's not safe here and worries every time I go into town for supplies.

I'd thought her fear unjust, but now I too am afraid. Today at the markets I overheard a man saying the council has started selecting girls for trialling ...

Chapter Twenty-Eight

At school I tried to be invisible. I kept expecting someone to come forth and declare my fate, but it didn't happen.

From my seat in the biology room, I had a clear view of the car park. A police car had just pulled in, and Britta stepped out of it wearing a pale blue gown that could have belonged to her great-grandmother. I wondered what trouble she'd gotten in for her to need an escort.

I drew pointless spirals across my page while my classmates copied what was on the board. Britta swept through the door, taking a seat without so much as even acknowledging the teacher.

"Miss McLeod," he said in a voice laced with sarcasm. "How nice of you to grace us with your presence."

She merely nodded, which infuriated him even more. The argument that followed disrupted the class, but I'd suddenly tuned out.

McLeod. Sergeant McLeod.

The realisation hit me so hard my palms started to sweat. By staging Claire's death to seem accidental, Britta's father had gone against everything his title stood for. And he'd only risk something like that for good reason.

I thought back to what Jake had told me – how the girl's body had appeared unharmed, the only peculiarity being how wet she was.

With a jolt I thought of Sophie. Poor drowned Sophie.

McLeod had been so nervous on the beach that day Brie found the body.

My head was spinning with scenarios and questions. Had Claire's real cause of death also been from drowning?

I glanced over to where Britta was rearranging her long satin skirts. Was her eighteenth-century attire a subtle hint that the past was still very much alive?

I decided to spend Friday night at Angel Bay, spinning an intricate web of lies in the process. When I asked Amber if she'd account for my whereabouts, her eyes lit up.

"You're going to stay with Jake, aren't you? Of course I'll tell your mum you're with me! See you Sunday, okay?"

"Sunday," I repeated, trying to sound excited. The weekend of her party had finally arrived.

After school I rushed home, hoping no one would be there. I had just finished stacking blankets into my boot and was raiding the pantry when Emily appeared.

"Where are you going?" she questioned, yawning sleepily, her hair a tangled mess at the back of her head.

"To stay with Amber."

"Before you go, some teacher left a message for Mum," she said, handing me the phone.

My geography teacher breathed heavily down the line between frustrated sentences. Had I really not done the latest paper?

Delete.

Emily watched as I quickly scribbled a note to Mum.

"Are you really going to Amber's?" she asked carefully, eyeing the pillow under my arm.

I nodded, avoiding eye contact, and signed the note in big, happy writing.

"You don't have to tell me where you're going, just tell me you're all right," she urged.

I tacked the note to the fridge and told her what she wanted to hear.

☼

Waves swilled over gleaming white sand, and I breathed in the smell of briny vegetation. As usual the beach at Angel Bay remained deserted. I always tried not to dwell on why that was—it was just too grim.

Gazing up at the ominous cliffs, I wondered which point the girls had been pushed from.

I needed to know.

Wet grass slapped my jeans as I hiked upwards, and I stubbed my toes on half-buried rocks. Eventually I stumbled onto a well-trodden path that was clearly being used by animals. Had it initially been carved by people's footsteps? Perhaps the footsteps of frightened girls as they were dragged to their deaths?

I pulled off my heavy jacket, stopping to catch my breath. From here I could see the little cottage perfectly. It nestled lovingly into the land and its surrounding gardens.

"Evelyn's gardens," I whispered as I thought back to a diary entry I'd read the night before. She had spent countless hours down there, weeding and pruning and planting—fulfilling the old woman's last wishes. Marlene had died within two months of meeting Evelyn, who stayed on and made the place her own. She grew herbs beside the kitchen, buried various seeds and bulbs in the wet earth and planted blue and white forget-me-nots in loving memory of the woman who took her in.

I tore my gaze away from the cottage and continued climbing. When I neared the top, beads of perspiration rolled from my hairline. A smattering of scraggly trees grew amongst rocks now jutting from the path, and the ground began to level. I didn't know where I was going, but as I followed the winding path through the trees, I had the strangest feeling I'd done this before. Wind plucked at my thin T-shirt and ruffled my hair. The smell of salt was all around me.

I came across the ledge so quickly I almost stepped off it. My scream flung echoes back and forth across the water until it sounded like the bay was full of terrified girls.

Little bits of the path crumbled and fell—and there, far beneath me, lay the sea. I inched backwards, dropping down at the base of an old tree, my heart beating quickly from exertion and fright. I could hear the deep rumbling of the ocean swelling against the cliffs, and something in me stirred.

I'd stood here before—in precisely this spot. I peered over the ledge, trembling on hands and knees. Foam sprayed high into the air, fanning out like an exotic flower.

The dream.

My vision swayed, and I took a steadying breath before looking out once more. Yes, I had dreamt of this island-studded sea—felt the ice-cool water surging against the foot of these cliffs. I'd felt the terror of falling too, but only inside the safety of a dream. This was the very ledge so many had been thrown from. I could barely imagine the horror.

Where strong currents met, the water churned angrily. Amber was right; it would have been impossible for anyone to swim to shore from there. I doubted even I'd make it.

I shuffled backwards, tearing my gaze from the haunting deep. Sometimes it was so cold—so huge and unloving. The sun was going down, and in a few hours I'd watch the moon float out of the sea. Still shaking, I grasped a lower branch of the mossy tree and hauled myself up. I kept my eyes on my feet, determined not to look at the sheer drop any more, and that's why I saw it. Half-buried in the dirt was the surface of something polished.

Using my fingernail, I picked it from the soil, then let it roll into the palm of my hand. A pebble? No, it was too shiny—more like a shell—but it was almost perfectly round. I rubbed the dirt off with my shirt and brought it closer to my face. It was pale; the exact colour of the moon.

A pearl! Hadn't Evelyn handed me a necklace made from pearls identical to this during one of my many dreams?

I dropped to my hands and knees again, scratching desperately at the hard ground. There were more—dull little orbs scattered in the earth, their sheen softened by the dust. I continued sifting through the dirt, glad no one could see me. They'd think I'd lost my mind—and maybe I had. The thought of leaving even one behind was not an option, yet I couldn't know how many there had originally been. The string once holding them together had long disintegrated into the land.

Finally I gave up, tipping the pearls into my pocket and brushing the dirt from my knees as I stood. Why was Evelyn's necklace on top of this cliff?

That night I lay curled in my blankets, the floorboards hard and cold beneath me. Rain lashed against the fragile windows and a draught found its way inside, making me retreat deeper into my improvised bed. It wasn't ideal, but at least no one would find me here.

The candles beside me flickered, their orange light dipping low before swelling and making the room glow again. I eased the tattered diary out of my pillowcase and as my eyes adjusted to the wavering light I fell back into Evelyn's life.

The hunt for this girl continues.

I hear everything from our cottage. The heavy, compassionless footsteps and the sobbing that eventually fades to sea and wind. I know what comes next and I do everything I can to distract myself, but their screams tear through the night and scrape raw wounds across my heart.

What's worse is the terrible silence that follows. I can never sleep on these nights, so I don't mind the physical task I've taken upon myself. With shaking hands I lift the shovel from its place by the door and walk to the huge tree where I've chosen to bury the bodies. When it flowers, the tree will cry pink tears onto the graves of the innocent. Sometimes I'm out all night, digging the sandy earth.

I feel the life inside me move, and I wonder. Do I really want to bring something so pure into a world so corrupt?

By the time I finish preparing the graves it's often daybreak, and I sleep before facing what the tide washes in. Some mornings the girls' family members are down there before I am, pulling their daughters from the sea. Other times not. These are the ones I bury – the ones whose families can't bear coming out here. They take comfort knowing I'll deal with it for them.

It's the least I can do, and I try to convince myself I couldn't

possibly be the one Pytheus wants. Surely the legend isn't real,
and surely he's not the one I'm hearing?

I swiped at the tears tumbling down my cheeks and
blew out the candle. It had been a long day.

☼

I walked the beach at sunrise and was tempted to swim,
until my eyes fell on an ancient-looking tree near the end
of the lawn. From where I stood, I could make out the pink
buds that adorned its sprawling branches. I thought about
the drowned girls who lay buried beneath it—how they
had washed up on this very beach.

Heart thudding, I wandered back to the cottage and
through the garden. Underfoot, the grass was damp. I
loved this place, and as I righted fallen pot plants and
lined them up against the house, I imagined moving my
belongings here and making it my home. I'd sleep in the
first room and take comfort knowing it had been Evelyn's.

It took hours to weed the flowerbeds and heap together
all the dead leaves. The more I worked, the less I thought.
After clearing the path of fallen branches and standing the
angel statue up, I was sweaty and dirty.

By the time I bid the house goodbye, pastel pinks of
early evening stained the sky.

At home I filled my basin with water, scrubbed the
pearls until they shone and strung them onto a thin cord.
As lovely as they were, I didn't dare wear them. They'd

provoke less questions hanging from my mirror.

I had dreamed of this necklace, and now it was here.

Chapter Twenty-Nine

As I sat at my dressing table, I had to keep reminding myself it was the night of Amber's party. I longed to swim out to the islands, but my reluctance to socialise lately hadn't gone amiss and if I failed to show tonight, Amber wouldn't forgive me.

Besides, one of the patrol boats Lexie had mentioned was at that moment chugging through the bay. The beam from a massive spotlight swept across our house, flooding my room before continuing across the water. They were obsessed.

I turned back to my wardrobe, sighing. Jeans, green jacket, old Converses, whatever. Straightening my hair took almost an hour. It was so long now and much thicker. My skin was perfectly smooth, every imperfection softened by saltwater. In certain lights I even looked airbrushed, and that wasn't me being vain. It was merely an observation.

As I piled on makeup, I listened to the sea. Without realising it, I swayed in time with the lapping waves, the ocean luring me into its rhythm. When I caught sight of myself in the mirror, my eyes were huge and staring, my hand motionless as I held the wand of mascara to unfinished lashes.

Brie's door slammed shut in the wind and I jumped, suddenly attentive. I closed the window before plugging in my iPod. Chaotic rock music filled my room, and I settled back in front of the mirror, mind on task again.

I pulled a pot of eyeshadow towards me and brushed silver powder onto my lids. It felt so unnatural. The desire to swim was strong, but Amber was my friend and I wouldn't let her down.

As if she'd somehow sensed my scattered vibes, I found she'd sent a text reminding me to pick up the alcohol. It was really her way of saying, *You'd better be on your way*.

I typed a quick reply, disconnected my iPod and flicked off the light. Moonlight filtered in through my lacy curtains, caressing me like a bubble bath. I drew a shuddering breath. I'd forgotten it was full tonight. The tides would be more fun than usual. My skin was radiant in the glow, as if it held the light — absorbed it even.

Irresistible, persuasive, a lover's touch — the moon was pulling me as it did the ocean. Waves crashed loudly on the beach, making it impossible to think straight. The tide had turned and was on its way in, rushing over dark rocks and surging up the shells, closer, closer. This was dangerous.

"Sunlight."

Shutting my eyes, I tried to block out the voice floating in off the ocean.

"Don't resist it."

I imagined cold, soothing water against my skin, the salt permeating my cells and altering every sense. No, I couldn't swim tonight.

"Yes, you can."

"Stop," I whispered.

"Don't you want to touch the currents?"

"Stop it,"

"Don't you want to feel the tides wash over you?"

I gritted my teeth and shook my head, but the word that escaped my lips was *yes*. I dropped my bag and crossed over to the window. Like a new coin, the moon shone silvery bright. I unlaced my shoes without a second thought, tiptoed along the landing and let myself outside.

Crowds of locals stood on the beach, and the ocean sighed with me. I didn't take my eyes off them as I moved carefully down the jetty. But they were too busy sky gazing to notice me. Everything swayed slightly, and the wooden planks were smooth beneath my bare feet. In a moment I'd be swimming in the cool, moonlit sea.

Lexie's words darted into my head like scared fish. *The moon brings back to the ocean what it rightfully owns.*

I wouldn't drown tonight. This would just be a quick swim before Amber's party. I stripped off, leaving my clothes in a crumpled heap at my feet. Gripping the edge of the jetty, I peered into the depths before diving in.

307

Water flowed around me like silk sheets, and everything I'd ever feared left me. I floated on my back, a smile playing on my lips.

Yet as I swam lazily around the jetty, I felt something wasn't quite right. At first I ignored it, pushing every worry from my head and enjoying the looseness of water around me. The moon shone into the sea, and I swirled my fingers through patches of light. It wasn't until the ocean had become too still that I acknowledged how strange the tide was behaving. Currents that had been racing inland were now holding back, changing direction, and I was being encouraged out into the bay.

"Sunlight."

His voice sent shivers down my spine.

"Sun ... light, Sun ... light." It seemed to come from all around—in the wind that rushed on silent wings, and on the growing waves that carried me out deeper. It was time to leave. I'd had my fix.

But the pulling tide was strong, and I made little progress despite my powerful stroke. The change in weather scared me, and adrenaline flooded my system. I was no match for these conditions.

"Don't fight it. I can give you what you want."

The usual feeling of freedom vanished, and hot flames of panic rose inside me. Now, more than anything, I wanted to be on my way to Amber's party. Old fears returned with a vengeance as I was dragged under. Fighting against twisting currents, I clawed my way back to the surface. The wind picked up, the waves blackened, and I knew a storm brewed on the horizon.

Again and again I was pulled under and tossed up, choking on water, then choking on air, unable to transition to either. Was Pytheus going to drown me, properly this time, just as he had my ancestors?

I'd become so cold I barely noticed the sensation working its way up my legs. Perhaps I was getting tired and starting to cramp. But it quickly turned into entire body aches. My legs felt so heavy.

I envisioned the creature Lexie was so intent on painting — the girl whose lower half consisted of something much different from skin. Was the sea god trying to claim me?

Pushing the breath from my lungs, I dived deep beneath his controlling waves. The air weakened me, yet the water made it so easy for him to entice me — so easy for him to fray my earth ties, making me forget. As the ocean swept through my lungs, I tried keeping thoughts of land in my head. Picturing the forest I sometimes ran through, leafy and green, helped remind me of my earth blood. Thinking of Jake made me stronger.

I resurfaced only when I was clutching the jetty ladder, and the water pushed me out like rough hands. Dark clouds rolled into the bay, blocking out the moon as I fell onto salty planks. Painful gasps racked my already trembling body. Janie had said living in both worlds was never an option, and now I believed her. *Your earth ties are weakening, can't you feel that?* she'd asked.

I could, but I wasn't prepared to choose ocean — to give up the life I had.

It scared me to admit that Pytheus was indeed becoming harder to resist. I wasn't in control like I thought I'd been. If I hadn't escaped his hold tonight, what might have happened? It wasn't worth the risk of finding out.

My ocean days were over.

☼

When I woke to my alarm the next morning, I assumed I'd set it wrong. The seven o'clock sunshine that usually warmed my room was absent. Brie stirred next door, turning her radio on as she always did. I opened the curtains, yawning.

Outside it was bucketing down. Raindrops dimpled the ocean's surface in thousands of perfect circles, and I sighed; there was no point even plugging in my hair straightener. After dressing in jeans and a hoodie, I laced a heavy pair of black boots and trudged downstairs.

Mum wasn't angry at me any more. She hugged me while I slouched at the sink, filling the jug and staring out to sea.

"Sunny?" She turned off the tap as it overflowed. Water sloshed over the rim and onto the floor.

"Mmm?"

"What's wrong with you?" Frown lines creased her

forehead and I noticed silver threads in her blonde hair.

"Nothing." I couldn't tell her about the dreams that left me emotionally hung-over every morning, or that a group of people had met in secrecy to discuss my whereabouts. This town was crazier than most people knew.

To what lengths would they go to fulfil their ancient promise? Unwanted images of Sophie's body continued to plague me.

"Are you doing drugs?" Mum asked.

"Only coffee," I assured her. Maybe I'd feel better once I'd had a cup.

Brie skipped into the kitchen, dressed so brightly I felt even more of my energy slip away. She wore a purple dress and had flowers in her hair, despite the weather, which had begun to deliver gusts of wind so strong I could feel the house groaning. I had angered the sea god.

Sloshing our way to the car, we unsuccessfully shielded ourselves with folders and were drenched within seconds. Brie slid in beside me, wringing out her hair and leaving pools of water on the leather seat around her. She flicked the heater on, shivering. As we followed the road into town, gales swept through the valley, battering the car from side to side. Trees on either side thrashed frantically, reaching out as if to snatch us into the forest. I had to concentrate hard to stay on the road.

"Wild," Brie muttered, reapplying her mascara. Rain tumbled like waterfalls from high slate roofs, making the houses even more foreboding in the dim light. When we pulled into school, the car park had been transformed into a rainbow of umbrellas.

"Where were you?" Amber demanded the instant I stepped into the building. Lexie stood sulking at her side.

I was so distracted it took a moment to remember what I'd missed. My heart sank. How could I have forgotten? "Amber, I'm so sorry —" but she cut me off.

"Enough with the excuses!" Her eyes blazed fiercely. She'd never be able to understand my battle, even if telling the truth was an option.

"I was ready to come," I stuttered, and she looked at me expectantly.

"There'd better be a good reason why you weren't at my party."

I picked at my fraying jeans, quickly trying to think up a believable story. "I got really sick —"

She held up her hands to stop me. "Whatever."

I was left alone in the hallway.

☼

All week we woke to dark mornings. Half the time I couldn't even remember driving to school. Everyone walked with heavy hearts through the dreary days and forgot about the sun. Our classrooms were cold, our clothes always damp, and I tried telling myself they were wrong — that this wouldn't last — but rain tipped relentlessly on the strange little town by the sea.

And I was lost.

I'd be halfway through something, then find myself staring restlessly out at the bay. I missed the ocean so much it hurt—literally. My muscles cramped painfully from lack of salt and my lungs ached constantly. The longer I stayed away, the more I felt like something inside me was dying.

My withdrawals were all-consuming, to the point where I didn't even try making things right with Amber. I often saw her in the corridor between lessons and in the car park after school, but she wouldn't look at me.

The rain was never ending, and only Britta's eyes sparkled.

Chapter Thirty

Jake met me in the school car park one Friday morning and escorted me indoors beneath a black umbrella. "Where's your magic gone?" he asked breathlessly, shaking the rain from his clothes.

"Magic?" I asked nervously while Taylor scowled at me through running makeup and limp hair.

"We need some of that sunshine you brought on your first day," he explained. I hauled books from my locker.

If only you knew who I really was.

The bell rang, and he reached for my hand. "Will thou, beautiful Sunlight, meet me in the tallest tower when the shadows are long and the clock striketh six?" he asked dramatically.

I laughed. "You mean the abandoned post office? Sure."

He kissed my freezing hand and disappeared into the crowd.

I forgot to meet him. It wasn't until much later, when I found my phone blinking amongst a pile of clean laundry, that I wondered who was trying to reach me. The only person who talked to me these days was Jake …

Appalled, I fumbled with my shoes and dashed through pouring rain to my car. Darkness was falling when I pulled away from our brightly lit house and into the stormy night. I was forced to drive slowly; the rain had made deep pools on the road, which sucked at my tyres and threatened to pull me off course. I chastised myself for being so forgetful.

After several wrong turns I eventually ended up on the right street. Abandoned brick buildings loomed before me. I exited my badly parked car, nervously scanning the unlit road. How could half a town just lie forgotten? And for so long? It was eerie.

I hurried down the alleyway, wishing I had a light. On entering the cobblestone courtyard, the impression of stepping back a hundred years overwhelmed me. Fog swirled, making the post office and its scaffolding barely visible in the rainy night. Climbing in this weather was too dangerous. There had to be another way in.

I was drenched by the time I found it—a door with lower panes of glass missing. Without hesitating I squeezed inside. A stack of newspapers resting on an impressive oak desk distracted me, and I lifted one curiously, searching for the date. They'd been printed early in the eighteenth century, left here undelivered. I had chills, thinking of the people who once worked here.

You don't have time for this!

My footsteps echoed as I tore up a narrow staircase, and

several times I convinced myself I was being followed. Long lines of windows blurred by. Would he still be here?

Heart thudding, I climbed the fourth flight of steps, roughly aware of the direction I should be heading in.

I wound higher and higher until the stairs finally ended, then hurried down the short length of passage towards a wooden door. This had to be it.

Disappointment filled me when the handle didn't budge. I rubbed a patch of dust from the glass and peered in. Scraps of paper littered the floor – or was it confetti? Straining my eyes, I tried to decipher what it could be.

Flowers.

Jake had been and gone. I swallowed hard, my gaze following a trail of petals to the middle of the room. Candles dotted a tartan rug, and I could smell the smoke that had spiralled from their blackened wicks. I ran back the way I'd come, guilt tugging at my heart as the rain fell harder.

My tyres squealed away from the curb, and I only just missed hitting a dishevelled man who'd appeared beneath some leaky guttering. I don't think he noticed as he tilted a paper bag to his mouth and staggered on down the road.

My phone lay quiet beside me, and I drummed my fingers impatiently on the steering wheel before swinging onto the main road. I made a beeline for Jake's house, glad his parents were away tonight. I'd say sorry and tell him how he meant the world to me – how maybe I even loved him. But I didn't pull into his driveway. Not when I saw

Taylor's car there.

I pulled over, wishing I was mistaken. With my car still idling I watched his house, waiting for her to leave. I don't know how long I stayed. The old me would have kicked down the door and confronted them, but instead I drove home, reminded of why I hadn't wanted a boyfriend in the first place.

You knew it couldn't last. Just breathe, you'll be fine.

But I was kidding myself. I'd let down too many walls and was in too deep for it not to hurt. The thought of them together ate away at me. How was this possible after everything Jake and I had become?

I rang Amber, despite her still being angry at me.

"Mmm?" She was half asleep, groggy with tiredness.

"Amber, it's me."

"What do you want?" she muttered irritably. "You really let me down."

"Jake's back with Taylor."

And that's when I started crying. My nose ran, my body shook, and I felt like throwing up. There was shocked silence from her end.

"Really? Are you sure?" I could hear the disbelief in her voice when she finally spoke. I wiped my eyes on my duvet, trails of watery mascara staining it, and nodded, even though she couldn't see me.

"I'll be over soon," she promised.

I met her at the door, and our awkwardness was palpable. It had been weeks since we'd talked. I was

317

blurting out apologies and verging on another meltdown when she hugged me.

"If I'd known the reason you'd been hiding away was because your relationship was ending, I could have helped you!" She'd come to that conclusion herself, and I didn't correct her as she pushed her way into my messy room.

"Maybe you were right," she complained loudly, flinging her sleeping bag onto my bed. "Maybe guys are all the same." Two bottles of wine rolled from her pillowcase and she thrust one at me, grinning. "We'll be fine, we've got wine!"

I had to keep reminding her we were in a house full of others sleeping. The alcohol numbed my system and made my head spin. I needed fresh air.

We stumbled down the stairs and into the cold night. At first we just sat by the letterbox while Amber chain-smoked, but then she had an idea.

"Let's go to Jake's!" Her eyes sparkled. "We'll see if that home-wrecker's still there."

If I'd been sober I would never have agreed to it.

Walking the four blocks to his house took ages, and the sight of her car still glinting in his driveway set a fresh wave of tears flowing.

Amber wanted to slash the tyres but I wouldn't let her. Instead she started hurling abuse from the footpath. "Jake, you scumbag!" she yelled, and I pulled her back into the shadows.

"It's fine, Sunny," she slurred.

A dog began to bark close by.

"Come out here, skank," she screeched. I cringed as someone's porch light flickered on.

Amber giggled as we ducked behind some wheelie bins.

"I need to pee," she whispered loudly, then shouted, "You're such a mongrel, Jake!"

When his light came on I scarpered, but she was ready to take on the world.

He appeared in the doorway, wearing just his boxers, running a hand through sleep-tousled hair. "Amber?" He squinted in the dim light, making sure his eyes weren't deceiving him.

She zigzagged across the road towards him, an empty wine bottle swinging from her hand. I crouched behind a hedge that bordered a field, praying she wouldn't give me away. I couldn't quite hear what they were saying, but Amber was pointing accusingly at Taylor's car while Jake stood there scratching his head. I wondered if he was denying it or telling Amber how it was my fault. In the end I turned my back on them and slumped into wet grass.

Eventually I heard doors closing, and the pool of light that had spilled from his house was sucked up by darkness.

"Sunny?" Amber whispered.

"I'm here," I called back softly.

She squeezed through the hedge and reached for my hand. "He's not back with Taylor."

"What?" I was suddenly aware of my heartbeat.

"I really need to pee," she told me, disappearing behind some trees. The wind was starting to pick up again, causing the nearby woods to groan and sway. I wished I'd brought a jacket.

"So why is she there?" I demanded.

"She isn't. Apparently little Santorini is Charlotte's best friend." An owl swooped silently in the air above us.

"Huh?"

"Taylor has a sister," Amber explained, zipping up her jeans and turning to face me. "She's like an exact freaking replica of her, only smaller and less blonde. She borrowed Taylor's car to get here."

I looked at her doubtfully.

"He's not lying," she insisted. "They came to the door to see what was happening."

We walked slowly back through the wet field, our shoes soaking up the rain. As we meandered through backyards and random streets, which Amber claimed to be shortcuts, I drifted, weightless. I didn't care that it took twice as long to get home, or that it had started pouring again. It didn't matter that I'd be dead tired tomorrow and possibly have pneumonia.

We were drenched right through by the time we got to my house, and the blanket of alcohol was long gone. I wasn't even bothered when I realised Mum was waiting up so she could tell me I was grounded for the rest of the month, or that she began the drugs and alcohol spiel at

320

half past two in the morning.

All I cared about was that Jake and I still had a chance to work things out.

But if getting to bed at three wasn't bad enough, sleep brought with it disturbing dreams I didn't need.

I was transported straight to the cliffs at Angel Bay as Amber slept peacefully beside me.

Chapter Thirty-One

Through ice cold water I drift deeper and deeper. Darkness is everywhere — heavy and suffocating. The weight of ocean presses in from all around, imprisoning me inside a watery fist. It's getting harder to breathe …

I woke slowly from haunting dreams, clutching Evelyn's diary beneath the pillows.

"Thank God it's Saturday," Amber murmured, easing herself off my bed.

Outside it was just getting light, and fog as thick as candy floss spun beyond my windows. I pulled on jeans and a grey jacket, wishing we hadn't gone to Jake's last night. The sooner I apologised, the better. My head throbbed as I opened my door and peered out.

Emily breezed past in a cloud of perfume. "Wouldn't go that way if I were you," she advised. "Mum's been up since five."

"Five?" I mouthed incredulously, and she nodded. I pressed my fingers to my temples, knowing I was in for an exhausting lecture the second we crossed paths.

Hoisting up my window, we climbed into the tree. Wet leaves slapped my face, and the branches were slick with rain. Amber laughed as she swung recklessly to the ground, mud splattering up her jeans.

"I'll see you at school on Monday," she said, leaping onto her scooter and disappearing into fog.

I leant against my car, considering my options. If I walked to Jake's and returned via the tree, my absence might go unnoticed. But it was quite a hike for so early in the morning, and the apology needed to happen with a degree of urgency.

I cringed as the Mustang roared to life; Mum was going to kill me. I quickly turned my phone off and shoved it into the glove box.

My heart beat madly as I rang Jake's doorbell. What could I say that would make up for our behaviour last night?

Charlotte appeared, and I wondered if she knew why Amber had turned up in the middle of the night, angry and loud enough to have woken the neighbourhood. She seemed a little frosty towards me, so maybe Jake had told her. I eyed the new stud sitting crookedly in her swollen nose.

"Cool piercing."

Her eyes lit up. "Kimmy did it last night."

I bet I wasn't going to be the only daughter in a mother's bad books today. We stood in awkward silence for a while.

"Is Jake here?"

She sighed. "Let him down gently, okay? He really likes you."

"Huh?"

She stepped aside and I padded down the hall, confused by her comment. Jake was still in bed, emerging bleary-eyed from beneath the covers at the sound of his door opening.

"Sunny, hi," he muttered, rubbing his eyes.

"Jake, I'm sorry about yesterday. I lost track of time, and when I got to the post office you were gone. I came here to see you, but then ..."

"But then you thought Taylor was here. I know."

"I'm sorry." I desperately needed him to believe that.

He paused, eyes wandering over my tangled hair and tense shoulders, then nodded. "Come here." His voice was thick with sleep, and I breathed a sigh of relief when he slid his arms around me, pulling me into a hug. He was warm and golden.

"I thought you were going to be really mad," I admitted.

"Well, I was, but you look so sad."

I spent the morning at Jake's house. Kimmy may have looked like her sister, but they were complete opposites. I had to keep reminding myself I didn't hate her.

Eyeing the blood-splattered tissues that lay scrunched in the lounge, I told Charlotte to put antiseptic on her nose. Then I taught her how to make blueberry pancakes. Hours passed before I reluctantly stood to leave. What would I be going home to? Jake walked me to the door, interrupting me when I apologised for the third time.

"I always forgive the ones I love," he whispered, gently pressing his lips to mine.

My whole body tingled as I registered what he was telling me.

☼

"Give me your car keys."

I stared at Mum's outstretched hand. She'd been waiting for me in the lounge, looking oddly nervous. Up on the landing, my sisters lingered. Emily drew a finger across her throat in a swift slicing motion. Brie looked worried.

"I had to fix some stuff with Jake—"

"Keys," she interrupted, voice shaking slightly, and it occurred to me she wasn't used to disciplining us like this. Emily had always been a handful, but her dramas were minor, never lasting longer than a week. I clutched the keys anxiously. If she took back the Mustang I would surely die.

"Mum, please!" I begged.

"Sunny, you don't know how much it scares me to see you acting like this!"

And you don't know how much worse you're making everything, I felt like yelling. Just the thought of being housebound beside the ocean was torture.

"While you're grounded you can drive to and from school. That's it."

I slowly surrendered the keys. When had our relationship gotten so bad?

"Phone. Seeing as you don't answer it anyway."

"You're kidding?" I almost choked, but the worst was still to come.

"I don't want you seeing Jake any more." Her eyes didn't meet mine as she said this; she was focused on smoothing out a crease in her blouse.

"What?" I cried, indignant now.

When she looked up, her mouth was a thin line of determination. "Sorry, but it's for your own good!"

I shook my head. "He's the one thing you can't take away from me."

☼

To kill the time spent shut away in my bedroom, I examined every one of Janie's photos, reread each tragic obituary and wove Evelyn's pearls through my hair as I read her diary. And night after restless night I called a storm into the bay. That's where I found solace.

I'd sit at my window behind the billowing lace and only feel relief when my green-tinged clouds decorated the sky. Sometimes I played with the weather for hours until I was exhausted, other times it left me feeling so invigorated I'd creep through dark gardens and silent streets to Jake's house. I'd slip noiselessly through his window and into his bed. He was a beautiful distraction.

The first night I did this he'd been taken totally by surprise, but as I became more unsettled my late-night visits weren't so unexpected, and sometimes he'd be waiting up for me. During these moments I seemed to discover myself over and over; it was almost as addictive as drowning and I'd lose myself in him. His slow, deep kisses were like swimming beneath a full moon, his fingers on my skin like gentle waves.

Occasionally I wondered how he'd react if I told him my secret. Would it change the way he felt? Would he even believe me? I tried not to dwell on it.

Often I'd fall asleep in his embrace, only waking when he'd gently shake me and point at the brightening sky. I'd stumble home, heavy-lidded and tired until the next storm revived me.

And most nights I dreamed. Sometimes they provided insight, filling gaps in my family's complicated history, and other times they were so disjointed I couldn't make sense of them. One morning I woke to Jake stroking my damp face, his eyes full of worry as I struggled to unravel myself from Evelyn. It seemed she was very much alive in me.

"What do you dream, Sunny?" he asked, but I couldn't tell him. I knew how crazy it would sound.

Thankfully he wasn't a witness the following night

when Pytheus interfered with one of my many nightmares.

☼

Evelyn laboured through the water towards me, face blurring as if the ocean had gotten beneath her skin. Her mouth was open in a silent scream, her eyes frantic, trying to warn me.

"What happened?" I asked fearfully, but she was disappearing before my eyes — dissolving into the water.

"Evelyn!" I swam hard against the pulling current, attempting to reach her. Then, through the muffled water that pressed in from all around, I heard something else — something new to these dreams. It was distant, so very distant. I could have sworn it was someone laughing.

I wasn't mistaken. With increasing volume, laughter rang so loudly it hurt my ears. Evelyn's terror grew, before the ocean burst through her and she was gone.

I woke in a cold sweat, the night still dark outside.

"What did you do to her?" My voice was just a whisper. Quelling my fear, I pushed back the duvet and thrust open my window. "What did you do to her?" I had to yell over his laughter that still filled my head. Had I really only dreamed it?

"I made the ocean too cold inside her. She was feeble—a disgrace unworthy of such blood—but you ... you are much stronger."

"Strong enough to resist you." I ground my teeth

together, pulling the window shut before crawling back into bed.

"You can't resist me. You belong to me."

"I don't belong to anyone," I retaliated, at the same time wondering if that was true.

The house went eerily quiet. He replaced my thoughts with warm currents and salt, with phosphorescence and moonlight. I was standing, even though I didn't remember getting up, and walking out of my room as he lured me on. I barely noticed the carpet underfoot, or the owl that called her warning outside the lounge window. I stumbled from the house like a confused sleepwalker, vaguely aware of the hooded men halfway along our beach. I stepped onto the jetty, breaking into a run. My mind was fog and I couldn't think straight. Not a rational thought penetrated my brain. When I reached the end of the jetty, I didn't stop. I fell into the ocean, spluttering, hopelessly trying to claw my way back to the surface.

"You do belong to me."

My terror was Evelyn's as I slipped through the water. Maybe I would truly drown this time. Pain ripped open my lungs, the water like ice inside me. It didn't ease, and I wondered if he'd been toying with me the whole time. His hold on me was terrifying but I refused to give in, and for about an hour we battled like this—me unable to surface, yet determined not to sink.

Eventually I felt his grip on me slacken and I fought my way up to the ocean's skin, drawing in fiery mouthfuls of air. Crouching on the jetty, I caught my breath.

Dawn lit the edges of the islands when I made my way inside. Unfortunately it was only now that I looked down into the yard and saw Britta. She had her face tilted up to my window, and panic shot through me. Had she been there earlier when I'd flung it open, shouting questions into my dream-filled night? Had she seen me beneath the half-moon, barefoot and disorientated, running along the jetty? Had she stared in silent wonder as cold water swallowed me? Her hungry eyes told me yes, she had indeed seen everything.

I lay shivering in bed that night, cold and scared. It certainly wasn't what I needed the night before an English assessment.

Mum handed me my keys the next morning, and I took them without a word. I was so tired.

"It really is for your own good," she said tentatively, as if we were no longer comfortable being in the same room together.

I shook my head. "You have no idea what's good for me. Jake is great."

She didn't say anything to this, which meant she disagreed.

"Sunny, I know what it's like to give up everything for a guy."

I choked on the coffee I was sipping.

"I know I've made bad choices!" she snapped before I could say anything, and I turned to leave.

"Sunny," she tried again, resting her hand on my arm. "You'd tell me if you were in any kind of trouble, wouldn't you?"

"Things aren't easy right now!" I yelled, frustrated. And then I was crying. Giant tears pushed through my eyelashes and spilled into my coffee. "The only good thing in my life is Jake, so why would you try to keep me from him?"

I swiped angrily at my tears before pouring my coffee shakily down the sink.

I was first to leave the assessment. Ignoring my teacher's reaction as I handed her my almost blank paper, I hurried outside to my car, which was beneath some old redwoods on the far side of the car park. The sky had filled with more black clouds, and strong gusting winds had me huddling inside my jacket. At least it had stopped raining—even if it was only for ten minutes. I hoisted my bag to my other shoulder as I unlocked the Mustang.

"Sunny!" The voice was friendly.

"Yeah?" My response came automatically, but when I turned, my breath caught in my throat.

Stepping out from behind a tree was the man who'd

spoken my name in the stone building. *Our children have given us a name ...*

His eyes held me, anchoring me to the spot.

"So, you're the one they call Sunlight." It wasn't a question, and I couldn't exactly deny it—not now. Chills crawled down my spine.

"Yes."

As he approached, his intense gaze never left my face, immersing me in an emerald sea and making it impossible for me to look away.

"Of course," he murmured. "So pale, like something that shouldn't see daylight." He took another step closer and I couldn't put any more distance between us, my back already pressed against the car. I trembled as he drank in my features, committing me to memory. The door handle I gripped was slick beneath my hand.

"Such dark hair ..." He reached up to caress a curl that had come loose, and I shied away, yanking open my car door and dropping into my seat.

"Can I help you?" My voice was far from level.

"Yes, actually, I think you can. I think you can help all of us."

I cast a nervous glance over the car park, afraid he might have others with him, but he seemed to be alone.

"Do you know much about your ancestry, Sunlight?" He eyed me eagerly and leaned in close—so close I could smell his sour breath and see the pores like craters in his skin.

"No." I shook my head. "Can't say I do." I was ready to take off at any moment.

"Levi!" he called abruptly, and the boy I'd been avoiding for weeks appeared. He looked apprehensive, obviously not here by choice, but his expression changed the minute he saw me. Recognition flashed on his face, his mouth dropping open as if he couldn't believe I was real. The man would have seen this had he been able to take his stare off me for even a second.

Levi was totally composed when my tormentor finally turned to him.

"Well?"

"This isn't her." He lied with confidence, and I could have leapt up and hugged him. "No, the girl I saw was much taller, and her eyes were—" he leant forward as if to examine me "—green, like yours. You've got the wrong girl."

The man ground his teeth violently. "Are you sure?" His eyes had narrowed to angry slits and he roughly took hold of my wrist. "I need Lyle. You remember him—don't you, girl?"

I had a fleeting image of the man who'd chased me up the cliffs and through the streets. "Don't touch me!" As I pulled free of his grasp, he made a lunge for me, but I managed to slam the door and lock it. He connected painfully with the window.

"Don't think this is over!" His face was contorted with rage, and flecks of spit splattered the glass. I fitted the key into the ignition and fled, well aware he'd spoken the truth. It'd be naive of me to believe otherwise.

My secret wasn't just getting the better of me. It was destroying me.

Chapter Thirty-Two

As exams loomed closer, the teachers inundated us with mountains of reading that I pushed to the very back of my locker and left there. Usually I would have studied for weeks beforehand, stapling charts to my walls and memorising a hundred different dates, but school held little importance now.

I struggled just getting up in the morning and knew all my energy was being spent on resisting what I wanted most. I'd stare listlessly at the ocean, and sometimes hours would pass without me realising. Instead of feeling restless, I became tired, and I stopped visiting Jake at midnight. He picked up more shifts at the garage and I saw him less and less, despite no longer being grounded.

The battle inside me raged on, keeping me awake at night. I often slept with my headphones in, and while it did help to block out Pytheus, it didn't stop me dreaming.

The constant call of the ocean in my head consumed me to the point where it was all I could think about. I kept to my room and only went downstairs for meals, though if

Brie hadn't knocked on my door each night to tell me it was time for dinner, I probably would have forgotten to eat.

And I considered dropping out of school for good. I filled out my leaving form and carried it around with me, but Mum's inevitable disappointment always stopped me from handing it in.

Sometimes I found tightly folded notes from Jake inside my locker, and every night he'd text me 'sweet dreams'.

One day I arrived home to find a bunch of white lilies on the doorstep. I put them in a cracked vase and cried, bewildered by my reaction. It would have been so easy to go and see him—even just call him—but I didn't. By harbouring my secret, I felt like I was lying to him. How would he feel knowing he'd been with someone not entirely human? I became certain the person he loved wasn't really me, and I wasn't sure how to break it to him.

I stopped visiting Janie too, and she went back to sending me letters written in her unsteady hand. Was I okay, she wanted to know, and when would she see me again? Guilt nagged at me each time one arrived; I knew how long they'd have taken to write. But I did nothing about it.

Rain pelted the classroom windows. My car remained damp. And Lexie's pale friends complained more than ever, stalking around with permanent scowls.

Mum continued to worry about me. She wasn't even mad when she discovered I failed my English assessment, or when the history teacher rang to say I hadn't bothered writing the latest essays. Again she told me it scared her seeing me like this, and that I should spend time with friends.

After weeks of not seeing Jake he stopped by unannounced, asking if I'd meet him for dinner in town. I agreed, although the thought of leaving my room, let alone the house, was daunting.

"So you'll be there?" he asked again, as if I hadn't heard him.

I saw the uncertainty that dwelled in the blue of his eyes, and the questions that trembled on his lips.

"Yes," I promised, and he kissed my forehead before he left.

☼

I really had planned to go. I borrowed one of Brie's dresses, washed my hair — I even painted my toenails. But I was forgetful and unfocused. I'd just listened to yet another voice message from the rest home — Janie wasn't doing so well, and would I please visit?

Rain splashed my bedroom windows, and the wind found its way in through one of the frames. I'd been meaning to see her …

I still had a few minutes to spare before dressing, so I flipped open Evelyn's diary to distract myself from my guilt. I'd almost read it from cover to cover. Her entries were fewer and much shorter now, written so messily I often had to reread each sentence. I imagined her hurriedly scribbling it all down, attempting to document her messy life. Did she know her time was running out? I cringed at the thought. If the prophecy was true, how much time did I have left? I ran my fingers over the faded ink.

I had my baby. He's perfect and tiny with the darkest eyes I've ever seen.

I glanced at mine in the reflection of my mirror. They were so dark I'd seen some people look twice. Did all of us have such soulless eyes? Gently, I lifted the string of pearls from where they hung and fastened them around my neck. They were cold against my skin. Wearing them made me feel closer to Evelyn, which somehow made me feel closer to myself.

Mum arrived two weeks ago, and I would honestly be lost without her. I didn't know it would be this hard. I thought that if anything could keep me from the ocean at night it would be my son, but the call is even stronger. Now, more than ever, I'm finding it almost impossible to ignore. The voices in my head are disturbingly real, and sometimes I find myself on the verge of obeying them. I manage to resist, but only just. Imagine believing the stuff of fairy tales. I dream of letting the ocean into my lungs, which surely means I am attracted to death. Maybe this is what it's like to be depressed. This is a cruel world, Procellae has taught me that.

Closing my eyes, I took a calming breath, afraid of what the next entry might hold. Tiredness crept up on me as I lay there, threatening me with dreams I couldn't escape.

I didn't hear Jake's bike through all the rain and opened my eyes to him standing wet in my doorway. Despite the lack of sun his skin was still golden, and I admired his loveliness as I watched him speak. His voice hung like velvet in the air around me, his lips forming words that didn't quite reach my brain. It took me long moments to realise it was well past the time he'd asked me to meet him, and that he was angry. How had I let myself fall asleep?

"Sunny!" He tore the diary from my hands, tossing it into a pile of clothes on the floor.

"How dare you!" I shrieked and immediately regretted it.

"How dare I?" he repeated in disbelief. "Did you even plan for a second to meet me tonight?"

I pushed my hair away from my hot face, wondering if this was the end of us.

"What's going on with you?" He cast his eyes over my dishevelled state and the mess in my room.

"I lost track of time—"

"In general, Sunny! Why do you lock yourself away up here? Why, when I talk to you, do you act as if I'm not here?" His angry blue stare held my dark one, and I thought of waves against black rocks.

"There are so many things I want to tell you." I bit nervously at the inside of my cheek and tasted blood. He didn't say anything, which meant I had to continue. "But some of it I can't right now."

"Why not?" he demanded.

What could I tell him?

"And don't lie to me!" he cried, as if my expression had already betrayed me. "Is there someone else?"

"What? No, of course not!" I was stunned to think that would even cross his mind.

"Well, I've been wrong before." His eyes burned into me, and I swallowed hard, trying to get rid of the lump forming painfully in my throat.

"Do you know how I feel when I swim and the moon touches my skin through the salt?"

It was the last thing he'd been expecting me to say. I wanted to elaborate on that by describing how I would let the ocean push into my lungs and twist into my veins.

"Huh?" He looked baffled, and misery pulled at the corners of my mouth. More than anything I wanted to say something that mattered.

Clearly frustrated, he asked, "What does that have to do with anything?"

Again I let the scenario of me telling him run through my head. My hesitation had him standing to leave.

"Don't go," I begged as mascara-coloured tears pooled beneath my eyes.

"I'm gone until you decide to trust me."

The sound of his bike leaving tore a great ravine in my heart. I listened as he drove out the driveway and down the street until he was too far away to be heard. I mopped my face with the duvet and looked outside to where rain fell harder. The dark figures that had been guarding the beach were now leaving, obviously not prepared to spend the night out in such conditions.

I was already off my bed and running through the yard. Thick mist hung in the air, and I clambered blindly over dark rocks, falling hard at least twice. It didn't slow me down. I pushed damp hair off my face and dropped onto the beach, out of sight, where I ran, calling to the sea.

"Waves!" Hurling myself across broken shells, I felt the ocean listening.

"Wind!"

Even before the word had left my lips, it was lost in gusts now blowing off the water. The bay was dark and salt stung my face. I licked it from my cracked lips, shuddering at the taste.

"Yes." I laughed like a crazy girl, and the ocean crashed at my feet. On the cliff tops, trees were bent over, their roots creaking as they pulled free from the earth. Chunks of dirt tumbled down the rock.

"Yes!" I stretched out my arms, turned circles until I was dizzy and fell to the sand. I hadn't felt like this in so long. Waves grew and grew, the wind screaming like something fierce. The rush of the storm was inside me now, the energy a ball of fire in my stomach, and this time I didn't hold back. I hauled the waves so high they soared above me like walls of marbled glass. Wind flung foam at me, begging me to feel salt on my skin. In the distance, waves swallowed the islands, their beaches lost. When the water surged even further up the beach, I took shelter near the cliffs and watched my storm rage on.

It took immense willpower not to walk into the sea and never look back.

Chapter Thirty-Three

Later that night as I tried to finish Evelyn's final entry, thoughts of severing my earth ties stirred. Initially they were elusive and fleeting, my brain barely registering them, but then they lingered and grew until it was all I could think about.

After abandoning the diary, I massaged my temples. I could escape all of this and embrace all of that. At first I would miss everyone, but I'd soon forget them. Pytheus had made that quite clear.

I listened to the waves hugging the beach. I was drawn to the ocean like a flower is to light. Resisting was too hard. It had stolen the very essence of who I was, just as it had done to Janie. She was proof we couldn't prosper here.

Thinking of her brought on a fresh wave of guilt, but I shoved it away.

The thought of spending endless nights in the ocean and having the freedom to build storms made me smile. Imagine doing both at the same time! Why had I never thought of that before? It would be fantastic.

"You have no idea what we are capable of."

My eyes shot open and I pulled the window shut with a crash.

"You can't shut me out, Sunlight. You let the ocean in, and you let me in. I'm inside your head."

It was so hard not to be distracted as I finished reading the diary.

Last night the baby wouldn't stop screaming and I had to leave. I left him there to cry. What a terrible mother I've turned out to be. On nights such as these I stand in the shallow waves and imagine giving in to the voice in my head. I am crazy beyond help. I picture Mum lifting my baby from his cot and whispering words of comfort into his ear. I have failed everyone. I could slip away from this world and no one would care. My destiny is beneath the waves, where I shall surely drown. I can't seem to escape this, and refuse to believe the tales these people tell or the dreams I dream. I will welcome death to banish my madness and die with a broken heart. I cry for hours but have made my decision. My lover's pearls will mark the end. I'm sorry, Baby, I really did try.

Even though I was exhausted, it still took hours to fall asleep.

When I finally did, I dreamed. There was no avoiding it.

☼

I can see Evelyn, and our resemblance is unnerving. It's as though I'm watching myself up on that cliff. She is crouching there, contemplating something much bigger than herself.

The moon casts soft light on her face, embracing her in its glow, but I don't think she notices. Her eyes are dark and brooding.

She reaches into the pocket of her colourless dress and pulls out the string of pearls. In the moonlight they are radiant, casting pools of silver onto her white face. For a moment she pauses, admiring their beauty as I would have done. She runs them through her fingers, presses them to her cheek, and when she reaches up, her face is stained with tears.

Sobbing, she loops them onto the old tree that marks the ledge where so many before her have fallen. She looks broken-hearted and defeated. On trembling legs she pushes herself up, forcing herself to the edge. Not once does she look down.

My heart is hammering in my chest when I realise what she's about to do. "No!" I scream. "Evelyn, no!" But she can't hear me.

I see her take a deep breath and step from the cliff. As she falls, I fall too—but I'm the lucky one, for now.

I woke with a fright, one hand clutching the pearls at my throat. If these dreams were showing me the past—which I was now quite certain they were—why was everyone so convinced this town was cursed? I'd seen Evelyn clearly abandon her earth life, and regardless of whether or not she'd believed any of it, she had in effect chosen ocean.

I dragged myself out of bed, motivated only by the fact that I needed to talk to Jake. Yawning my way into the kitchen, I relived the dream.

What had gone wrong?

I made the ocean too cold inside her ... Remembering Pytheus' chilling response caused my hands to shake as I poured extra strong coffee into a mug. When I finished it I brewed more. It was barely enough to wake me up; only the briny deep could make me feel alive again.

Brie came grumbling down the stairs, and when she tripped on the last couple she swore loudly. That was so unlike her.

"I think I have seasonal affective disorder," she mumbled, pouring herself a black coffee. "I googled it, and there is such thing."

The weather was starting to get to her—as it was to everyone else. Outside, the waves were white-crested and tempestuous, pushed in every direction by the wind. Our little jetty trembled as water heaved against its posts. Brie spread out some complicated-looking maths sheets on the table and set a scowl on her face.

"Any coffee left?" Emily slumped down opposite me and twisted her hair into a bun. "Seriously, what is up with the weather? Maybe this place really is cursed," she muttered, emptying the pot.

The lights flickered for a second and we were left in darkness.

"Great," Brie cried sarcastically, throwing up her hands and sending her coffee cup flying. In the dim light we watched coffee soak through her almost finished worksheet.

"I'm going back to bed," she said, defeated.

☼

The ride to school was especially quiet without Brie beside me, and the day was so dark it felt like night; no wonder people were so irritable. I wouldn't admit it to anyone, but I enjoyed the energy within the storm clouds, and the powerful lightning that flickered across the sky.

That's because it's your fate, the little voice niggled. Sometimes I couldn't tell if it was Him or just my chattering mind, and it frightened me.

In class we all sat in silent rows, heads turned mechanically towards the board, but while the other students tried to concentrate, I didn't bother. In fifth period I was aware of eyes on me, and as I turned Jake quickly looked away. A trigger of panic darted through me. It was my own fault he'd given up. How long had I thought he would put up with my lies and deception?

I heard his words as if he had spoken them again just now in the classroom. *I'm gone until you decide to trust me.*

Tears stung my eyes but I blinked them furiously away.

He couldn't understand why I felt so distant—no one could. I'd try to talk to him after class, explain that I really did love him, though what would it change?

The bell rang but as I left my seat the teacher held me back.

"Are you okay, Sunny?"

"Yeah, why?"

She looked at me with uncertainty, as though it should have been obvious. "You were getting top grades at your old school, but I haven't seen an essay from you on my desk in weeks. Exams start next month, and I want to see you pass." She eased off her glasses and laid them carefully on the desk. "Is everything all right?"

She seemed really concerned, and I didn't know where to look. If she knew who I was she'd throw me to the ocean herself.

"Uh, I'm just not sleeping well?" It was such a bad excuse it even came out like a question. Although it was partly true, it definitely wasn't the reason I was failing.

She rubbed her tired eyes and glanced out the window. Rain slipped easily down the glass, warping the dark trees beyond it.

"Neither am I, for that matter. I think this weather is getting to all of us."

Sighing, she gathered a pile of essays together and stood up. "Sunny, if you ever need to talk I'm always here." She patted me on the arm before sweeping out into the corridor.

I stood in the empty classroom, willing away the tears that seemed to be on call the last few days, then made my way to yet another after-hours detention—this one from the history teacher for not doing the homework he'd set.

Stopping briefly at my locker, I thought of Jake. He'd probably be on his way home by now.

It was Britta, whose locker was a couple of doors down, who made me forget about finding him. She was muttering under her breath and I closed my eyes, trying to separate her voice from the others.

"It is in the bay we'll find her."

Goose bumps crept along my arms and up my neck; she was quoting that chilling poem. The words she spoke were now perfectly audible in the hallway. It was as if everyone else had ceased to exist.

"Tempted by your silken waters indeed," she muttered.

I opened my eyes to find her staring directly at me.

"I've finally found you."

I had no idea she'd be waiting for me in the car park. It had gotten dark while I'd sat in detention, and I didn't see her until it was too late. Britta was leaning against my car, smoking, her gleaming eyes fixed on my face. Equally alert friends flanked her.

"So, pale one, why is Pytheus so angry?" she asked through a cloud of smoke. I had to take a step back to breathe. My heart was already beating like it did after a ten-kilometre run, because even though the overcast skies obscured it, I knew the moon was almost full.

And I knew what that meant.

"I don't have a clue what you're talking about. Excuse me." I pulled my keys from my bag but she jerked them out of my hand and hurled them to Seth.

"You know exactly what I'm talking about."

Just then the clouds above us parted and she tipped my face up at the moon. "You can't resist him forever."

Her skin was cold on mine and I threw her off. "Go to hell, Britta! You and your old stories and your messed up little town are insane!"

I was on the ground so fast I barely had time to register what was happening. Gravel bit into my back and she pressed the spike of her heel into my cheek. I could taste blood.

Behind her the moon was a halo of light, and all I could make out in her dark face were those smouldering eyes. I knew in that moment she wouldn't hesitate to kill me, but I reminded myself that wasn't what she wanted.

Her voice was calm when she spoke again. "I'll trial you myself. Pytheus wants blood and so do I. My ancestors made a promise, which means we never should have stopped searching. I will find her, even if it's the very last thing I do."

The boys stepped closer now, their excitement flagrant. They circled us, as if expecting a struggle, then yanked me up and shoved me heartlessly into the back seat of my car.

"Darcy, meet us there," Britta ordered, and one of the boys nodded obediently.

If Seth hadn't driven so erratically I would have considered leaping from the car, but escaping wasn't the only thing on my mind. I wanted a confession. As they rummaged through the glove box and discussed my taste in music, I discreetly extracted my phone and hit record.

I drew a deep breath. "So when I'm dead your daddy's just going to cover up for you again?"

It was a big accusation, but Britta looked unfazed as she curled a long strand of hair around her finger. "Claire was pathetic—she was only underwater for a minute. I've seen kittens hold their breath longer."

I felt cold as the conversation went on around me. Seth swung violently off the road, and my phone slipped out of my hands to sit blinking beneath the passenger seat.

"Good, here's Darcy now," Britta said, gracefully exiting my car as it came to a stop. "Park the cars out of sight," she instructed before disappearing.

Through the windows I recognised the woods that, in this light, concealed the old stone building. Why were we here?

"Get out," a burly guy ordered, and when they began binding my wrists with rope I panicked. I lashed out and ran, and for a couple of moments I was free. All I needed was for a car to drive past and someone would help me, but then I was slammed into the dirt and I lost consciousness.

☼

When I woke, it was the sound of the woods groaning that reminded me of my current predicament. I was in a field with a group of maniacs who had bound my wrists so tightly I wanted to cry. After staggering to my feet, I was pulled roughly through the trees towards the building.

Britta was nowhere to be seen, but I guessed it was she who had left the door open. My vision blurred as they led me to a hole in the floor, and I hoped I didn't have a concussion. A long flight of stairs descended into darkness. My head throbbed with every step I took. I hated to think where we were going. The air was damp and I started to shiver. When Seth lit a tall white candle, I realised we'd arrived in some kind of dungeon.

Then I saw Britta. She had her palms pressed against cracked stone walls and was staring up at the ceiling. Moss covered everything.

"Sunlight," she muttered without turning around, and the boys who held me paused.

"Sunlight, Sunlight, Sunlight!" She screamed out my name only to have it thrown back at her by the haunted walls. When she finally turned to face us I could see just how damaged her mind was. A smile played on her cold, pretty face as she pointed across the room.

When I spotted the baths set deeply into the floor, I

knew exactly where I was and what was happening. *Historic texts describe baths as the preferred method.* Isn't that what Lexie had said?

My heart raced frantically as they walked me towards one. Sets of rusty manacles were chained to the stone.

Without warning, Britta pushed me in and I fell hard on my knees. My headache worsened and the room spun alarmingly. She jumped in after me, replacing the rope at my wrists with the iron shackles. I didn't have it in me to fight her. Seth kicked on the tap. Freezing water pulled from an underground source gushed onto the smooth stone, and I struggled feebly—unable to stand—as it soaked into my jeans. Now I was truly scared. The water flowing from the tap was fresh, which instinctively I knew would drown me. Properly. They weren't to know it was the salt I needed. It was like putting a saltwater fish in a pond. It just wouldn't survive. Their ancient trials had been a total waste of time, but wasn't that always the case?

"Not tonight, idiot!" Britta snarled at Seth. "The moon isn't full until tomorrow, and I'm all about following tradition."

A splinter of a chance sparked up in my chilled body. They left with the promise of returning, but I didn't plan on being here when they came back.

I called a storm from where I crouched.

Usually I needed to be near the sea, but I had so much fear inside me it wasn't hard to channel my power. Even though I was far beneath the ground, I could hear the wind starting to claw at the building.

Energy surged through me, heating the metal that encircled my wrists, and I imagined the sky outside turning green. What now? Should I destroy the entire building? If that's what it took to be free I would, but I was struggling to concentrate. The shackles were getting so hot I could smell my flesh burning, and I lunged forward in pain. Again I fell hard, and it was the force of the fall that broke one of the deteriorated brackets I'd been chained to. The restraints were more damaged than I'd realised. I thought of the ocean, ferocious and unstoppable, and wrenched the remaining bracket effortlessly from the stone. My wrists were still confined within the manacles, chains hanging heavily from each, but I was free.

I climbed out of the bath, body aching, and looked around. This was where Claire, Sophie and many before them had spent their last nights on this cruel earth. What a way to die, I thought miserably.

I lifted the candle, and its light pushed into the far corners of the chamber. There were four baths in total with old chains in each. I made myself walk around the room, even though every step I took terrified me. Flung over one of the taps was a denim jacket I recognised from Sophie's picture. I pressed it sadly to my cheek. It was unfathomable to me how Britta could take someone's life with absolutely no guilt.

☼

I guessed right that they'd leave the Mustang parked hidden in the woods. It was unlikely anyone would have found it there.

I ran through blinding rain and fumbled with the door, the chains swinging uselessly and slowing me down. My hands were freezing but I didn't wait to warm up. I blasted the heater on hot and got the hell out of there. I was pretty shaken up but it had gotten me thinking straight. I knew how to fix things with Jake.

As soon as I got home, I swallowed some painkillers and locked myself in the bathroom. The shackles were ugly antique-looking things, and I felt sick knowing other girls had died wearing them. I wasted almost an entire bottle of conditioner trying to slip free of them. My wrists were bruised and tender when I finally gave up. While I showered awkwardly and combed out my hair, the chains clattered noisily. Back in my bedroom I tried to take deep, even breaths. I didn't have to worry about Britta for now — as far as she was concerned, I was crying and powerless beneath a derelict building. Rust-coloured water dripped from the chains onto my duvet. I'd have to deal with them tomorrow when no one was home.

I charged my phone and played the recording back. Goose bumps erupted on my arms, and I rubbed them away before easing my tired body into bed. This confession would hopefully free Jake of Taylor's relentless blackmail. The longer it remained a secret, the longer she would use it against him.

I had to expose McLeod.

☼

I slept until Brie charged into my room. "Can I—" she started, but I didn't let her finish her sentence.

"Wear whatever you like. I can't go to school today—I have to do something else." I pulled up the blankets so she wouldn't see what was attached to my wrists and silently begged her not to ask what my plans were.

"Are you in trouble?" she asked, wriggling into a pair of my jeans. They were way too long for her but she just turned up the bottoms and swung around to face me.

"Maybe," I admitted. "But don't worry, I'll be fine."

When the house fell silent I dressed in a heavy coat that concealed the manacles, grabbed my phone and ran to the Mustang.

☼

I drove past the police station multiple times before actually working up the courage to go in. If I saw any cops with green eyes I'd be running straight out. I walked to the front desk, hoping I was doing the right thing. "I need to talk to Detective Santorini, please."

"Name?"

"It's Sunny. I don't have an appointment."

She looked up at me, exasperated. "The detective is a very busy man. If you want to speak to an officer I can try to get you a slot with Sergeant McLeod."

"No," I blurted, and I must have been feeling fragile because I started crying—loudly. My uncontrollable sobs made the receptionist very uneasy.

The door behind her opened and a tall man with dark eyes looked me up and down.

"It's okay, Sandra. I have half an hour before I need to interview the Smith boy," and Santorini led me into his office. "Take a seat, miss."

He handed me a glass of water but my hands were shaking so badly I slopped it over my jeans and had to set it back down on his desk—chains rattling.

What if my plan didn't work? What if I ended up making things worse for Jake and his father?

I was relying on Taylor staying quiet about what she and Jake had seen, on the basis it would make her own father look bad if she didn't. As the detective's daughter, surely she felt some obligation to uphold his reputation. And surely she knew how bad it would look if people discovered she, of all people, had withheld crucial information regarding such a serious crime. Wasn't that in itself an offence?

"Are you okay?" The detective was a kind man, I could

see that. How had Taylor turned out so mean?

"Can you get these off?" I pulled back my sleeves, and a brief look of shock registered on his face. He examined the locks.

"Wait here."

I expected him to come back with a bunch of keys—not bolt cutters. When I was finally free of them, I massaged my painful wrists.

"What happened?" he asked.

"Last night some students drove me out to the woods and left me chained up in an abandoned building. But that's not why I came."

"No?"

"I came because I know Claire Maine didn't die in a car accident. She was murdered." It was probably the last thing he'd been expecting me to say, and I wondered if he was asking himself how he'd wound up with a delusional girl in his office at nine-thirty in the morning. I looked at him through bloodshot eyes. Would he believe me?

He stared at me gravely before calling out to the receptionist. "Sandra?"

She popped her head into his office, ignoring me.

"Reschedule my interview."

☼

The detective led me down a carpeted hallway and into an interview room. It was one of the blandest spaces I'd ever

seen. At the table where I sat there was a small black box —
apparently it would record our conversation — and an
expensive-looking monitor was fastened to one wall.

He ushered me to a chair and turned on the equipment.
I tried not to look at the miniature version of me that had
popped up near the bottom of the screen. All of this was
making me more nervous. The detective pulled a thick
notebook out of a drawer and flicked to a fresh page. "Start
by telling me about last night."

"Well, there are a lot of superstitious people in this
town," I said quietly, and he assured me he understood
what I was talking about.

"Half of them think I'm the one responsible for all this
rain." I looked out at the flooded lawn and told him they
wanted to prove it by holding a trial.

He asked me to explain what I meant, so I described the
hidden room beneath the ash trees.

"They think you're still down there?"

I nodded.

"And they're planning to return tonight?"

"Yes."

He scribbled in his notebook, his writing so messy I
couldn't read it.

"Who will I be expecting, exactly?" he wanted to know.

"Britta McLeod, amongst others."

He paused for the briefest of moments, his pen
hovering above the page. When he poured himself a glass
of water his face gave away nothing.

Outside, the sky was so dark it felt as though night was falling, and thunder rumbled in the distance.

"That must have been quite an ordeal for you," he said sympathetically, photographing my wrists with a large camera. I bet he had all sorts of horrific photos on there.

"It was worse for Claire. That's where she was killed, and everyone thinks she drove off a cliff."

"Why are you so certain she was murdered?"

"I've got a confession. Here—listen." I pulled out my phone and played the recording from last night.

"I'm going to need to keep that as evidence," he finally said.

Chapter Thirty-Four

I'm walking along the beach. It is early morning and Angel Bay is full of light. Everything is slightly blurred in this dream world that I'm getting so used to and the colours are dull, almost sepia.

I make my way along the tideline, lifting my feet over bulging piles of seaweed. Up on the lawn is the cottage; its paint is new and marigolds smile from chipped clay pots. The sweeping lawns are well kept and I try to make out if there is anyone home, but the sun glints off the windows, reflecting the water. My feet sink deep into wet sand as I avoid mounds of dirty sea bubbles, dark green and gleaming.

In the distance I see something in the shallows. The tide holds it, rocking it back and forth against the beach, but I struggle to make out what it is. I walk a little quicker, wondering if maybe a dolphin has been separated from its pod and is in trouble. If I hurry, maybe I'll have time to help it back out into the bay.

As I get closer I pause. Netting swirls gossamer-like

from the creature, concealing its identity. I start to jog. The sand swallows up my ankles, but I keep pushing forward. Just metres away I stop again. I realise it's not netting at all—it's fabric that clings to whatever is floating there. My stomach churns.

Clothes.

The waves reveal her to me, and I drop to the sand. Minutes pass before I dare look again, and when I do I wish I hadn't.

Her dark hair is alive in the current that tugs her to shore but her face is white with death. Her eyes are gently closed, her lips colourless. She is beautiful, even now. Salt has started to harden on her eyelashes, and the bay is peaceful, quiet. The only sounds are the waves rolling gently over the sand. I rock back on my heels and press my fingers to my temples.

But then something else is happening. Juniper is running towards me. Her blonde and silver hair streams out behind her, and a smiling baby bounces on her hip.

Her face is frantic as she sets the baby onto the sand and hurries to Evelyn. She is crying, screaming, pulling her from the water and lugging her up the beach. All I can do is watch.

A seagull wheels over the cliffs, gliding on an invisible current of air, and I hear Him. It starts quietly, then it's right inside my head. Cold laughter reverberates off the islands and pulses through me.

I woke up and lay totally still. The answer came to me

without having to ask. It slithered through my room like a poisonous snake.

"I had no use for a heartbroken girl just drifting in the shallows, not really alive or dead. Her filthy earth blood made her weak. She was so like her mother it made me sick! I soon pushed her back to shore where she belonged," he spat. His laughter still rang in my ears, cold and full of malevolence.

"But you. You are all ocean."

The next day I went to school solely to make things right with Jake. I'd wanted to find him after leaving the police station, but the detective had told me to stay home and keep a low profile. I was pretty sure Britta would be under interrogation at the station today. Even if she wasn't, the need to see Jake overrode the risk of running into her.

He was standing by our lockers, and I pushed through the crowded corridor towards him. What would I say?

Taylor appeared, which stopped me dead in my tracks, and someone crashed into me from behind.

"Watch what you're doing," the boy muttered angrily, but I didn't bother turning to see who it was.

Taylor was gliding over to Jake, fanning her hair evenly about her shoulders and fluttering her eyelashes. She leaned against my locker as they talked, and I felt him slipping further and further away from me. He pulled on a heavy jacket and closed his locker door.

As he made to leave she stopped him, leaning forward to whisper something in his ear. I watched her lips, sticky with gloss as they formed words I couldn't make out. Blood pulsed loudly in my ears.

Now wasn't the time to lose control. I turned to stare down the busy hallway at the clock on the wall. The bell would ring any minute, and I really needed to talk to him. When I looked back at them my heart momentarily stopped.

She was pressed into him, their heads joined in a kiss.

I walked numbly into history and sat at the very back where I would be left alone — not that anyone besides Amber tried talking to me any more. There I hid behind my folder and let the tears slide freely down my face.

☼

Once Emily pulled the wings off a butterfly, and now — sitting in that classroom — I knew exactly how it felt. I was ugly and helpless, as though everything that was ever precious to me had been stolen. Inside I was sinking to a dark place I was afraid I wouldn't come out of.

On the other side of the room, Taylor was draped across her chair, the trace of a smile never leaving her lips. She pushed back her blonde hair and turned to face me. *Game over*, I could almost hear her saying. *I win.*

I turned away and squeezed my eyes shut, trying to

block it out, but the scene was already on replay. I curled my hands into fists until my nails cut my palms.

Then I heard it—a whisper from somewhere deep within my mind. *Call your storm.*

Black waves crashed through my thoughts, and I stumbled blindly from the classroom before anything could happen. I ran to the Mustang, and the sky overhead was already thick with impenetrable clouds. As I pulled away from school, rain splattered my windscreen.

I didn't want to believe that Jake would do this to me. I had trusted him, even if he had thought differently. If only he'd waited just a tiny bit longer, then I could have worked out a way to tell him who I really was, or rather, what I was. What I could be …

I wiped a tear off my chin, trying not to remember him and Taylor together, how her blonde hair mixed with his dark. Again I saw their lips touch. I let out a cry of anger, and lightning touched down just metres from the bonnet.

My hands shook when I saw the patch of charred road in my rear-view mirror.

When I reached my turnoff, Angel Bay was a chamber of darkness. Tears flowed harder as I parked the car. Like a peaceful cat the ocean slept, and I stumbled towards it.

"You don't need that boy."

I shuddered when I heard him, even though it was what I'd come for. I took a deep breath. "I accept who I am!" My heart was pounding uncontrollably, and a light wind lifted my hair from my shoulders. "Didn't you hear me? I accept it!" I touched my toes to the water, and my blood sang as the storm inside me grew.

The current changed for me, pulling against the rhythm it had abided by since the beginning of time. I reached out my arms, drawing it to me, and breathed deeply. I was afraid, but I gathered the storm to my side. The water rose and I shuddered with pleasure.

"Wind," I whispered. It flew over the bay towards me, whipped the surface into turmoil and screeched through the trees behind the cottage.

"Waves!" I screamed, and they grew and grew until they were black towers above me.

Jake

Her eyes were wild. Wilder than the sea, which had formed waves so big it was a miracle she wasn't being swept away. I'd followed her out here, aware of the storm clouds chasing her car, and the lightning that punched down at her from the green-tinged sky. There was one hell of a storm coming, and she'd headed straight for it.

She looked ethereal standing there—tendrils of hair dancing in the wind—and it was a moment before I found my voice to call out to her again. So far, she'd barely acknowledged my presence.

"Sunny?"

I shivered as she turned to me, seemingly dazed. It was as if I were a transparent figure from her imagination, perhaps a memory just there to haunt her. Again she focused hungrily on a point way out at sea. What was she doing?

I waded in after her.

"Sunny!" I reached for her hand and she swung around to face me.

"Get out of here," she growled, and I took a step backwards.

"I saw you and Taylor!"

"It's not what you think, I promise."

But she threw back her head and laughed. Everything

about her had changed.

"Promises are for fools!"

"Taylor caught me off guard! Didn't you see me push her away?" I took a deep breath. "Even though you and I barely have a relationship any more, I can't love anyone else but you!" Taking a tentative step forward, I rested my hand on her shoulder.

"Traitor!" she screamed, and her eyes made my blood turn cold. They were black and empty, like she had no irises at all. How could I even begin to make her see reason?

The waves seemed to grow and swell closer to us, the wind urging them forward.

"We need to get out of here. It's wild!" I told her, but she stepped deeper into the turmoil, the sea sucking at her legs and soaking the hem of her jacket.

"Don't!" I warned. However, she wasn't listening.

I tried again. "Sunny, let's go back to the car."

She thrust her hands out in front of her—as if to keep me away—and I fought against a gust of wind that threatened to push me into the water. She didn't give me a second look, just turned back and stared out at the horizon, searching. Wind was tearing through the bay, shaking the little house behind us and causing its old deck to creak dangerously. My jeans were heavy with water, and I was already shivering from cold.

"I accept my destiny!" she screamed.

Huh?

The desperation in her voice intensified. "Pytheus!"

Realisation hit me harder than the wind I was battling against. She was calling the sea god. But why? Surely she didn't believe the stories …

The waves grew darker, taller, and the wind whipped the ocean to foam until it was a seething whirlpool.

"Sunny, please!"

She looked at me, properly now, as though she had only just realised I was there.

"Everything they're saying about me is true, Jake."

I opened my mouth to argue, but my breath caught in my throat when Britta's words came back to haunt me. *Someone saw a girl walk straight out of the ocean! She took off, running …* And then something Sunny had said just days ago. *Do you know how I feel when I swim and the moon touches my skin through the salt?* That line had been keeping me awake at night.

"Everything," she repeated softly.

I didn't want to believe it, but certain things were beginning to make terrible sense.

She froze for a second, like she was listening to something, and I stepped forward. "Sunny, don't," I cautioned again, but at the sound of my voice she waded out further. The water swirled around her waist, and even though it was freezing I don't think she could feel the cold. Could she really be the fabled creature from the legend?

"This isn't who you are!" I shouted above the noise of the wind, which was howling like an injured animal.

"This is what you all wanted," she insisted.

"No!"

"I'm bad, Jake. I want this. I welcome it, even."

"Sunny, you're a good person," I argued.

She abruptly spun around as though she could hear something I couldn't. The tide was coming in fast now. Towering waves broke gently around her, which was impossible.

"You have a choice!" I yelled, like I knew what I was talking about.

Her eyes flickered with light and for a moment I recognised the girl I loved. She took a step towards me, and I could tell she was fighting some inner battle because she paused again, torn.

"You pretended to love me." Tears were rolling down her face, mixed with sweat and salt and betrayal. My heart broke right then and there. This was my fault.

She clutched her head in frustration—was there really some voice I couldn't hear?—and let out a cry of anguish. Lightning flashed across the sky as the storm moved closer.

"Goodbye, Jake." She pressed her palms heavenwards and a cold mist descended slowly upon us before she collapsed into the gurgling ocean. Her eyes rolled back and the waves rose up, pulling her under.

"No!" My voice cracked and was torn away by the wind. I couldn't see her but dived in anyway.

The cold almost completely immobilised me, and the

tide was so strong I struggled to stay above the waves. My jeans weighed me down and it was almost tempting to let them. There was no way I was going to find her, and it was because of me she had resorted to this. If only I had tried harder to understand her misery. That's the thing about life. There are a lot of if onlys.

"Sunny!" I screamed for her, dived down again and again, but it was so dark I couldn't see my own hand when it was right in front of my face. The ocean became rougher and wilder and I let it take me whichever way it pleased.

An hour later I washed up on the beach, where I lay shivering and riddled with guilt. I had abandoned her in every sense.

All night I watched the ocean, praying I would spot her. When the sun crept over the islands, I stumbled into the cottage—numb and frozen—knowing I had finally and truly lost her.

Sunny

I woke to absolute blackness, completely unaware of how much time may or may not have passed. I couldn't even recall the excruciating pain when I switched from air to water.

I sucked the ocean deeper into my lungs and then pushed it out slowly, trying to remember. Why was I here? I floated, weightless, the water rocking me like a cradle. How long had I been here? No answers came to me, my confusion growing with every second.

I swam slowly to where I thought the surface should be, every part of me hurting. It felt like I'd spent the night being pummelled in the surf. I carved my way upwards, and when I saw the gleaming skin I swam faster, feeling more fluid than the sea herself. I didn't want to be here any more, but back in my bed, warm beneath the covers.

When I burst through the surface, water running off my skin, I drew in a deep breath. It was hot and fiery as if I'd stepped into a furnace, and I cried out in pain. It stung at my cheeks and scratched its way down my throat. It had never been so bad. I swallowed hard and ducked back beneath the surface for a moment, thinking, thinking.

I resurfaced, paused and tried again. The water was smooth like black glass and a slow breeze slid over it, cooling my face. I opened my mouth to let air trickle into my airways but it didn't seem to be reaching my lungs. I gasped now, desperate for the sea to come pouring out like all the other times, yet it didn't. My chest was full to the point of exploding; I needed air! I clutched at my neck, unsuccessfully trying to gulp oxygen. While my lungs caught fire, stars burst around me and I fell gasping beneath the water.

I pressed my fingers to my forehead and listened to the sea while it pulsed like something alive. This was horribly familiar but I couldn't work out why. What was I doing here?

"You came home." His voice spread through the water.

I felt my heart jolt, and uncertainty was replaced with fear.

"Oh, no!"

"Oh, yes."

I had driven out to Angel Bay in a state of madness and called him. I remembered standing on the beach, and the waves growing at my command.

"Another storm. Well done."

I shuddered in horror as I realised that meant I'd made my decision. The water seemed to blacken around me and something cool brushed against my side. In a flurry of bubbles I lashed out, panicked. All I could think about was that I had chosen this and then I remembered why.

Jake.

Once again I saw him with Taylor in the hallway. It felt like someone had wrenched out my heart and slashed it brutally in half. Yet he had been on the beach with me, I'm sure he had.

I drew in a salty breath, the pain fresh like an open wound. Hadn't he told me just weeks before that he loved me?

I stared up at the stars, understanding that the air would now kill me. I couldn't feel or taste the tears but I knew I was crying.

"You should be thanking me."

"For what?" I demanded.

"You chose this, and I have given you the most precious gift of all!"

"Huh?"

"You mean you haven't even noticed?"

He went silent and I floated hopelessly beneath the surface, unsure what to do. Could I really never see anyone again? I pictured Brie's laughing face and thought of Jake's husky voice as he sang along to the radio. My chest tightened and my heart pounded uncomfortably. The ocean closed around me, and I fought away the terror that threatened to overwhelm me.

The moon came out from behind the clouds, bathing me in silver light. I took a deep breath and relaxed a little in its glow but then I opened my eyes and looked down. I'll never forget that moment or the feeling of horror accompanying it.

I gasped, slapped my face with icy hands to make sure I wasn't dreaming and screamed until my throat was raw. It was muffled in the water, bouncing right back at me, and my tears spilled into the sea.

"No!" Panic was tearing me apart. I felt my fingers tingle and my breathing become shallow. "Please just drown me," I sobbed.

"You can never drown, Sunlight."

I stole another glance down my body and quickly squeezed my eyes shut. Evelyn had warned me, or at least tried to. It was beautiful. Terrifying. Right, yet wrong.

The blood within me battled. Ocean. Earth. Earth. Ocean.

It was sleek and powerful-looking, the colour of tarnished silverware. My whole body shimmered with salt and moonlight. I couldn't bring myself to look again. I didn't want to believe I had become the creature from my nightmares, from Lexie's hundreds of obsessive paintings.

"My little mermaid," he chuckled.

Chapter Thirty-Five

I didn't leave the bay. I couldn't. In my mind it was the only thing that kept me connected to the world I had once lived in.

I'd swim to shore and, without breaking the surface, gaze at the cottage as it bent into impossible, watery shapes. Misery would wash through me. I was so close I could almost touch it, but never again would I feel the breeze as it flew through the trees or hear birds nesting in the old rafters. I'd taken all that for granted and now I'd lost everything.

What did my family think? That I had run away, or worse? Was my face on flyers lining the school corridors? Were people half expecting my body to turn up, just as Sophie's had? I tried not to think about it.

Sometimes I saw Jake, blurred from beneath the water. He'd sit on the sand for hours and I'd stay out of sight, watching him and wondering what was running through his mind.

At first I'd been tempted to call out, but I soon realised

there was nothing anyone could do. Did he understand what had happened that night on the beach? Again I tried to recall those final moments before drowning, but the blank spots in my memory remained. Was he aware now that this was the terrible secret I had been so carefully hiding?

The rocks eliminated any chance of him seeing me, and I never got tired of looking at him. He was sad — I could see that in the way he sat and in his eyes as they scanned the waters for my existence. Perhaps he was sorry, but it didn't matter because it was too late.

Jake's visits became less frequent until eventually he stopped coming. I had no way of knowing how many days I spent there waiting for him to appear. From the sloping seabed I cast my eyes one last time towards the beach — hoping, wishing, praying — but the sand was empty. He'd given up on me. I needed to move on just as he had.

I swam through Angel Bay, the last of the phosphorescence pale green against my skin. It was getting colder now which meant the little creatures would be gone within the week. I promised myself this was the very last time I'd look for him. I knew I needed to make some kind of decision, because this was forever. Lexie and Janie were right — they had been all along. I did belong to the sea, I always had, and Pytheus had proved that.

He talked to me constantly, trying to persuade me to embrace my dark side, but I was able to resist the temptations he threw at me. It frustrated him that he still didn't have complete control over me and that I refused to wreak havoc alongside him. He continued to batter the bay with strong winds and caused the rain to fall day after day. The locals had been so wrong to believe my return would fix everything. I was here, and yet as far as they were concerned, nothing had changed.

According to Lexie, Pytheus had once been good to her ancestors, but I knew those days were over forever. Juniper had angered him for all of eternity.

I took one last look at the house, the beach and the trees, swam to the bottom of the sea and left Angel Bay.

At the bottom of the ocean it is very dark.

I couldn't see but was able to sense the shape of things, which made me sometimes imagine I could. I understood what it meant to be blind, memorising every contour of rock that jutted from the seabed and discovering where the ledges dropped off to deeper water.

Time passed with no way of telling how long I had been here. I didn't fear the vast expanses of black or the seaweed that brushed against me, but I was constantly on edge. Creatures much bigger than me shared these waters and I wasn't exactly sure where I stood on the aquatic food chain. Occasionally I entered shark territory and would press myself against the rocks, hoping they wouldn't smell me.

I could have gone into shore where the meanest thing was a starfish, but I liked the darkness. I wanted to avoid the earthy currents that swept off the beaches and made me think of home. I wouldn't torture myself—and I especially didn't want to see the creature I'd become.

It was hard to distinguish night from day, but when I sensed the moon growing full again I swam into Procellae Bay. So I'd been gone a month, but it felt like six. I breathed in the salty moonlight and thought of Jake. If it weren't for the ones I'd left behind, I think I would have embraced my new life. But it was impossible to forget them.

I broke through the moonlit surface, just enough so I could peer across the waves towards land. There were the locals, lighting their candles. I dived back down into the deep. The pretty tea lights floated above me, and Evelyn's pain was my own.

I missed everything so much it hurt. Back when I'd been free to come and go as I pleased, I'd struggled to remember the ones I loved. How was it the opposite now? The only time I felt any sort of calm was right before I fell asleep, when my mind let go enough for me to enjoy my ocean world. In fact, a peace would fill me so deeply that I remembered why I had chosen it, but it really didn't last long. Anxiety flickered through me when I thought about the decision I'd made and in turn what I had lost.

It was on a particularly regretful night, swimming through Procellae Bay, that I found the cave.

I was diving down a wall of rock when I came to it. The gap was so narrow I had to squeeze in sideways, and I grazed my elbow painfully on the way in. It was even darker inside, but the gap gradually gave way to a large space. I wondered if it had been carved by the ocean over a long period of time and whether it would exist at all in another thousand years.

I felt safer knowing there was some kind of room I could come back to. I was well aware of the fishing boat that let out its great nets, and the powerful currents Pytheus conjured in the bay.

During the day, weak light would infiltrate my cave. I'd peer out at the moody surface or float on my back to stare at the rock ceiling, longing for the earth beneath my feet and the smell of sunshine.

How long had Evelyn survived this? She'd been here a while—I knew that much from the dreams. Going by her last diary entry, she'd thought that by jumping to the sea she was accepting death but it had been much worse. She'd become a prisoner here, more miserable than before. At some point the darkness and cold had become too much—her earth blood too strong for her to survive here. Unlike mine.

I was capable of new things, extraordinary things, yet I didn't want them. I wished more than anything that I was at Angel Cottage with Jake, where the bay seemed to capture too much light.

While I didn't understand why he'd gone back to

Taylor, I couldn't blame him for giving up on us. He'd trusted me with his secret but I hadn't once given him a glimpse into this world of mine. The only way he could have ever understood my chaos was if I'd told him, and I had chosen not to. Was it possible he would have believed I'd been possessed by an ancient sea god? I'd never know, and realised it was a miracle that Jake had tried to make it work for as long as he had. All I'd done was make it impossible.

He wasn't the only one I'd pushed away either, and so the guilt continued to niggle. My regrets closed in on me, and I felt defeated.

I was aware of the dark and gloomy days above sliding into weeks. Would the townsfolk ever see the sun again? Would there come a day when they would tear down their depressing houses and replace them with cheerful seaside homes? I didn't really care. They'd done nothing but make my life hell.

"We could tear the houses down for them," Pytheus whispered gleefully and I shuddered.

Suddenly my head filled with visions of wind ripping up the roads, and waves that flooded the houses.

"That is an irresistible idea."

I ignored him and fixed my gaze on a jellyfish floating in on the high tide.

"You have a brilliant mind—you just don't know it."

I refused to engage; he was still as bitter as ever, despite my return. The jellyfish projected itself slowly up towards the cavernous ceiling. Its pink tentacles trailing behind it were the prettiest thing in the whole room.

"Come on, my beautiful daughter. It'll be so much fun. Picture what I could create with you by my side." His hunger for destruction was insatiable and it scared me to imagine the outcome of a storm cast by the two of us. I knew the power he craved — on land I'd become addicted to it.

He wanted wild oceans that swallowed the land, claiming it as part of his kingdom. Every day he tried to tempt me with offer after offer of storms, but still I managed to resist him. He got bored and angry at my lack of willingness to create and destroy. I felt his restlessness all around me — in the waves rolling onto the beaches and in the currents tearing harder at my cave.

"Forget it." Not even bubbles escaped my lungs. The air had left me a long time ago, but he could still hear me.

"You don't need words down here," he taunted. *"I can hear your every thought."*

I couldn't fathom never being able to speak again. But there were a lot of things I wouldn't experience now, like hearing Jake sing along to the radio as he worked on his bike. The thought was crushing.

"I'm getting bored with this, Sunlight. You chose to be here and I have graciously made you a true ocean child."

I took a watery breath, grateful I couldn't see myself when I looked down. He disappeared from my head and I was left alone with my longings and regrets, aware of the rain he pulled from the skies. I don't know if it was the earthy currents that made me dream that night or the full moon, but I found myself walking through the most beautiful garden.

☼

The moss is damp and springy beneath my feet, and around me everything is in bloom. I step over a clump of wild violets and breathe in the sugar-scented air. What is this place?

I follow a path, staring up at the branches of budding trees and at the endlessly trailing orchids. Suddenly I'm mindful of someone walking beside me. The girl can't be older than five or six and she has the most amazing dark eyes I've ever seen. She smiles up at me and we walk on in silence. I don't know where I'm supposed to be going but the little one beside me does.

When we come to a hedge I pause, and she takes my hand, leading me on. The branches snag at our hair, and I reach down to untangle the hem of her dress when it gets caught. Someone else takes hold of my free hand and pulls me through to the other side.

We've entered a rose garden with trellis archways and I stare at the young woman before me. She is slender and tall with milk-white skin and I wonder if she and the little girl are sisters. Their eyes are so similar. We set off across the petal-strewn lawn towards a leafy oak that is growing big and strong in the middle of the garden.

A dark-haired girl is sitting peacefully beneath it, gathering acorns into piles. When she sees us she stands, her face breaking into a smile. Her hand slips into mine and I feel the smooth, worn wood of an acorn she is holding.

We carry on past rows of purple lupins and others continue to join us. They are happy to see me. Some of the girls are really young, and the older ones occasionally stoop down to pick them up, balancing them on their hips as we meander through the fields. At some point I realise who these dark-eyed girls are. They are my fore sisters — the ones whose ocean blood has drowned them.

I search for Evelyn's face amongst them but she is nowhere to be found. Desperation fills me. A girl whose eyes are black like coffee watches me.

"Lift the curse and set her free," she says softly, and around her the others nod.

"Where is she?" I ask.

A pretty girl steps forward, and in her long white dress she reminds me of an angel. "Her soul is caught somewhere between your world and ours. You can lift the curse."

The little girl who has been holding my hand the whole time smiles at me encouragingly.

"How?" I ask them, but the field we are in is starting to fade. I am waking up, the colours of my dream running into each other in one great blur.

"Tell me how!" I cry urgently, but it's too late.

Chapter Thirty-Six

It was Pytheus who had woken me, pulling me from the garden and back into the nightmare that was my life.

"It's time. I'm going to show you what you're missing."

I felt disorientated from the dream, the soft pastures and flowers still vivid in my mind. Was Evelyn's soul really lost somewhere? I brushed my fingers over the pearls at my throat.

I was suddenly distracted, unsettled by how quiet the ocean had become. I'd heard people talk about that—how a great storm was sometimes preceded by a certain calm. My skin crawled with goose bumps as I remembered back to my birthday. It had been the same then. I imagined Pytheus out there, wherever he was, stilling the ocean while he gathered his anger. How devastating would it be this time?

It took up until then for me to realise I was nervously rolling an acorn back and forth across my palm. Impossible, yet here was a little piece of earth in my hand, far beneath the ocean. It gave me a burst of strength. I wouldn't let him endanger my family. I balled my hands into fists. "They're not just something you can play with!"

The water around me seethed and spun. Suddenly I hated him.

"That's it, use your emotion!"

Below me the ocean floor lifted into turbulent clouds of seaweed, and I took a steadying breath. My anger was exactly what he wanted. His ruthless energy filled the water so quickly I felt nauseous. I backed deeper into the recess of my cave. Lightning set the sky ablaze, illuminating my rocky interior before plunging me back into darkness. My family didn't deserve this.

"Work beside me and I'll spare them," he offered, but I didn't trust him.

When that didn't work he tried to make me angry, putting images in my head of the ones who had hunted and despised me. I wouldn't have been able to let it go so easily in the past but he struggled to control my mind here, and while it infuriated him, it suddenly gave me a flicker of hope. As he called the wind to his aid and tore the ocean into soaring waves, I watched from the entrance of the little room I now called home. The sky twisted into terrifying formations of black cloud, and the rain fell harder. If I was going to undo this I'd need to concentrate. When the rain began falling, softly at first, I closed my eyes and turned inward.

If it was possible to create a storm then it must also be possible to create the opposite.

Tuning out the external in every sense, I focused instead on the salt swirling through my veins, and the water I pulled into my lungs. Feelings of regret and heartache tried to re-emerge but I let go of what didn't serve me. There was no point dwelling on the mistakes I'd made.

While the ocean churned wildly beyond the cave, I thought of warm evenings and cobalt skies. My arms floated loosely at my sides, palms facing upwards. I just wanted a night of stillness. He'd been hinting at this storm for weeks, and the water had held a certain heaviness that set me on edge. I took a deep breath and raised my hands over my head, reaching for the waves far above and urging them to settle. At first I was sure it hadn't worked, but then I felt a weight at my fingertips and I drew the waves back in towards the surface as if they were attached to my fingers by cords. It didn't compare to what I'd created in the past, when I'd thrown my energy into a disorderly array of wind and lightning, but the peace that started to fill me was gratifying.

I could visualise the locals waiting for the moon to rise, probably watching in confusion as tranquillity started to replace turmoil. The peace didn't last long. Pytheus' voice was like the crashing of boulders in a landslide, thunderous and angrier than ever.

"Don't test me!"

He hauled the waves out of my grip, carving them into towering monsters so dark and powerful I trembled with fear. Panic danced in the water around me and I struggled to find my calm. There was no way I could stop him when he was like this, and now it wasn't just boredom that motivated him—he wanted to prove to me exactly what he was capable of.

He wrenched the tides from their outgoing pull and they surged in with such ferocity I was shoved to the back of the cave, my ribs connecting painfully with an outcrop of rock. Adrenaline soon numbed the pain but nothing could ease my fear. The houses that rested so peacefully were about to be obliterated and I felt helpless. I wouldn't be able to forgive myself if anything happened to my family, especially now that Pytheus' fury was because of me. The weather was worsening by the second.

"As if you could defeat me, Sunlight," he mocked, and hearing the name Janie had chosen for me made me think of the conversation I'd had with her months earlier.

I'd been perched on the chair beside her, my face tight with worry. *Sometimes I want bad things, really bad things,* I'd whispered, my mind on a storm I'd called just the night before.

It is only light that can banish darkness, remember that, she'd said in an attempt to hush my demons.

It was a well-known saying, but at the time I hadn't given it much consideration because I'd believed I was dark beyond help. Pytheus had gotten inside my head, warping my thoughts as he pleased.

In the world above me I heard the wind howl, no doubt battering the town with icy sheets of rain. The locals would be huddling together, determined to stay.

I thought of my fore sisters who had smiled encouragingly from within the dream. We hadn't deserved the darkness that had filtered down from one generation to the next. How many had understood it was our own blood betraying us? That it was our very blood that drowned us? Did they all feel the salt so thick in their veins that on the full moon it was all they could do not to go insane with longing? With the dreaming? I wondered if they too had woken with the sense of never having slept.

The acorn was still clenched tightly in my fist and I tried to relax, rolling it through my fingers and pressing it to my cheek. My ancestors were trying to help me, and the message was clear enough: I had earth blood too. Perhaps they knew that was what could make me strong, despite the fact I'd chosen ocean.

So I thought of flowers, and how it felt to crush leaves beneath my feet once they'd turned red and gold and fallen from the trees. I could almost smell the pungent-sweet scent of the forest floor after a rainstorm and hear the birds calling within the canopy of green. It helped me remember who I was, as if in making room for such memories I'd had to briefly push aside all thoughts of ocean.

Keeping these memories in my mind, I focused all my energy on reversing the racing tide, knowing it wouldn't be long before waves crashed over the shore towards the houses. I closed my eyes, reaching for the surging tide with curled fingers, and slowly but surely the sea became tight. It was like a line going taut after it had been previously slack, and somehow I'd become attached to it.

The tide now sat in the centre of the bay, uncertainty holding it there. Pytheus was furious, but I didn't let his anger touch me. Lightning shredded the sky into an inferno of ribbons and the thunder was deafening, but it seemed I was in control of the water.

Long strands of hair drifted in front of me, and I imagined them picking up the currents, bringing back to me the information I needed. My heart beat so slowly I could count just one or two beats a minute, but the energy I felt flickered through me like a live current and I tugged the tide from his grasp.

"Girl, you are foolish!" he snarled, but I'd found my calm and the ocean was listening.

I pictured the locals standing soundlessly, wondering at the weather as it behaved so unnaturally and marvelling at the green light creeping into the sky.

I thought about everything that had made me feel safe—Jake's smile, my soft denim jacket, Mum's coloured towels rolled neatly beside the bath—and after that it was easy. The clouds disappeared beyond the horizon, and the debris that had been flung from the seabed drifted back to rest on the shells. I could hear it all landing, muffled thuds that made me think of footsteps on ash. The waves levelled out until the ocean was a sheet of pressed steel, and I shook out my hands as if I could rid myself of the energy now coursing through me.

The cave had started to lighten and I swam out into moonlight. It was so still I almost felt myself relaxing, but I was anticipating the return of Pytheus and his incessant string of whispers that would inevitably fill my head. The longer he stayed quiet, the more I realised how much room he'd been taking up. I'd gotten so used to hearing him, his thoughts flowing constantly beneath my own, that my mind now felt pleasantly empty.

No, it was more than that. I felt free.

My heart beat faster as I considered the possible reasons why I couldn't hear him. I swam further out into open water. Where was he? Usually I could sense him all around me.

"You were wrong," I said softly, knowing he could hear me. "I don't belong to you and neither does Evelyn."

I hoped it was true and swam to the surface. It had been weeks since I'd been up there and my chest was pounding. I'd try one more time.

When I emerged, the breeze stroked my face and I held my breath. If this didn't work, the disappointment would be unbearable. I looked at the land that punctured the sea, and then inhaled deeply.

Water flooded from my chest and it seemed as though the whole sea came pouring out of me. Could it really be happening? I took another tentative breath and the air trickled sweet and soft into my lungs. It didn't burn or choke me—it just came and went like it had a million other times. I cried giant sobs of relief that took over my body.

The moon was radiant and I could just make out the locals standing awestruck on the beach. I sent their candles back to shore so they would understand.

I made my way swiftly towards Angel Bay, holding my breath and keeping the wonderful air in my lungs. Even though I would always be a creature of the sea, maybe someday I could go to the jetty and explain to Mum that I'd never meant to leave them.

When the sand scraped my belly I let the air leave my lungs in a stream of bubbles. I surfaced and looked in at the bay that had become so familiar to me. I'd give anything to feel the dry sand against my skin and sleep once more on the beach where I'd fallen in love.

I used my hands to drag myself slowly out of the water. The shells grazed my skin but I pulled myself up to the white sand and pressed my cheek to the ground. Night sounds that I had quickly forgotten came to me from the sleeping forest behind the cottage. I had broken free from Pytheus, even if I couldn't resume my human form.

I turned away from the sea, which was perfectly flat, and faced the land. My Mustang was still there, barely visible amongst the trees. I'd left it in the driveway and knew it must have been Jake who had moved it. Where did everyone think I was?

☼

I woke curled up on the sand. It coated my body like sugar on a doughnut and I smiled. In the ocean it would have floated right off. As the sun warmed my skin, which was so pale from being in the dark, I worked my fingers through my tangled hair until it was loose.

Maybe this would be okay. I could still have some of my old world. A tear traced a delicate path down my cheek. I'd never feel Jake put his arm around me though, or feel the way his lips met mine and sent my heart into a frenzy. He was with Taylor now anyway, I reminded myself. Jake would never love me like this. I'd turned into something from ancient mythology, a creature almost no one believed in.

I forced myself to look at what I'd become. My skin merged into a dazzling white fantasy that glittered in the sun. I brushed my hand over the gritty substance it consisted of. It was like sugar, like … salt.

I sat up to look closer, running my finger gently over the part where my stomach melted into what now looked like salt crystals. It began crumbling under my touch, and I looked down horrified when a chunk came loose under my hand. I gasped, holding in my palm a lump of the fine white material.

A crack had formed in it where it met my flesh, like a plaster cast that had been on too long.

I groaned. Even though I didn't want this new part of me, I knew I'd be destroyed without it. The crack deepened, spreading all the way down to where I gracefully forked.

"No!" I cried, easing myself down to the tide that was slowly creeping in. The sea swirled over me, and I hoped it would heal me like it had all the other times.

Instead I watched as I started dissolving in the cool water. Clouds of salty particles washed away from me, and I swept my hands desperately through the ocean, trying to catch them. The sun and the land must have destroyed me. I would die!

Panic and fear and all the other feelings I'd become so used to were threatening to engulf me when I saw something else that made me painfully happy. Through the salty foam emerged something I never thought I'd see again.

Chapter Thirty-Seven

I stumbled from the water, unstable on my legs which were still swaying in time to the sea, and collapsed on the soft grass in front of the cottage. I laughed and cried. I shouted out to the bay like a mad person and spun in circles with outstretched arms. I was dizzy from the light.

Before going home I needed to come up with a conceivable story. I wasn't even sure how long I'd been gone, and I hated to imagine the rumours going around.

Popping the boot of my car, I pulled out an armful of clothes and dressed in the cottage. I was definitely paler from my stint under the surface but I could come up with some plausible excuse for that. Blue veins stood out like rivers beneath my skin, and my hair was so long now it fell past my waist.

Outside in the sun I cut it as straight as I could with a rusty pair of scissors. I roamed restlessly through the house after that, unsure of what to do next, and then suddenly, urgently, I knew I had to see Janie.

When I reached the rest home, I parked my car out of

sight and snuck in through a window to avoid staff.

Janie was sitting where I'd left her, and I saw straight away that she had almost drifted into the life beyond this one. My heart started to hurt all over again as I remembered the last few letters she'd sent.

"Grandma," I whispered, squeezing her hand fretfully. There were important things I had to tell her.

Movement flickered beneath her eyelids.

"It's me, Sunny." I felt her fingers move slightly under my hand as if she understood. "I'm sorry I didn't come sooner."

I started to cry and my tears rained down on her. I felt so bad for leaving her here alone.

Her lips moved as she tried to comfort me.

"It's okay," she whispered. "You came to me when I dreamed." She took a shallow breath and I could tell she hadn't spoken in weeks. "I knew you were okay."

I wiped my face and tried to pull myself together. "I lifted the curse!"

Her lips curved into a smile. "That's my girl."

It was almost impossible to leave, because I felt certain it was the last time I'd see her. I kissed her goodbye and cried the whole way back to Angel Bay. There I wandered through the garden, still unable to put together a believable story, and eventually fell asleep on the back lawn.

"Sunny?"

Even in my dreams Jake's voice was charming. He was running towards me, sweeping me off my feet and taking me into his arms. I was smiling, laughing, breathing in his cinnamon scent, and then suddenly I was being shaken awake.

He was crouching over me, the sun bright behind him, and I wanted to jump up to hug him but I was caught in the confusing space between dreams and sleep. How had I not heard his bike? My vision wobbled slightly, though whether from shock or my time in the ocean I wasn't sure.

His eyes expressed disbelief, and he reached out a hand as if to make sure I was real. The touch of his fingers on my arm made me shiver. I hadn't had physical contact with anyone for so long. A bird resumed its song from the hedge nearby and I could hear the roar of the high tide as it pushed its way under the cliffs at the end of the beach.

"Jake?" My voice came out trembling, and then he had his arms around me, pulling me roughly to my feet.

"Are you okay?" he questioned hastily, brushing hair away from my face and searching my eyes for some kind of answer. His hands were shaking and I took a step away from him.

"What's wrong?" he asked, looking so worried. Did I really have to spell it out for him?

"I'm her! Don't you get it?"

"None of it matters," he breathed.

"Yes, it does! I'm the one everyone wanted gone."

"Not everyone, and I don't care if you're the girl from a legend I've spent my whole life not believing. I don't care if I never see the sun again. The only thing I care about is that I be with you, always."

"What about Taylor? I saw you with her."

He shook his head. "*She* kissed *me*, Sunny. I don't want anything to do with her."

There was silence after that. We both had a lot to think about. Eventually he gestured out to the ocean and back to me, his eyes full of questions.

"What ..." he started but then shook his head. "I almost couldn't live without you," and I saw he meant it. He wiped the tears off my cheeks and led me around to the front of the cottage.

We sat on the grass and talked for hours, me trying to put my experience into words that could never do it justice, and him trying his hardest to understand. It was a relief to finally tell someone the whole truth. The sky above us was the clearest cerulean blue, and as it began to fade I soaked up the last of the sun.

"Where does everybody think I am?" I asked. It pained me to think of the state Mum would be in.

Jake looked at me carefully as though he didn't know what to say, and I knew there must have been some pretty gruesome rumours. I was grateful he chose not to repeat them.

"Well, Lexie's freaky mates are saying you finally

accepted your destiny, but most people think you've gone looking for your father."

I stared at him doubtfully. "What? Why?" I didn't even know what country my father lived in, and I'd certainly never felt the urge to go and find him.

"I wrote a goodbye letter from you."

"You did?" I unconsciously plucked grass from the lawn.

"I hope you don't mind. All I could think was—what if you did somehow make it back? What would you tell them? Not the truth, obviously. So I spun a story about how you needed to find your roots. It was something you could fall back on if you ever made it home."

"Are you serious? And they believed it?"

He nodded. "And every night I wished it really was as simple as that."

While it wasn't far from the truth, it was certainly far from simple. In a way I had gone to find my roots, and Pytheus was a father of sorts, however nothing was simple about the fact he was an ocean god.

"We should go back and put them out of their misery," he said, but I shook my head, exhausted. Around us the air was still, and the sky had that strange pinkish hue that always comes on right before dusk.

"Let's stay here, just for tonight—it's already getting late."

☼

I half expected it to be raining when I woke the next morning, but the sun was creeping through the cottage's old shutters, warm and bright. I rolled over, smiling at the sight of Jake. He had one arm underneath me, the other resting in the groove of my waist. His face was peaceful while he slept and his hair hung down past his eyes.

I tried to unravel myself from him but he pulled me in tight.

"Stay," he murmured. I rested my head against his chest and listened to his heart beating. It was as rhythmic as the tides I had grown so used to.

The ocean was right up at the banks when we got up, washing against the grass. While Jake parked his bike out of sight behind the house, where we would come back for it next week, I stood on the lawn in my bare feet, absorbing the sunshine and wondering how I could still think the ocean was so beautiful. It was aqua blue today, the sun splitting its surface into blinding mirrors.

I listened closely, sure I would hear the voice I'd become so accustomed to, but heard nothing. Not even the faintest whisper of my name.

Where had Pytheus gone?

Jake walked noiselessly over to me and slipped his arm around my waist. I wasn't ready for my morning with him to end. Moments like these were precious—I knew that now. I thought about what I'd soon be facing and bit my lip nervously.

Jake squeezed my hand reassuringly. "Let's go."

☼

We pulled out onto the road and I wound down the windows to breathe in the warm, muggy air. The damp earth was finally starting to dry out.

There was just one other thing I needed to do before going home. The idea had come to me in my sleep and I hadn't been able to shake it.

"I know which cemetery she'll be in," Jake had said after I'd explained what I wanted to do. "There's one that no one ever goes to any more — the graves are apparently really old. We'll find your Evelyn."

So instead of going the usual route, we turned onto a road running parallel with the highway, then twisted off into a maze of barren orchards and gravel roads.

I tried to tune into a radio station, wondering if Britta would be on the news. She, along with her friends, had apparently spent the last two months in a juvenile detention centre while they waited out the agonising lead-up to one of their many court hearings. Last night I'd insisted that Jake fill me in on everything I had missed.

"What about your father?" I'd asked anxiously.

"He came clean. He's testifying against McLeod."

Jake pulled into a car park overgrown with weeds and led me through the grass towards a grove of trees. Mossy headstones poked out from fallen branches and long grass.

He was as patient as ever as I scraped the moss away from each stone, reading the inscriptions. I recognised some of the surnames and finally found her at the base of a sleepy pine. Years of neglect had made her name almost illegible, and I started to cry. Jake rested his hands gently on my heaving shoulders.

I scratched away a shallow patch of dirt from her site and pulled the pearls from around my neck. With a tiny thud I dropped them into the earth, and they shone brightly from their new home before I covered them over. They belonged to her, not me.

"The man she loved gave her those," I said softly.

Jake didn't say anything. He just stood there with me before eventually pulling me to my feet and leading me back to the car. "You okay?"

I wiped my face on my sleeve and nodded. I knew I wouldn't dream of her again.

☼

Emily was the first to greet me. I paused before pushing the door open and took a deep breath. I'd been gone for two months.

I just had to get through this afternoon, and even though I'd been through much worse, my heart beat unsteadily.

I let the door bang loudly shut and made my way to the lounge. She was deeply engrossed in a magazine and didn't look up. I was relieved it was just her here for the moment; Mum wouldn't have finished work yet and Brie would still be at school.

"Hi," she said and flicked to the next page.

"Hey."

She jerked her head up to stare at me. At first she couldn't speak but then she leapt up and threw herself at me. "Oh, my God, you are in so much trouble!" she said after she'd finished hugging me. I was then bombarded with an unanswerable string of questions.

I remained fairly vague.

"Well, I made the most of your clothes and makeup," she confessed. "And I broke your hair straightener. I'll get you a new one."

Right now that was the last thing I cared about. Mum would be home in an hour. In a desperate attempt to keep my mind occupied, I gutted out my room and cleaned everything until there were actual clear surfaces. By the end of it I was sticky with perspiration and still just as nervous.

When I heard the car pull into the driveway I slunk downstairs. Brie burst into tears the moment she saw me. Mum just stood speechless in the doorway and turned almost as pale as me. More grey hair mingled with the blonde, and deep lines creased her pretty face. I'd put them through hell.

I hugged her tightly and the questions tumbled from her mouth. Where had I been? Why hadn't I told anyone I was leaving? Didn't I know it was the most selfish thing anyone had ever done?

Brie didn't leave my side, and that night she questioned me to the point where I admitted I hadn't actually gone looking for my father.

"I just had to get out of here." I knew I'd hurt her by disappearing. She didn't understand why I hadn't said goodbye, but it was in her nature to forgive.

It was late when she finally went to bed. I opened my window and let the ocean sounds put me to sleep. I didn't dream, and I woke at dawn when the tide was high.

While I'd been sleeping, the bay had filled with thick, wet fog. Unable to get back to sleep, I sat at the window and watched the sky lighten.

When I saw a person on the beach—wandering listlessly through clouds of mist—I didn't think much of it. In any other town it would probably be cause for concern, but not here. It was most likely just another troubled local. As he got closer though, I realised he was very old. I could tell by the hunch of his shoulders and his slow, heavy footsteps. A person could meet their death down there in the cold if they weren't careful.

Teeth chattering, I pulled on my robe and hurried to the beach. He was wading in the shallows ahead of me, barely visible. He must have been freezing.

"Are you okay?" I called, voice trembling, but he kept on walking. Sometimes I lost sight of him entirely, as if he were as insubstantial as the mist he stumbled through. He didn't hear me until I was right behind him.

"Sir, are you lost?"

405

When he spun around to face me I saw in an instant that he was a man who'd lost his mind. He was distressed and disorientated, madness gleaming in his black eyes.

"Have you seen her?" he asked urgently, and at the sound of his voice my blood ran cold. It wasn't possible …

Fog swept in from the sea, filling my nose and mouth until it seemed to suffocate me.

"Seen who?" I managed to whisper.

He clutched my shoulders, only I barely felt the contact. I could see his bony hands on me but they were weightless like a bag of feathers.

"Juniper!" he answered feverishly.

My heart raced as I stepped away from the ghost of Pytheus. Did he even realise who I was? When I didn't answer he carried on down the beach, wailing her name. The mist started swirling right through him, tugging him deep into the clear water.

For a minute I was too shocked to move. My hands shook uncontrollably.

I took a shaky breath, ran across the sand towards home and slipped into bed beside Brie.

☼

There was only a week of school left, and I went in the next day to empty out my locker. I tried to keep a low profile but to no avail. When Lexie and all her friends saw me their eyes grew wide with astonishment, and for once they didn't have anything to say.

"See!" Amber said to them smugly. "Still human—hasn't morphed into a mermaid!" She rolled her eyes at me. "They won't know what to make of things now you're back. Some are convinced the curse has been lifted. Don't know how they came to that conclusion."

"You weren't there at the full moon!" Lexie fired back. "You didn't see what we saw." She turned to face me. "So you really just went looking for your dad?"

I nodded.

"I can't believe we actually thought you were her!" she laughed, and it took everything within me to smile back at her.

"You could have texted me!" Amber kept on insisting as we stood at our busy lockers, and I was apologising for the fiftieth time when Jake came striding towards us. His blue eyes radiated through me. I saw Taylor making a beeline for him, and I stepped into her path. She stumbled, but it was my hand he reached for and my hair he ruffled playfully.

☼

The news of Janie's passing came that night. I'd heard the phone ring and then Mum's slow footsteps as she climbed the stairs to my room.

For a moment she stood at my doorway, her tired eyes looking in, and I wondered how often she'd done this in my absence. I moved a pile of clothes off my bed and patted the space beside me, thinking she wanted to talk.

We sat side by side and when she didn't say anything I tried to fill the silence with apologies. She placed her hand gently on my arm, interrupting me.

"It's your grandmother, Sunny. I'm so sorry. The woman from the rest home said you'd be upset …"

The room became blurred through my tears and she hugged me tight, no doubt surprised to discover I knew Janie.

"The funeral's in a couple of days. I'll come with you."

The service was small and simple.

We laid bright-orange carnations on the freshly dug earth, and Mum held my shaking shoulders. Afterwards we drove to the rest home. Someone had packed all Janie's belongings into two boxes, which I placed carefully on the back seat of my car. As we went to leave, the receptionist handed me an envelope with my name on it. One last letter.

I opened it much later that night and it wasn't a letter at all. I leafed through official-looking documents and realised with incredulity that she'd left Angel Bay to me.

A shiver of delight ran through me.

"Thank you," I whispered, and a gust of wind rushed in to stroke my cheek.

☼

The sun was low in the sky when Jake and I made our way down to the beach where the band was setting up. Guys from school were stacking driftwood haphazardly into a pile below the high-tide mark, and girls were soaking up the last of the sun, flaunting their bikinis. We dropped down beside Amber and Lexie on the sand and they passed us plastic cups filled with warm beer.

"To boys, booze and blue skies." Amber raised her cup, sloshing beer over all of us.

Jake wrapped an arm around me and hooked his finger through a loop in my jeans. We talked about summer and made plans for our holidays that were just around the corner. Amber wanted to go on a road trip but I had other ideas. Jake was going to help me paint the cottage, and we'd even talked about getting some furniture up there.

The sky faded to dusk, and soon the bonfire spat shards of light high into the air. It was a hot night and people took to the tide. Amber was letting a boy from the year below us persuade her into swimming, and Brie was slung over someone's shoulder near the water's edge. Jake had to leave to get Charlotte home in time for her curfew and promised to meet me tomorrow. He said he had a surprise.

After pouring out the last of my beer, I picked my way over couples lying in the sand and headed for the rocks at the very end of the beach. I clambered up them, the half-moon casting enough light for me to see by. Behind me, the beach party was dying down.

Embers from the fire sank low in the sand, and the band

began taking down their makeshift stage. I peered down through velvety water, at the gently swaying seaweed that clung to dark rocks. In the moonlight it was so beautiful.

I stripped off my clothes, felt my hair brush softly against my back and dived in.